SIDEBAR

What Reviewers Say About Carsen Taite's Work

It Should be a Crime

"Law professor Morgan Bradley and her student Parker Casey are potential love interests, but throw in a high-profile murder trial, and you've got an entertaining book that can be read in one sitting. Taite also practices criminal law and she weaves her insider knowledge of the criminal justice system into the love story seamlessly and with excellent timing. I find romances lacking when the characters change completely upon falling in love, but this was not the case here. I look forward to reading more from Taite."—*Curve Magazine*

"This [*It Should be a Crime*] is just Taite's second novel…but it's as if she has bookshelves full of bestsellers under her belt."—*Gay List Daily*

"Taite, a criminal defense attorney herself, has given her readers a behind the scenes look at what goes on during the days before a trial. Her descriptions of lawyer/client talks, investigations, police procedures, etc. are fascinating. Taite keeps the action moving, her characters clear, and never allows her story to get bogged down in paperwork. *It Should be a Crime* has a fast-moving plot and some extraordinarily hot sex."—*Just About Write*

Do Not Disturb

"Taite's tale of sexual tension is entertaining in itself, but a number of secondary characters…add substantial color to romantic inevitability"—Richard Labonte, *Book Marks*

Nothing but the Truth

"Author Taite is really a Dallas defense attorney herself, and it's obvious her viewpoint adds considerable realism to her story, making it especially riveting as a mystery. I give it four stars out of five."
—Bob Lind, *Echo Magazine*

"As a criminal defense attorney in Dallas, Texas, Carsen Taite knows her way around the court house. This ability shows in her writing, as her legal dramas take the reader into backroom negotiations between the opposing lawyers, as well as into meetings with judges. Watching how Carsen Taite brings together all of the loose ends is enjoyable, as is her skillful building of the characters of Ryan and Brett. *Nothing But the Truth* is an enjoyable mystery with some hot romance thrown in."—*Just About Write*

"Taite has written an excellent courtroom drama with two interesting women leading the cast of characters. Taite herself is a practicing defense attorney, and her courtroom scenes are clearly based on real knowledge. This should be another winner for Taite."—*Lambda Literary*

The Best Defense

"Real life defense attorney Carsen Taite polishes her fifth work of lesbian fiction, *The Best Defense*, with the realism she daily encounters in the office and in the courts. And that polish is something that makes *The Best Defense* shine as an excellent read."—*Out & About Newspaper*

Slingshot

"The mean streets of lesbian literature finally have the hard boiled bounty hunter they deserve. It's a slingshot of a ride, bad guys and hot women rolled into one page turning package. I'm looking forward to Luca Bennett's next adventure."—J. M. Redmann, author of the Micky Knight mystery series

Beyond Innocence

"Taite keeps you guessing with delicious delay until the very last minute…Taite's time in the courtroom lends *Beyond Innocence* a terrific verisimilitude someone not in the profession couldn't impart. And damned if she doesn't make practicing law interesting." —*Out in Print*

"As you would expect, sparks and legal writs fly. What I liked about this book were the shades of grey (no, not the smutty Shades of Grey)—both in the relationship as well as the cases."—*C-spot Reviews*

Battle Axe

"This second book is satisfying, substantial, and slick. Plus, it has heart and love coupled with Luca's array of weapons and a badass verbal repertoire… I cannot imagine anyone not having a great time riding shotgun through all of Luca's escapades. I recommend hopping on Luca's band wagon and having a blast."—*Rainbow Book Reviews*

"Taite breathes life into her characters with elemental finesse… A great read, told in the vein of a good old detective-type novel filled with criminal elements, thugs, and mobsters that will entertain and amuse."—*Lambda Literary*

Rush

"A simply beautiful interplay of police procedural magic, murder, FBI presence, misguided protective cover-ups, and a superheated love affair…a Gold Star from me and major encouragement for all readers to dive right in and consume this story with gusto!"—*Rainbow Book Reviews*

Switchblade

"I enjoyed the book and it was a fun read—mystery, action, humor, and a bit of romance. Who could ask for more? If you've read and enjoyed Taite's legal novels, you'll like this. If you've read and enjoyed the two other books in this series, this one will definitely satisfy your Luca fix and I highly recommend picking it up. Highly recommended."—*C-spot Reviews*

"Dallas's intrepid female bounty hunter, Luca Bennett, is back in another adventure. Fantastic! Between her many friends and lovers, her interesting family, her fly by the seat of her pants lifestyle, and a whole host of detractors there is rarely a dull moment."—*Rainbow Book Reviews*

Courtship

"The political drama is just top-notch. The emotional and sexual tensions are intertwined with great timing and flair. I truly adored this book from beginning to end. Fantabulous!"—*Rainbow Book Reviews*

"Carsen Taite throws the reader head on into the murky world of the political system where there are no rights or wrongs, just players attempting to broker the best deals regardless of who gets hurt in the process. The book is extremely well written and makes compelling reading. With twist and turns throughout, the reader doesn't know how the story will end."—*Lesbian Reading Room*

"Taite keeps the stakes high as two beautiful and brilliant women fueled by professional ambitions face daunting emotional choices… As backroom politics, secrets, betrayals, and threats race to be resolved without political damage to the president, the cat-and-mouse relationship game between Addison and Julia has the reader rooting for them. Taite prolongs the fever-pitch tension to the final pages. This pleasant read with intelligent heroines, snappy dialogue, and political suspense will satisfy Taite's devoted fans and new readers alike."—*Publisher's Weekly*

Lay Down the Law

"Recognized for the pithy realism of her characters and settings drawn from a Texas legal milieu, Taite pays homage to the prime-time soap opera Dallas in pairing a cartel-busting U.S. attorney, Peyton Davis, with a charity-minded oil heiress, Lily Gantry." —*Publishers Weekly*

"Suspenseful, intriguingly tense, and with a great developing love story, this book is delightfully solid on all fronts. This gets my A-1 recommendation!"—*Rainbow Book Reviews*

Reasonable Doubt

"I was drawn into the mystery plot line and quickly became enthralled with the book. It was suspenseful without being too intense but there were some great twists to keep me guessing. It's a very good book. I cannot wait to read the next in line that Ms. Taite has to offer." —*Prism Book Alliance*

Above the Law

"…readers who enjoyed the first installment will find this a worthy second act."—*Publishers Weekly*

"Ms Taite delivered and then some, all the while adding more questions, Tease! I like the mystery and intrigue in this story. It has many "sit on the edge of your seat" scenes of excitement and dread (like watch out kind of thing) and drama…well done indeed!"—*Prism Book Alliance*

Without Justice

"Carsen Taite tells a great story. She is consistent in giving her readers a good if not great legal drama with characters who are insightful, well thought out and have good chemistry. You know when you pick up one of her books you are getting your money's worth time and time again. Consistency with a great legal drama is all but guaranteed." —*The Romantic Reader Blog*

"This is a great read, fast-paced, interesting and takes a slightly different tack from the normal crime/courtroom drama having a lawyer in the witness protection system whose case becomes the hidden centre of another crime."—*Lesbian Reading Room*

By the Author

Truelesbianlove.com

It Should be a Crime

Do Not Disturb

Nothing but the Truth

The Best Defense

Beyond Innocence

Rush

Courtship

Reasonable Doubt

Without Justice

Sidebar

The Luca Bennett Mystery Series:

Slingshot

Battle Axe

Switchblade

Bow and Arrow (novella in Girls with Guns)

Lone Star Law Series:

Lay Down the Law

Above the Law

Letter of the Law

Sidebar

by

Carsen Taite

2017

SIDEBAR

ISBN 13: 978-1-62639-752-1

This Trade Paperback Original Is Published By
Bold Strokes Books, Inc.
P.O. Box 249
Valley Falls, NY 12185

First Edition: August 2017

Credits
Editor: Cindy Cresap
Production Design: Susan Ramundo
Cover Design By Sheri (graphicartist2020@hotmail.com)

Acknowledgments

Big thanks to the usual suspects. Rad and Sandy Lowe for providing a publishing house where their authors are both comfortable and challenged at the same time. Ruth Sternglantz for your superb marketing. Cindy Cresap for making every book better with your keen editor's eye. Ashley Bartlett for your insightful critique of the first draft and pushing me to write, even when it's hard. And VK Powell—I think you read this manuscript about a dozen times as I wrote and rewrote and rewrote again. I can't thank you enough.

To Lainey, my amazing wife, cheerleader, and confidant. Thanks for making this wonderful life possible. Couldn't do it without you. Wouldn't want to.

A special shout out to my Cairn Terrier, Mollie. For almost your whole life, I've been writing books and you've occupied the space beside me—couch, chair, floor beside my desk—while I tell these stories. Although sometimes you snore through the edits, the way you wag your tail and widen your soulful brown eyes when I tell you it's time to write warms my heart. Every single time.

And to my readers. Your kind words of encouragement and loyal support are appreciated more than you can ever know. I write stories because you read them. Thank you, thank you, thank you.

Dedication

For Lainey—there's no one I'd rather have by my side.

Chapter One

West Fallon pushed through the revolving door and spun toward a future she'd been dreading all year. The long security line that greeted her once she entered the federal building only increased her anxiety. When she finally reached the conveyor belt, she dutifully placed her wallet and keys in the pale green dog food bowl provided by the security guard and removed her belt and placed it on top of the pile. She patted her pockets for good measure before walking through the metal detector. The absence of a loud beep meant she was safe from the second guard, waiting with a metal wand, and free to go. West shoved her stuff back in her pockets, but when she reached for her belt, she caught sight of a goddess who vanquished all thoughts of what lay ahead.

She was tall and dressed in a tailored suit that didn't completely hide her curves. She ran a hand through her chestnut hair, and West took in her tapered nose, full lips, and flawless skin marred only by a fierce frown that didn't quite diminish the brightness in her hazel eyes. "I have no idea what's setting off the alarm." Her voice was smooth despite the undercurrent of frustration.

The guard shrugged and pointed at her bag. "Sure you put all your electronics in there?"

"I'm positive." The woman pointed at the X-ray monitor. "Besides, shouldn't you be able to see whatever's in my bag?"

"It's your bra," West blurted out. Hardly able to believe she'd referenced this stranger's underwear out loud, she went all in. "Nasty underwires." A slow flush burned its way through her as she remembered the time she'd brought her pal Jill Martin here a few years ago. Jill's double D, full support brassiere almost kept her from entering the building. But this woman was no Jill Martin, interested in exploring the place where federal crimes were tried. No, she was older, late thirties at least, and the suit signaled she was probably here for court, not a curious look around. West cocked her head, assessing the woman's attire. "Are you an attorney?" A slight hesitation and then a quick nod. "Cool. Just show them your bar card and they'll let you in."

The woman stood still for a moment and then began rummaging in her bag. West stared, acutely conscious she was bordering on being rude. Her work here was done, but in a tug-of-war between what waited upstairs and this woman's beautiful eyes, the eyes won. When the woman successfully negotiated her way past the guard and collected her bag, she smiled in West's direction. "Thanks for the tip. Do you work here?"

"Not if I can help it."

"Oh, sorry." The brunette scanned her, lips pursed. West looked down at her casual outfit, jeans—not her best ones—a Ghostbusters T-shirt, and red Converse. She laughed. "Don't worry, I'm not some defendant, looking for free representation. I'm here to see a friend."

The stranger joined in the laugh. "I didn't mean to imply anything. Besides, I was the one who couldn't get through security on my own. I haven't been here in a while, but last time I was, I don't recall the machines being so sensitive."

"Where are you going?"

"Excuse me?"

West paused. She'd asked the question without thinking. It wasn't any of her business where this woman was headed, plus she couldn't quite decide if she was just avoiding the inevitable. For a second, she considered asking the woman to join her for a cup of coffee or an early lunch—anything to prolong the contact, but she squelched the impulse for the distraction it was. "I just thought I might be able to point you in the right direction. I'm headed upstairs." She pointed at the directory to their left. "Most everyone in the building is listed there."

"Thanks." The woman looked over at the directory but didn't move.

West glanced at the bank of elevators and then back at the woman, torn between wanting to escort her wherever she needed to go and an aversion to anything that would prolong her errand. They both had business to attend to, and the sooner she got hers over with, the sooner she could get out of this place and back to a summer full of the kind of work she really wanted to be doing. Her itinerary didn't include time for distractions, and everything about this woman screamed distraction. She shot her one last look. "Have a good day."

West rode the elevator with a couple of well suited men toting hefty briefcases. She caught them eyeing her in the reflection on the highly polished steel doors, no doubt wondering where she was going dressed like she'd just finished a shift at a local coffee shop. Unlike downstairs where she'd cared what the beautiful stranger thought of her, she didn't give a rat's ass about the opinion of these two. Until she was paid to show up here, she'd dress however she pleased, and even after things were official, she'd intended to push the boundaries, unwilling to be uncomfortable no matter what promises she'd made.

When the elevator stopped on the sixth floor, she followed the suits out of the car, and they all walked to the left toward the additional layer of security in place on every floor where courtrooms were located. The marshal at the desk stood and craned his neck past the men to call out to her. "West! I hear congratulations are in order."

The suits turned toward her, apparently deciding her outfit wasn't the only unusual thing about her. She ignored them harder than before. "Hey, Peter. Good to see you. He's in, right?"

"Yep. They're in the middle of a hearing, but should be done soon." He looked at his watch. "It's a pretty big case. Why don't you stick your head in?" He motioned for her to come on back.

"Thanks." She ignored the questioning looks of the suits and ducked around the metal detector, allowing Peter to give her a quick hug before she trudged down the hallway. Judge Henry "Hank" Blair's courtroom was the last one on the left. She paused before the closed double doors, considering her options. Should she continue down the hall to his chambers and wait for him there or should she slip into the courtroom and catch the last part of the hearing? Curiosity won out.

She eased open the door and tiptoed toward a seat at the back of the courtroom. The defense attorney was at the podium arguing vigorously that the defendant's estranged wife had no right to turn over the defendant's private video collection to the police while he was in custody. After she made her points, the attorney for the government stood and quoted a string of case law designed to punch holes in every argument he'd just heard. West settled in to listen to the spin, and when both sides finished their spiel, she was surprised to see that thirty minutes had passed and she'd actually enjoyed herself. Maybe this gig wouldn't be so bad after all.

When the assistant US attorney finished his rebuttal, Judge Blair asked a few questions of each side and then told them he'd have an opinion in the next few days. As the onlookers in the gallery started to scatter, she heard her name.

"West, come up here."

Hank Blair was standing behind the bench, waving to her, a big smile on his face. Despite her discomfort at being made the center of attention, she returned the smile and walked up the aisle, conscious all eyes were trained her way. It had been a long time since she'd denied Hank anything, but as she drew closer to the cluster of attorneys surrounding the bench, she wished she had.

"I want you all to meet one of my future law clerks, West Fallon. Just graduated first in her class from Berkeley Law. This fall, she'll be starting work right here in this courtroom."

West took in the jaw drops and raised eyebrows. She was used to people underestimating her based on her appearance. There was a time other people's opinions had power over her, but three years of battling her way to the top at Berkeley had cured her. People underestimating her was a sign of their weakness, not hers. She shook hands with the other attorneys, filing their names in her photographic memory for future reference, certain she'd run into them in the fall. If she was here.

A few minutes later, she followed Hank to his chambers, where once they were alone, he scooped her up in a huge bear hug that she pretended to merely endure. When he released her, he frowned and rubbed his chest.

"What's the matter?" she teased him. "Bear hugs getting the best of you?"

"You wish." He grimaced. "No, I think it was the patty melt I had for lunch. Love those onions, but they don't love me."

She stared a little harder, not entirely sure she believed his explanation, but she saw nothing specific to signal any alarm. He was paler and maybe a little thinner than he'd appeared a few weeks ago when he'd flown out to California for her graduation, but otherwise he was the same larger-than-life personality he'd always been.

"How was your trip?" he asked. "Can you stay for a few days? Diane would like to have you over for dinner and, of course, you're welcome to stay with us while you're here."

West noted his tentative tone. Dinner and an invitation to stay at the house was more than he usually asked for, and for a second, she considered changing her plans to give him what he wanted. "I'd planned to drive out tomorrow. I'm supposed to meet up with some folks about a place to stay during the summer." She watched his smile falter, and she tossed him a bone. "But I guess I could go a day later. And dinner sounds nice."

"Good. Food hits the table at seven sharp, same as always. It'll be nice to have you there."

"I'm looking forward to it." And surprisingly, she was. Her original plan had been to make this visit nothing more than a drive-by. She'd swing into the courthouse, drop her news, and hit the road again, but now that she was here, staring Hank in the face, gathering the nerve to be honest was proving harder than she'd thought. Maybe in the causal comfort of his home, it would be easier to tell him she couldn't possibly keep her promise to clerk for him this fall.

In a day or two, she'd continue her cross-country trek to Montgomery, Alabama, where she had a spot waiting at the Southern Poverty Law Center. There she'd do real work, tackling hate groups, championing civil rights—white knight stuff. The summer gig was a trial run, but she planned to do everything within her power to show the attorneys at the Center her commitment and dedication in hopes they would invite her to stay on for the long haul. She hadn't told Hank yet, but she'd taken a gamble and signed up to take the Alabama bar exam in July. Knowing everything he did about her, Hank had to understand why she couldn't let anything get in the way of this opportunity to make a difference in the world.

"So, what's up?" Hank asked.

"Excuse me?"

"As much as I'd like to believe you came by just to see me, I figure you didn't brave the lines downstairs just to say hello. Do you want to check out your office? Maybe measure the walls for some art and your diploma?"

She opened her mouth to ask him if he'd lost his mind, but before she could speak, she caught the sly grin and realized he was only giving her a hard time. "Yes, we starving college students often have lots of art worthy of hanging." He started to reply, but a rap on the door interrupted them. "Get that if you need to," West said.

"Sorry," he replied as he strode over to the door. Halfway there, he stumbled. West instinctively reached out to catch him, but he waved her away. "I'm fine. Just clumsy."

He paused with his hand on the door and a perplexed expression marring his face. West stared, trying to process his sluggish words and drooping face, but before she could make sense of it, he was in free fall, clutching his chest, the other arm flailing for purchase. West leapt toward him and barely made it in time to cushion his fall as her world came crashing down.

When she reached the sixth floor, Camille stepped out to find another security stop between her and her ultimate destination. She smiled to herself and looked around as if the young woman from downstairs might magically appear to give her tips. She hadn't been able to stop thinking about her, which was silly since their entire conversation had lasted no more than a minute and she didn't even know her name. But Camille had been intrigued by the juxtaposition between the woman's causal dress and her easy confidence about the inner workings of the courthouse. And then there was the flicker of interest she'd seen reflected in her gaze. *Too young. Not your type. But it's nice to be noticed.* The thoughts crowded her head, and when the marshal standing behind the desk cleared his throat, she figured she'd probably been standing there, lost in thought, for longer than she'd realized.

"Sorry." She placed her bag on the conveyor belt and patted her suit pockets one more time before walking through the metal detector.

"What's your business here today?" he asked, his expression unreadable.

She looked at his name badge. Peter Donovan. She hoped someday soon, Peter and everyone else here would know her well enough to waive her in. "I have an appointment with Judge Stroud."

"Phone?"

She stared at him, trying to decipher his question. "You need to see my phone?"

"More than see it. I need to keep it unless you have a bar card."

"Of course." She reached toward the conveyor relieved she remembered to carry the card she hadn't needed in years. She held it out for his inspection. "My phone's in my bag."

The marshal's demeanor shifted ever so slightly, but Camille still felt the cold shoulder that came with being an outsider. She'd never practiced in this building, so there was no reason for anyone here to accord her the respect that came with familiarity.

When she finally reached Judge Stroud's chambers, the mood was completely different. The matronly woman at the desk outside his door greeted her with a huge smile and an offer of coffee or tea.

"I'm fine, thanks."

"I'll let the judge know you're here."

Camille sat on the couch, but kept her feet firmly planted, resisting the urge to sink into the bulging cushions. Who put such a nap-worthy piece of furniture in their place of business? It felt like a test somehow, like if she managed to stay awake she would get the job. She suppressed a smile and picked up a magazine she could pretend to read, hoping the ruse would hide her sudden attack of nerves. She flipped idly through the pages, barely noticing the content until she spotted a picture of a young actress who'd recently taken Hollywood by storm with her edgy good looks and devil-may-care attitude. Camille barely remembered the actress's name, but she bore a stunning likeness to the young woman who'd helped her out downstairs. Of course, she didn't know that woman's name either, so it was possible…

No, it wasn't. The woman she'd just seen was actually more attractive than the starlet on the pages of the magazine. More intriguing and definitely more delicious. Besides, what would a Hollywood actress be doing here in Dallas, lurking around the federal courthouse? The idea fascinated her, but she ultimately settled on the conclusion that the woman she'd seen downstairs was only a doppelgänger for the actress. Or the other way around.

"Judge Avery?"

Camille looked up and tracked Judge Stroud's amused expression as he looked from her to the magazine. She groaned inwardly, wishing she'd been caught reading anything except *People* magazine, but there was nothing she could do about it now. She decided to spin. "I think it's great that you keep current pop culture reading materials in chambers. Helps to keep things human. For instance, I now know my horoscope says today has the potential to change my life."

Stroud pointed toward his office door. "How about we go talk about that very thing?"

The chief judge's chambers were spacious, and the walls were covered with evidence of his many years in service. Certificates of accomplishment, autographed photos with dignitaries, and a few pieces of museum-worthy original art signaled success. Camille imagined her own professional paraphernalia in this space and applicants meeting with her as the chief judge. She was here to start her journey to that end.

He motioned for her to take a seat on a leather couch in the ample living room type seating area, and he sat across from her in a high-back chair, dropping the formality he'd greeted her with in front of his staff. "Camille, it's good to see you. How's your father?"

"The same. Very busy, very accomplished. He's in Saudi Arabia this week, meeting a new client for the firm."

"And your mother?"

"She's doing the real work at the firm while Dad's out gathering new clients. It'll be another banner year for them."

"And you're not interested in following in their footsteps?"

As he spoke the words, he tapped a folder on the table next to him. She saw the lettering on the tab—her application and résumé. Was this his way of breaking it to her gently that she wasn't going to get the job? "Their dream, not mine. I was on the bench long enough to know that's all I want to do."

"Even if it means you'd be starting over again at the bottom? As a magistrate, you won't have near the influence and discretion you had in your prior role on the bench."

Camille bit back her first response. Saying she really didn't have a choice probably wasn't the best way to make inroads. She'd gotten this informal meeting because Judge Stroud was a longtime friend of her parents, but he wouldn't be the sole decision-maker about whether she'd get offered a position as one of the federal magistrate judges. She may as well start practicing polished answers designed to get this appointment. Without the job, she'd have to hang her own shingle, take a soul-sucking big firm job or, God forbid, work for her parents.

"I don't really look at it as the bottom," she said. "Just the first step on the ascent to something new and more challenging than what I've been doing. My time as a judge in state court provided invaluable experience, but the jurisdictions are wildly different. I think working as a federal magistrate will be a perfect opportunity to broaden my horizons, and one day maybe I'll be working alongside you as a district court judge."

Stroud's laugh was forced. "Perfect answer," he said. "Way to play down your expectations since we both know your real plan is to eventually take over my job."

"Maybe." She cracked a smile. "But you're safe until I learn the ropes."

"Duly noted." He opened the folder and flipped through the pages inside. "You've got the glad-handing down. Now tell me what made the good citizens of Collin County toss you off the bench."

"You don't waste any time, do you?"

"It'll be the first question most of the committee members ask. Be glad they'll want to hear your answer rather than relying solely on the news reports."

"Fair enough." Camille took a deep breath. She'd prepared for exactly this sort of question. "I made a tough call, but in state court, judges are elected, as you know, and despite it being nonsensical, the elections fall along party lines, without regard to qualifications. My opponent focused his entire ad campaign on one case—a defendant with a drug problem who I'd allowed to have a second chance on probation. The defendant threw away the chance I gave him and reoffended, but, unfortunately for everyone involved, this time his addiction turned deadly. He was driving under the influence, crashed into a young girl, and killed her.

"It was a tragedy and when he came before me again, I put him away for the rest of his life. Unfortunately, no one remembers that part because it didn't fit the narrative of my opponent who spent substantial amounts of his own money in his quest for a robe and a gavel."

"He outspent you two to one."

"Yes, he did. He could afford it."

"Is there a reason you let him do that when I'm sure your parents would have gladly funded a scorched earth approach?"

"I'm a grown woman. I don't need my parents' money to get what I need."

"And yet you let them set up this meeting."

Camille grinned. "Like I said, I don't *need* my parents' money, but I'd be crazy to turn down a healthy dose of their influence. Besides, I know you wouldn't hire me on their word alone."

"Smart woman." He pointed at his desk. "Your file is ready to go out to the committee. We've had a lot of well-qualified applicants and I can't guarantee anything. Are you sure this is what you really want?"

Camille reflected on the last five months. Since she'd been voted out of office, she'd lost her way. She had filled her time consulting on a few cases and serving as a mediator for mind-numbing corporate litigation. Her parents had encouraged her to join their firm, but she had no interest in selling her soul for corporate clients who thought they could buy their way out of any situation. After a full term running a courtroom and having the final say, the idea of spending her days doing other people's bidding, even at ten times the salary, seemed like a step down. Other girls dreamed of being president someday, but in her dreams, she'd been wearing a black robe and seated with eight other justices at the highest court in the land. This was just the first step, and she was determined to tread carefully. "Yes, I really want this. How soon do you think it will be before the committee reaches a decision?"

"Soon. We need to fill the spot. There's a tremendous backlog. The last administration had a difficult time getting any judicial nominations approved by the Senate, so we've been short-handed. Now, that the Dems control everything, things are sailing through."

"If it helps, I have the distinct advantage of not currently being employed, so I can start anytime."

"I'll let the committee know."

They both looked up at the sound of a rap on the door. "Sorry, I asked Joan not to interrupt, so it must be important. Come in!"

Joan, the woman who'd greeted her earlier, poked her head in the door. She looked flushed and scattered. "Judge Stroud, we have an emergency. Judge Blair collapsed in his office."

Stroud sprang to his feet. "Sorry, Camille, I need to go. Give your parents my best."

He dashed out the door, leaving Joan to escort her out. They stared at each other for a moment, while Camille fished for something to say. "I'm sorry to hear about Judge Blair. Do you think he's going to be okay?"

"He's unconscious, so it's hard to tell. The paramedics are with him now." Joan shifted in place. "I should go check on things."

Camille stood, acutely conscious her presence and the norms of politeness were keeping Joan from being where she wanted to be. She followed her to the door. "Go ahead, I can show myself out." She placed a hand on Joan's arm. "I hope the judge is okay."

"Thanks." She delivered the word on the run.

Camille stood in the reception area watching her go and feeling decidedly useless. A few seconds later, she was walking down the hallway, back toward the marshal's station, when loud voices shouted behind her.

"Clear the way! Move!"

She hugged the wall, transfixed, as a team of paramedics hustled a gurney down the hall. Their expressions were drawn and grave, and they were almost as pale as the man they carried, but before she could absorb any other detail, Camille's attention was drawn to the woman who ran alongside them. It was the brunette she'd met downstairs, the one whose advice had gotten her past security. She was holding Judge

Blair's hand, and the calm, confident expression she'd worn earlier had been replaced by fear and tension.

Was this stranger the judge's daughter or did she just know the judge because she worked in the building? Camille wanted to reach out to her. Tell her that whatever was wrong, it would be okay, but she held her tongue. Other than their few-second exchange an hour ago, she had no connection to this woman, no right to comment or comfort. Hell, she didn't even know her name. But she wanted to.

CHAPTER TWO

Three months later...

Camille rang the doorbell and hoped no one would answer. The last few months had been a whirlwind. The chair of the magistrate judge selection panel had contacted her to say they wouldn't be considering her application because Senator Armstrong had recommended her to the president to fill Judge Blair's newly vacated bench. The entire confirmation process had been a speedy blur, and now she was standing on the doorstep of the man she was about to replace. It wasn't her choice to be here. He'd requested this visit, and she figured the least she could do was honor his last official request. If she knew the agenda, maybe she wouldn't be experiencing this level of trepidation, but she had no idea why she'd been summoned.

A striking woman with medium length silver hair answered the door. Dressed in white linen pants with a sky blue tunic shirt, she looked like summer, and the smile on her face said she was happy about it. The woman swung the door wide. "Judge Avery, please come in."

"Please call me Camille." She walked in and let her gaze sweep the entry before turning her attention back to the woman who'd answered the door. As if noticing the inspection, the woman offered a hand. "Diane Blair. It's a pleasure to meet you, and I appreciate you making the drive. I know the suburbs can be a pain this time of day."

"No trouble at all," Camille lied. Judge Blair's house in Southlake was far from the courthouse. The traffic snarls had been monstrous and the suburban streets wound around in a confusing fashion, but curiosity fueled her, and now that she was here, she was anxious to find out the reason for the trip. "Have you lived here long?"

Diane's face was briefly marred by a frown. "Not long at all. We moved here last month. We loved our house in Oak Cliff, but it was an older, historic home and there was only so much we could do to accommodate…"

She let the words trail off, and Camille scrambled to find a way to change the subject. Good thing she was done interviewing, since she seemed to have completely lost any sense of tact. "It's a beautiful home and this is a well regarded area. I'm sure you'll settle in nicely."

"Thanks." Diane looked over her shoulder. "Hank is just finishing up with his physical therapist. Why don't you follow me to the kitchen and I'll get you something cool to drink?"

Camille wasn't thirsty, but she took the tall, icy glass of lemonade and politely imbibed small sips while Diane pointed out some of the features of the expansive kitchen. Camille heard the edge of nerves in Diane's voice and doubted she really cared about the convection ovens or the built-in wine fridge, but she played along as if she was here for a regular social call instead of what was likely to be some strange passing of the baton. After what seemed like an eternity, she heard a buzz from a box on the wall. Diane grimaced an apology, picked up the handset, and listened to the voice on the other end. When she hung up, she said, "Hank's waiting in his office. I'll show you the way."

Camille followed her down a long hallway on the other side of the kitchen, marveling at the size of the place. When they reached the doorway at the end of the hall, Diane paused in the entry shooting her a look that said prepare yourself.

Judge Blair was slumped in a wheelchair behind his desk, the left side of his face slack as if straining to pull the other half down. She'd heard the news from Stroud that Judge Blair had had a stroke and wasn't returning to the bench. Her first thought had been she wouldn't let a little stroke keep her from her passion, but she hadn't clued in to the severity until just this moment.

Which brought her back to the reason she was here. He'd specifically requested her presence. Not a phone call, not a note. An in-person visit. Now that she was here, she was even more desperate to know why he'd insisted on meeting in person. After Diane excused herself, she strode into the room, determined to act like this was a perfectly normal visit. "Good afternoon, Judge Blair."

"Hello." He strangled out the word with a clear force of effort. She hoped he wasn't planning to have a long conversation with her, because if he was, it was going to be painful for both of them. He pointed at the computer on his desk and motioned her over. While she walked, he typed with one finger of his right hand. When she was alongside his desk, he pointed at the screen.

This is easier, yes?

Relieved they had a better way to communicate, she nodded. "How are you doing?"

He shook his head and pecked out another series of words. *Not about me. Clerks. Have you hired any?*

She did a double take at the words. The question was completely unexpected, but she had given the subject some thought. Some of the other judges had given her their leftover stacks of résumés and applications for the position, and she'd been going through them while she boned up on federal law and procedure. At first she'd been concerned about the pile of castoffs, but when she realized the district received hundreds of applications for the one or two coveted spots per judge, she realized everyone else's castoffs still amounted to the top talent from the recent graduating class. "I haven't hired anyone yet, but I have a few prospects. Judge Stroud is letting me borrow one of his clerks until I get my bearings."

Blair barely waited for her to finish her sentence before he started pecking at the keyboard again. *I need a favor. It's important.*

Like she was going to deny this man anything. Within reason. "Name it."

More typing. *West Fallon. Best there is. Ready to start on day one. She knows the court inside and out. You won't do better.*

The name didn't ring a bell, but it wouldn't. Most clerks were young lawyers, at most a few years out of school, some not even admitted to the bar yet. She'd had a few interns when she was on the state court bench, but federal judges had the luxury of one or two paid full-time lawyers at their disposal for research and other random tasks. The clerks generally worked for a district judge for a year or two before using the experience as a stepping-stone to either a position with an appellate judge or to open doors at some of the more prestigious firms. She was already inheriting a secretary and a bailiff, and she had been looking forward to the opportunity to hire her own clerks as a way to make her mark. What was so important about this clerk that he felt the need to personally ask her to keep her on? Figuring she knew the answer, she asked, "Family friend?"

Yes, but it's more important than that. Promise me you'll keep her on?

One look at the judge and she knew she couldn't deny him. Whatever the reason, keeping this clerk was very important to him, and it wouldn't hurt to have another clerk by her side who knew the courtroom inside and out. "Okay. I promise."

Satisfied at her answer, the judge visibly relaxed, and they spent the next hour going over details about the court. Camille was impressed with his willingness to share information about his staff and procedural details about the court. By the time they were done with their visit, it was clear to her he truly cared that she was successful in her new position.

Before she left, Diane stopped her at the door. "Thanks for coming by. The first month we were inundated with visitors, but everyone's gone back to their lives, as to be expected. He was on the bench for so long, it's been hard for him to adjust to a life without it."

"I understand."

"You're welcome to come back anytime. He'd be happy to answer any questions you have."

"I might just take advantage of that offer."

"And by the way, I voted for you. I get that you had to make a tough call." Diane pointed in the direction of the judge's study. "He had to make plenty during his career. He was just fortunate enough to have the safety net of a lifetime appointment. Now you'll have that too."

"Thanks."

Camille reflected on their conversation as she walked down the street to her car. Maybe Hank Blair could be a mentor of sorts. Judge Stroud would be the natural fit to take on this role, but he was so connected to her parents, she wasn't sure she would trust him with questions that exposed her own insecurities. She liked Hank, and he had a way of making her feel like there were no dumb questions. Deep in thought, she didn't notice the woman standing beside her until she was inches away.

"Hey, I remember you."

A second of surprise was followed by a surge of warmth at the familiar face. When Camille had last seen this woman, she hadn't seen the tattoo snaking up her arm, but she'd never forget that face, those eyes. She grinned. "I remember you too. Courthouse. Last spring. I was setting off alarms on the metal detector and you were dispensing advice."

"That's me." She scrunched her brow. "You live around here or are you following me?"

"No and no. Besides, I think I was here first."

"Fine, but if I'd known you were going to be here, I'd have shown up sooner."

"Are you always a flirt, or just with women you meet at the courthouse?"

"Depends."

"On?"

"On a lot of things. Let me buy you a coffee and I'll tell you more."

Camille drew back slightly. Flirtatious banter was one thing, but a date, even a casual coffee date, was another. All her focus needed to be on distinguishing herself at the job ahead, and random dates with total strangers, especially young, tattooed ones, wasn't on the agenda. "I'm afraid I have plans, but thanks for the offer."

The stranger cocked her head and gave her a smug, knowing smile as she pulled a card from her wallet. Camille watched, transfixed, as she scrawled a note on the card and handed it over. "When you're ready, give me a call."

Camille watched her saunter up the walk toward Judge Blair's house, and the memory of her running alongside the stretcher at the courthouse flashed in her mind. She wondered now what she'd wondered then—was this Blair's daughter? She glanced down at the card. *Good for one cup of coffee.* The offer was followed by a phone number and then a scrawled, but legible signature. *West Fallon.*

West Fallon. The clerk she'd just promised to keep on her staff. She stared at the phone number written in a neat row beneath the invitation. An hour ago, before her conversation with Judge Blair, she might have called the number on the card and taken West Fallon up on her invitation, but now that possibility was off the table. She was going to spend every workday with West for the next year, and the prospect brought equal parts dread and excitement.

West stood on Judge Blair's front porch rethinking her semi-slick move with the card and offer of coffee. What she should've done was flirt a little more, get the woman's name and number instead of the other way around. Now she was at the mercy of this stranger who might or might not ever call.

Truth was she was out of practice. It had been a long summer and she'd had no social life to speak of. After Hank had started rehab, she'd finally taken off to Montgomery for her stint at the Southern Poverty Law Center. She'd spent her days working her ass off and her nights studying for the bar exam certain if she worked hard enough on both fronts, they'd offer her a permanent position. Her bosses at the Center had gushed about the quality of her work, but budget cuts meant they'd put a moratorium on hiring. Apparently, the wildly successful Democratic sweep in the last election cycle had left people feeling passive about making donations to organizations that champion civil rights. With her dream job on hold for now, she'd decided she might as well fulfill the promise she'd made to Hank.

She glanced back at the woman who was pulling away in her Lexus. Just because she was about to start a drudge job didn't mean she couldn't have a little fun on the side.

"West, I thought that was you. Have you been standing out here long?"

West grinned at Diane Blair who stood framed in the open doorway. "Sorry, I guess I forgot to ring the bell. I haven't been here long."

Diane looked past her and then shook her head. "Well, come on in. Hank's in his study waiting for you and dinner will be ready soon." Her voice dropped to a whisper. "Do me a favor?"

"Sure, whatever you need."

"Don't wear him out. He's already had one visitor this afternoon and he won't admit it, but any amount of conversation really takes a toll."

"Okay," West said, but Diane's comment made her feel she'd missed something important. "I'm a little confused though. I thought he'd already gone back to work, but you're telling me more than one visitor is a hardship?"

Diane didn't meet her gaze, but West could tell by the duck of her head and a slight reddening on her cheeks, she was holding something back. "Diane, he is back at work, isn't he?"

Diane waved her hand. "Go on back. He's waiting for you."

West gave her one last hard look before following Diane's directions back to Hank's study. The wall along the way was covered with family photos. Hank and Diane. Hank and Diane and their kids. Soccer games, birthday parties, and weddings. In the sea of sentimentality, she found the few framed photos she sought out on every visit. She and Hank, standing on the steps of McFarlin Auditorium at her high school graduation. She wore her cap and gown, and Hank had his arm around her shoulders, beaming like a proud parent. The next one was her college graduation. Same pose, but both Hank and Diane were in the picture, flanking her like she was their own. She lingered for a moment, taking time to savor the closest thing she had to a family photo album.

The study door was slightly ajar, but she knocked out of habit.

"Come in."

She froze at the sound of his voice, recognizing the tone, but not the slurred speech. When she'd left for Montgomery, the doctors were promising a fast recovery. Maybe it just hadn't been fast enough. Bracing herself, she pushed the door open and stepped over the threshold, determined to deal with whatever greeted her inside.

Hank looked small, hunched in a wheelchair, but more than that, he looked frail, exhausted, and worn, nothing at all like the vibrant man in the pictures lining the hallway. Diane's words flooded her mind. Hank hadn't returned to work yet and he might not ever.

"West, it's good to see you. Come in."

She understood him, but only because she'd known him for years and knew the natural cadence of his voice. A stranger would probably have a much harder time ciphering through the slur caused by the paralysis on the left side of his face. She met his eyes. He knew exactly what she was thinking, and the last thing he would want was her sympathy. She walked over to the desk, using the length of her steps to search for levity. "Oh, this is pretty handy. Now you can say mean and nasty things about the attorneys appearing before you and they won't report you because they're not even sure what you said. Right?"

Hank laughed, and half of his face smiled weakly while the other half remained still and devoid of affect. For the first time since May, when she'd ridden in the ambulance with sirens blaring, her gut twisted at how close she'd come to losing him. She reached around his chair and pulled him into a tight hug, hoping the unusual gesture wouldn't send his heart into arrhythmia. The embrace lasted several seconds before she was satisfied her fears were no longer real.

"Sit," he said, waving his good arm toward the couch near his desk. "How was your summer?"

Unable to imagine engaging in small talk while the big question loomed over them, West said, "I will, but first I have to ask. Are you really back at work?"

"No."

One simple word, but it changed everything. She'd come back to Dallas for the clerkship. She'd found a place to live and abandoned other possibilities, all for a job that apparently wasn't hers anymore, but the thing that mattered most was Hank hadn't told her before now. Anger bubbled up, and she breathed deep to keep from giving in to its tempting pull. "I'm assuming you just found out or you would've let me know. Right?"

Hank had the decency to meet her stare head on, but he didn't sugarcoat his words. "Known for a while. Chose not to tell you."

"Because you knew I wouldn't come back."

"Yes."

"And now there's apparently no job to come back to." She shook her head, no longer bothering to hold back her aggravation. "I was first in my class. I could work anywhere."

He started to answer, but the sounds that came out were less and less like words. He pointed at the laptop in front of him and began pecking at it with his right forefinger. He jabbed at the screen, and she turned it so she could read his response. *Sure, you could. Are you ready to take one of those fancy big firm offers? In one year, you'll make five times what you'd make at a nonprofit.*

"I don't care about the money. I had a great internship this summer. I could've stayed there."

He tapped out more words. *Were they even hiring?*

West could tell he already knew the answer. "That's not the point. Even if they aren't, there are other places. Now, I'm behind the curve and I'm going to have to hope my roommate will let me slide on the first month's rent until I find a new job."

You don't have to do that.

"I'm not taking your money."

I'm not offering. The job is still yours. I've already spoken to my replacement. Nothing has to change.

"Oh, no. I only agreed to this clerkship because you asked. I'm not going to fetch coffee and do research for some brand new federal judge who doesn't know their ass from a hole in the ground."

Hank chuckled and then typed a novel. *This one might actually know a thing or two. Our agreement was you'd do the clerkship. One year. That was our deal and I'm holding you to it. Yes, I planned for you to be my clerk, but that wasn't the most important thing for me. This clerkship will open doors for you that your stellar grades won't. You want to change the world? You need to see how it works first.*

"I know how the world works. I've had plenty of experience."

Hank nodded. *Yes, you have, and I'm not trying to minimize everything you've been through, but the more you learn the judicial system from inside, the better equipped you will be to make it work for you. Trust me, I know what I'm talking about.*

She did trust him, as much as she trusted anyone, but she couldn't help but feel ambushed by this news. "Who's the new judge?"

Camille Avery. She was a state court judge in Collin County.

"Interesting. Does she have any federal experience at all?"

Matter of fact, she does. Right out of law school she worked for the solicitor general's office, under Addison Riley.

"The Addison Riley who's now chief justice of the Supreme Court?"

One and the same. After Avery worked in DC, she moved back here and worked as an AUSA for a while in the Eastern District. Her family has a lot of connections and she ran for and won a state court bench on her first try.

"Her family must have a lot of connections if she got confirmed so quickly."

Avery had already started the interview process to become a magistrate, so Senator Armstrong fast-tracked her into my seat. I just met her. Judge Avery is sharp, personable, and immensely qualified.

"You just met her?" West thought about the woman she'd given her card to not more than fifteen minutes earlier. "Here? Tall, brunette, legs for days?"

Hank narrowed his eyes and nodded.

"I think I may have just asked your replacement on a date. She was getting in her car when I got here."

"Lovely." He spoke the one word and then typed. *Please tell me she managed to resist your charms.*

"Jury's out on that one, Judge. Seriously, if those are the kind of judges the Senate is confirming these days, sign me up to clerk for a few more years."

Hank typed even faster now. *Good thing I know you're all talk. Promise me you won't hit on your employer anymore. She's going to make a good jurist, and I imagine she has her sights set on more for the future, so she'll need good, solid clerks to help her along the way.* He wagged a wavering finger. "That's your job. Understood?"

She hung her head in mock dejection. "Understood."

He grinned. "But you're right. Her family connections probably didn't hurt."

West nodded. She knew all about family connections, but not from personal experience. Many of her less qualified law school classmates had landed cush jobs due to the influence of wealthy and powerful relatives. Most of them thought she was just like them, taking advantage of her relationship with Hank to land a coveted clerkship. Little did they know, she dreaded a year of being a lackey when she could be out in the real world making a difference with her degree. Now that Hank wasn't going to be her boss, she dreaded it even more.

It's important to me that you do this. Hank typed as if reading her mind. *Now more than ever. It would mean a lot to me for someone I know to carry on my legacy. At least for a little while.*

West rolled over her options. She could find another job or fulfill the promise she made, but there really wasn't a choice. Her own dreams could wait. She owed him this.

CHAPTER THREE

Monday morning Camille rushed through the lobby of the Adolphus Hotel toward the Bistro. The maître d' held up a hand while he spoke to the two people standing in front of her examining the menu. Camille looked over her shoulder and said, "Never mind, I see them." Ignoring his fluster, she strode through the restaurant to the table where her parents were waiting. "Sorry, I'm late. Parking downtown is a nightmare."

Her mother motioned to the empty seat, and her father glanced up from the bound set of documents in his hand. "Not a problem," he said. "We've got an expert witness hearing over at the George Allen building and we used the extra time to prepare."

Camille hovered for a second by the empty chair. Years of experience taught her he didn't mean anything by the remark, but it still stung that both of her parents always put work first. Roger and Nancy Avery had built an empire specializing in toxic tort litigation, but empire-building came at a cost, and their family had paid the price. Camille thought about her older brother and wondered, not for the first time, if his death had indirectly been a result of being virtually abandoned by over-achieving parents who couldn't summon compassion for their drug-addicted son. She'd expected her own devastating election loss would impact their view of her, but meeting here, steps away from the courthouse, on the morning of her first day as a federal judge, had been their idea not hers, so she decided to stick around and make the most of the rare familial outreach. "Have you ordered?"

"Just fruit and yogurt for me," her mother said, patting her waist. "And oatmeal for your dad. Doctor says his ticker isn't what it used to be."

Camille nodded, certain her father's health report had more to do with the stress level of his job than his physical condition. Both of her parents were in perfect shape. They'd probably been halfway through a rigorous spin class before her alarm had gone off this morning. Their obsession wasn't genetic. She was all for good physical fitness, but she wasn't crazy about it, preferring recreational exercise like hikes and kayaking to the close, sweaty quarters of a gym. When the waiter came, she stubbornly ordered bacon and eggs, ignoring her mother's raised eyebrows.

"Where did you park?" her mother asked.

"After driving around and around, I decided to valet here."

"You'd think they'd have a spot for you somewhere at the courthouse."

"They probably do. I'm sure there's some secret judge's lot somewhere that I'll find out about today." Camille took a sip of her coffee. The whole summer had been a whirlwind, from the phone call the week after Judge Blair's collapse to the speedy confirmation. She'd barely had time to register the fact she was about to assume a seat in the federal judiciary. Little details about where to park and whether there was a secret entrance in the building seemed unimportant. She'd do like she always did—show up and act like she knew what she was doing until she figured it out. In the meantime, she'd try to enjoy breakfast with her parents whom she barely saw anymore.

Once everyone started eating, she said, "I can't remember the last time we shared a meal together." She took a bite of bacon. "Actually, I do. It was a year ago. At Uncle Randy's wedding," she said, referring to her father's brother.

"That was quite a spread," her father said, looking up from his papers and oatmeal. "My brother's wife knows how to throw a party."

Camille ignored the sarcastic remark. Her father had never approved of what he dubbed his younger brother's irresponsible choices—throwing away his law degree to become an author and marrying a woman half his age. "I was thinking of having a dinner party soon. Us, Randy and Evelyn, and maybe a few others. Nothing too fancy, just a smallish celebration."

"Oh dear, we'll actually be traveling a lot in the next month, and that's why we asked you here this morning," her mother said, raising her glass of grapefruit juice. "Congratulations, to the first federal judge in the family."

Camille looked over at her father, who absentmindedly raised his glass in response to her mother's toast. She hadn't expected any kind of celebration really, but somehow this afterthought of a breakfast seemed like a waste of time for all of them. It was clear her father would rather be working and her mother was only trying to placate. She didn't need parental approval or praise. Their connections might have gotten her the initial interview, but it was her experience and hard work that had closed the deal. Let them go to dinner parties and professional conferences and brag about their daughter the judge. In the meantime, she'd celebrate with people who truly appreciated how far she'd come and the sacrifices she'd made to achieve this success. Every step forward, up the ladder, would be her own.

She left her car at the valet stand and walked the two blocks to the courthouse. There might indeed be some secret entrance, but today, she'd walk through the front doors and pass through security exactly as she had when she'd come here back in May, looking for a spot as a magistrate judge. No one knew her today, but she was determined that in a few years, everyone would know her name.

❖

West poured hot water over the grounds in the French press and gave the mixture a strong stir. Three more minutes and she'd have a perfect cup of coffee. She was counting on it since good coffee might be the only good thing to come from her first day of work at the courthouse.

"Is that what you're going to wear?"

Her best friend, Bill, stood in the doorway to the kitchen of their apartment. Or rather Bill's apartment that he'd graciously allowed her to crash in until she found a place of her own. She and Bill had attended Berkeley Law and had gravitated to each other by virtue of having both grown up in Dallas. Bill had graduated a year before her and moved back to Texas to work for the regional office for Lambda Legal. When she'd found out there was no chance she'd be staying on at the Center, she'd reached out to Bill, and he'd generously offered to let her bunk with him for the year she'd be in town. In the course of moving she hadn't thought much about whether she'd need new clothes for the job. "What's wrong with what I'm wearing?"

Bill shook his head. "If you have to ask, then you might be beyond help."

West looked down at her outfit—rust oxfords, tan chinos, a sky blue and pale green plaid shirt, and a Wembley tie she'd found in a fifty-cent box at a garage sale. She gestured the length of the tie. "Uh, this is vintage."

"That's code for I bought it at a thrift store. You're going to federal court, not federal prison," Bill said, as he rummaged through the fridge. "Is there any milk left for cereal?"

West answered his question by flipping him off. She'd dressed as conservatively as she could stomach, and she'd much rather be sporting jeans, Chucks, and a T-shirt. What she had on would have to do. She'd promised to work the job, but she wasn't going to let it work her.

"So, tell me about this new judge. What's she like?"

"I don't know much about her other than what I could find on the Internet. She worked for Justice Riley a long time ago, did a stint with the US Attorney's office up in Plano, and she was a state court judge."

"Who got voted out of office after that guy she let slide killed a little girl. How in the hell did she get a federal bench?"

West shrugged. "Hank likes her and insists I will too. I guess we'll see."

"She sounds like she's been around a while. Old gal?"

"Not even close. Late thirties, forty tops. And she's pretty hot."

Bill jabbed her in the shoulder. "And here you were acting like you've never met her. Or did you just find a pinup photo online?"

"No, I've met her, but it was before anyone knew she'd…it was before Hank went into the hospital. It was that day in fact. I helped her get through security at the courthouse. She was downtown interviewing for a magistrate position the day Hank collapsed. And then I saw her on Friday at the Blairs' house. Guess he was passing the torch."

"What's she like?"

West considered the question. She didn't have anything concrete to say, but her gut told her under other circumstances, Camille might be a fun date. A little uptight, a bit slow to unwind, but when she let her hair down…For a few seconds, West imagined Camille's silky brunette waves fanned out across her chest and sucked in a breath while searching for the vaguest possible answer to Bill's question. "She seems nice."

"Nice? I saw that look in your eye. Nice doesn't even begin to cover what you were thinking just now."

"Lay off, perv," she said, swatting at his arm. "She's my new boss. Full stop."

"In your world maybe. Now I'm just thinking about whether she's wearing any clothes under that robe."

West drank the last of her coffee and put the cup in the sink. "I'm outta here. See you later."

The courthouse was close, but not close enough to walk to in the oppressive Dallas heat that lingered late into August. After circling the main downtown streets a few times, West finally managed to squeeze her Jeep into one of the last spots in a pay lot several blocks from the courthouse. The lot was tucked between two buildings on the east side of downtown that used to be more warehouse and less office space. Things had changed. She spotted several signs of gentrification, from imposing three-story townhouses to a farmer's market that boasted more restaurants than fruit stalls. The only thing that hadn't changed was the number of homeless people present on the streets. Some were curled on curbs, leaning against buildings, but some were entrepreneurs, offering an array of services to earn a buck.

"Wash your windows while you're working? Pay me what you think is fair."

West appraised the tall, lanky man who'd appeared out of nowhere and immediately pegged him as one of the homeless. Even at ten feet away, she smelled the sour stench of sweat and his stained and tattered clothes only bolstered her conclusion. His eyes were tired, but kind. How long had he been on the street, begging for work just to scrape by? She reached for her wallet, pulled out a five, and held it out to him. "The windows are pretty dirty, but I don't have a lot of cash on me." She grimaced as she spoke the last phrase, recognizing it all too well for the common excuse of the pedestrian accosted by the homeless. "I'm starting a new job today, and I can give you more when I get my first check."

"This is more than enough."

The man's smile was gentle and absolving, but it didn't diminish the guilt that her life had taken a different path than his. "It's not nearly enough. Thank you." She hurried off before he could say another word. The encounter stirred too many memories, and the first day of a new job wasn't the time to dwell on a past better off forgotten.

Early, but not too early to appear eager, she breezed through security and rode the elevator to the sixth floor where Peter greeted her with a big grin.

"First day?" he said. "Guess I'll be seeing a ton of you this year."

"Guess you're right." She reached into her back pocket for her wallet and set it and her phone on Peter's desk. "Don't have a bar card yet. You want to keep my phone?"

"Don't be silly. You're family." He waved her through the metal detector. "You know, I was a little surprised you were going to be here, considering…"

West picked up her stuff and jammed it back in her pockets. "Me too, but it's pretty hard to break a promise to Judge Blair. He's not big on the whole 'circumstances have changed' excuse."

"Well, you tell him we all wish him well. He's a great man, and we miss him around here."

"I will. Have you seen Judge Avery yet this morning?"

"She got here about fifteen minutes ago, along with her other clerk. You know him?"

"Nope."

"Name's Lloyd. Word is he's on loan from Judge Stroud. Seems like a bit of a pain if you ask me, but I'll let you make your own decision."

"Thanks, Peter. You have a great day."

West walked down the quiet hall, taking her time. She tried her best to arrive exactly on time, but she was ten minutes early. The idea of going into Hank's chambers and not seeing him there made her gut clench, but it was inevitable. After taking a deep breath, she tugged open the door and walked into the new world.

"Hi, West," the regal, sixty-something, African-American woman behind the desk called out. "You're early."

"Not on purpose." West smiled to soften the words. "Hi, Ester. Is Judge Avery in?"

"She's been here for an hour. New guy's here too." Ester jerked her head back toward the door behind her. "Go on in."

West looked at the door and mentally chanted the refrain she'd adopted to calm her unease. *Only a year. Only a year.* She could do anything for a short period of time, and as much as she didn't want to admit it, Hank had some good points. Working from chambers would give her insights into the judicial system she could leverage to get the kind of job she really wanted in the public sector. She straightened her tie and knocked on the door.

"Come in," a voice called out.

Camille Avery was seated behind the desk. If she was surprised to see West, she hid it behind a brief but knowing smile. West shot a look at the guy in the three-piece suit—who wore those, anyway—seated in front of Camille's desk and then nodded at Camille. "Good morning, Judge."

"Good morning, West. Have a seat. Have you met Lloyd?"

West slid into the seat next to three-piece Lloyd. "I haven't."

He stuck out his hand. "Lloyd Garber. Northwestern."

She stared at his hand for a minute, trying to decide if this guy was for real. When he didn't flinch, she shook his hand. "West Fallon. Nice to meet you."

"Now that you're both here," Camille said, her expression all business, "Let's get a few things out in the open. First of all, in case you weren't aware, this is my first day on the bench. I'm ready to hit the ground running and I hope you are too. We don't have a morning docket today, but the afternoon is full, and the first thing I'd like you to do is prepare a one-page memo to brief me on each of the matters scheduled for this afternoon's docket. When you're done with that, I'd like to start going through the rest of the current caseload and triage any cases needing attention. Some other judges have been filling in to decide pending matters since May, but there might be some motions still lingering and we'll need to reset any trial dates that were set over the summer. It'll probably take us a few weeks to get things running smoothly. Any questions?"

Lloyd raised his hand. West barely suppressed a laugh when she caught Camille trying hard not to roll her eyes. "What's your question, Lloyd?" Camille asked.

"Do you have some kind of template you'd like us to use for the memos? Maybe something you've had clerks use in the past. Judge Stroud hasn't had us write any memos yet."

"Short answer is no, I don't," Camille said. "Longer answer is that I'm new at this job, but I have done your job before, and I can tell you that wherever you work—judicial clerk or associate in a firm, big or small—brevity is always appreciated as long as you cover the salient points. Make sense?"

Lloyd nodded, but West wasn't sure he understood he'd need to start thinking for himself. Whatever he thought, she respected Camille's ability to get right to the point. She rose to follow Lloyd out of the room, but Camille stopped her. "West, do you mind sticking around for a minute? I need to ask you something."

She faced Camille and studiously ignored Lloyd's curious gaze. When the door finally closed behind Lloyd, Camille motioned for her to sit down again. "Nice to see you again," West said, keeping her tone even.

Camille nodded. "Nice to see you too. Circumstances have certainly changed, haven't they?"

"I suppose. I mean, I would still ask you out again. Nothing's changed about that, but I guess you decided not to use the number I gave you, so it doesn't seem like a winning proposition."

"Seemed a little inappropriate once I figured out you were going to be working for me."

West wondered when that had happened and then she realized Camille must've made the connection after she'd given her the card with her name on it outside of Hank's house. "So, you would've called?"

Camille rushed to answer. "I didn't say that."

"You're not going to tell me, are you?"

"We shouldn't be having this conversation."

West offered an exaggerated nod. "I get it. We should be all WASPY and ignore our feelings?"

"I don't have feelings." Camille scrambled to clarify. "I mean, of course, I have feelings, just not about you."

"Well, that sounded downright mean."

Camille cleared her throat. "I think you know that's not how I meant it. I just want to be clear now that we have a professional relationship, nothing that happened or might have happened before matters. Are we clear?"

West watched Camille's face for signs of her true feelings. She was obviously a tad flustered, but that could be attributed to first day jitters, but she suspected it was more than that. Camille was attracted to her. West wasn't entirely sure why she cared at this point since they couldn't do anything about it now. Maybe she just wanted to know, as if knowing would give her some kind of satisfaction, some kind of power.

"Oh, we're clear all right." West stood. "I better join your more experienced clerk before he finishes all the files and makes me look bad. Do you want us in the courtroom for the afternoon docket or would you rather we kept reviewing files?"

Camille looked surprised at the question. "It might be a good idea for one of you to be there. You can decide between you which one shows up."

"Okay." West turned to go, but Camille's voice stopped her.

"Do you mind if I ask how you know Judge Blair?" When West raised her eyebrows, Camille looked away, but kept talking. "It was pretty clear to me from talking to him that you weren't simply a new hire. He seems very interested in your future."

West met Camille's gaze and held it. Camille's expression was earnest, genuine, not predatory, like she was looking for gossip, but telling her the truth would open wounds long closed, though not remote enough to be painless. A moment ago, she'd had fun playing power games with Camille, but now she knew she'd been playing with fire. Camille was her boss for the next year and their every interaction had to be professional or she'd risk more than a reference on her résumé.

In the meantime, Camille was waiting patiently for her answer, so she delivered a response that would be honest, but share nothing. "I met him working on a case years ago and we became friendly. Nothing more to it." She waved as she walked toward the door. "Talk to you later."

She pushed through the door and breathed a sigh of relief when she was finally out of Camille's presence. She had no idea how she was going to make it through a year with Camille Avery and her devastating good looks and probing questions. If she'd known how hard it would be to keep it together, she wasn't sure she would've agreed to take on the job.

❖

Camille watched the door close, and when it clicked shut, she put her head in her hands. Damn. Everything about West distracted her completely. How in the world was she going to make it through the next year with West strutting around, oozing sexuality? And there was more to it than West's good looks. She had a mystery about her, and Camille was anxious to puzzle it out. West's vague detail about how she knew Blair was likely a watered-down version of the truth. She'd seen West's transcript and résumé. She'd graduated top of her class at Berkeley and held some prestigious internships while in school, so she was certainly qualified, but she was vastly different from the stuffy, pedigreed sycophants that often applied for such positions. In addition to the funky clothes and intricate tattoo hiding under West's sleeve, she was a couple of years older than most clerks, and the nonchalant manner suggested a take it or leave it attitude toward the job. She seemed like an edgy choice for a federal clerkship, and she had a strong feeling Blair's hiring of West Fallon was rooted in something deeper than a chance meeting while working on a case. No doubt she'd be able to find out more details from people who'd worked with Blair at the courthouse, but running through the gossip mill on her first day was a bit unseemly. The mystery of West Fallon would have to wait.

The phone on her desk rang. "Judge Avery."

"Judge Avery, Judge Stroud would like to talk to you."

"Thanks, Ester. You can put him through."

"Actually, he's right outside your door. He planned on busting in, but I told him we weren't going to start things that way."

Camille laughed at the protective tone in her secretary's voice. Ester had been with Judge Blair for a long time, and she'd expected it would take a lot longer than half a day to win her over. "Fair enough, but I'm available now, so you can send him in."

After a brief knock on the door, Stroud stuck his head in. "Mind if I come in?"

"Depends on whether you got the all clear from Ester."

Stroud sank into one of the chairs with a glance back toward the closed door. "I have to admit," he whispered, "I'm a little scared of that woman."

"Then I'm very happy to have her on my side." Camille leaned back in her chair. "To what do I owe this visit?"

"First off I want to congratulate you on your swift confirmation. I know Mark Hollis was in contention for the nomination, but Senator Armstrong really went to bat for you."

Despite his friendly smile, Camille heard a slight edge in his voice at the mention of Mark Hollis. Mark was a well-known lawyer in Dallas who'd made no secret he'd had his sights on a federal bench. It was also no secret Mark was an old friend of Stroud's, and she wondered if he wished his pal had been chosen over her, but acknowledging the rift seemed awkward, so she changed the subject. "I'm happy to be here and anxious to get started. You have any advice?"

He looked surprised at the question. "Me? No, you'll do just fine on your own. I came by primarily to make sure you have everything you need. You met West Fallon?"

Camille went on high alert. "I did. She seems very qualified."

"You sound like someone talking about a blind date. What is it they say—the prospect has a nice personality."

Camille squirmed in her seat at the dating reference. She needed to be very careful here. "I might've been a little surprised, that's all. She's not like any of the clerks I've met before."

"True. You won't find many like her. She was one of Blair's special projects," he said, shaking his head. "It was very nice of you to agree to keep her on."

"Actually," Camille said, "I'm not sure I need two clerks. I appreciate the loan, but if you'd like Lloyd back, I'm sure I can manage." She had a feeling Lloyd was going to be more of a drag on her time than helpful with the case load.

"Nonsense." He looked around the room. "This is a nice office."

Camille started to ask another question about West, but the abrupt change in subject signaled now was not the time. "You said primarily."

"Pardon?"

"You were primarily checking in. What else did you need?"

"I wanted to talk to you about your docket. We operate under a random assignment docket. The clerks dole out cases as they come in, but at times, as chief, I exercise my authority to reassign a case."

"O-kay." Camille strung the word out as she tried to figure out where he was headed with this information.

"I'm telling you this because I plan to reassign the Wilson case."

"Any particular reason?" Camille didn't try to hide the note of defensiveness in her voice. It might be her first day here, but she wasn't new to bench politics. When the presiding judge in state court interfered with the usual process of assigning cases, there was usually some implication the assigned judge either wasn't experienced enough or had some bias.

"It's not about you. It's a lightning rod kind of a case and it's set for trial in the next few weeks. You don't need that right off the bat."

"And when will I need that?"

"Excuse me?"

Camille leaned forward. "Barry, if you're trying to protect me, don't. I'm fully aware why I got voted out of office, but I don't regret the decision I made or the attention it generated. I hate publicity as much as the next person, but it's part of the deal. There will never be a time when having my judgment questioned in public is convenient. If you're going to pull this case from me now, at what point will you decide I'm ready to handle hot-button cases? And do you baby all the new judges or just the ones whose parents you vacation with?"

Stroud shifted in his chair. "Truth is we haven't had a new judge in a while."

"What kind of case is it?"

"Criminal. Drug counts, but one of them is a lifer."

"Well, I'd prefer if you'd treat me like everyone else. If it were a complex patent law case, I'd understand you wanting to reassign it until I had a little more experience, but I've handled plenty of drug cases and quite a few capital cases in state court, not to mention my time as an AUSA. You can safely assume I know what I'm doing. Okay?"

Stroud crossed his arms and frowned, but he apparently saw the logic in her words. "Okay, but come to me if you need anything."

"I will, but right now the kind of things I need are the password to the secret lounge and the code for the secret door."

Stroud laughed. "Ester will fill you in. She knows more about the ins and outs of this place than anyone else here." He stood up. "Would you like to join me for lunch?"

"Thanks for the invite, but I think I'd rather get settled in. Rain check?"

"I'll round up some of the other judges," he lowered his voice, "the ones I like, and we'll make a plan for later in the week." He walked through the door, calling out, "Have a great day!" over his shoulder.

Camille watched him go. She wished she knew what to ask him, but the truth was until she started digging into the case files, she didn't have a clue what she didn't know. Maybe when she got the memos back from Lloyd and West, she'd have a better handle on what she would be facing over the next few months.

West. Every thought circled back to her. Crazy really. Maybe she just needed a date. She'd had lots of offers and plenty of time to date after she was booted out of office last November, but other than her regular Sunday brunch with friends, an active social life had been at the bottom of her list of to-dos. Besides, first date conversations inevitably turned to topics that included career, a total non-starter for an unemployed judge whose only real prospect at the time had been work at her parents' firm.

But now she was a federal judge and she could hold her head high. Once she settled in, she could venture out and meet other eligible professional woman, maybe even one who wasn't an attorney. In the meantime, she needed to learn her way around the courthouse if she was going to fit in. She pressed the button labeled Ester on her phone and asked her to come in. The almost immediate knock on the door left her wondering if Ester had ESP.

"Come in. Have a seat. I need your help."

"Sure, Judge, whatever you need."

Camille didn't bother asking her to use her first name. Ester had worked at the courthouse most of her adult life and the title would be ingrained in her, but Camille vowed to break the ice in some other ways. "The list is long, but first I wanted to tell you I'm very sorry Judge Blair had to retire so suddenly."

"Thank you. We worked together for a very long time."

"And I know he valued your service. I'm sure I will too. There are a lot of things I need help with, and I'm depending on you to be my right hand."

"Whatever you need to know."

"For starters is there a special place I can park, and where can I get something good to eat around here?"

"Great questions. There's a cafe on the sixth floor, creatively named Cafe on Six. I can always get you food from there, but beware going in yourself because it'll be open season for attorneys to bug you with questions. A lot of the judges eat at the Adolphus down the street. I also have a list of places that deliver. Whatever you need, I can get it for you."

Ester's generous desire to be helpful spurred Camille to ask one of the questions she really wanted to know. "Do you happen to know when Judge Blair hired West Fallon? I couldn't help but notice you two seem very familiar."

The second West's name was mentioned, Ester's expression changed, closed off. "They've known each other a very long time. I think it was always assumed West would clerk for him when she graduated."

Camille wanted to fish for more information, but this was too obvious, too direct. Her obsession with the details about West wasn't becoming. West was well qualified for the job and it was none of her business if some sort of nepotism had led Blair to make her keep his promise to hire her. Camille vowed to let the topic go.

"Now, about that parking space."

Chapter Four

West shot a look at Lloyd who was completely consumed with a huge stack of pleadings in the file in front of him. He skimmed each page, sometimes thumbing back to reread a section. At the rate he was going, his one-page memo would be done in a week. She scanned the file in front of her and considered whether it was better to let him do things his way or throw him a lifeline. Unable to stand it any longer, she spoke up.

"I have a feeling she only needs a quick summary of whatever motions are on the docket today," she said, injecting her voice with what she hoped was a cheerful, I just want to help you out tone. "There should be a docket sheet from PACER in the front of each file." She reached over to point out the docket sheet from the e-filing system that listed all the pleadings that had been filed in the case, but Lloyd yanked the file closer to him.

"I'm good. I have been doing this longer than you." His voice was clipped and defensive.

"Sure. Fine." West shrugged and turned back to her own file. His loss if Camille wondered why in the hell he'd written one memo to her six. She dug back into the pleadings in the file in front of her. The case was pretty straightforward: felon in possession of a firearm. The defendant had been pulled over by a Mesquite police officer for making an illegal lane change. The hearing today was on the defendant's motion to suppress the subsequent search of his car based on his contention that not only did the officer stop him without cause, but also that the officer had no right to search his car. West had been to several suppression hearings during her time in the criminal law clinic at Berkeley, and she was up to speed on what to expect. The burden was first on the defense to rebut the presumption that the police acted properly without a warrant, and then the burden shifted to the government to show the search and seizure of evidence was reasonable. Camille probably knew the law on the subject, but West typed a quick summary of the motion and response, and included a bullet-point list of the things each side would need to show in order to prevail. In her opinion, the defense should win this one—illegal lane change was a pretty lame excuse for pulling someone over with lights and sirens, but ultimately the law was on the side of the government. No one asked for her opinion so she didn't go there in the memo.

She was on her fourth file when the door to their office swung open. Camille stood framed in the doorway, her hands on her hips and a smile on her face. "Who's hungry?"

West avoided the temptation to offer up a smart remark and looked at the time on her phone, surprised to see it was twelve thirty already. The afternoon docket started at two thirty, and Lloyd was only on his second file. "Is that a rhetorical question?"

"I'm starved," Lloyd said.

"Let's grab some lunch," Camille said. "I've just discovered the cafeteria and performed reconnaissance. Word is the food is good and fast. We can talk about the memos you have done so far while we eat."

Lloyd looked down at the files and back at Camille who shook her finger at him. "Come on. I'm not a big fan of skipping meals. Makes me grouchy. West?"

West closed the file in front of her. "Sure, I could eat."

The Cafe on Six served simple food from short order burgers and fries to a few home-style specials that rotated throughout the week like chicken fried steak and meatloaf. West grabbed a bottle of Coke from the drink cooler and joined Camille and Lloyd at the counter.

"West Fallon, as I live and breathe!"

West cringed at the sound of her name, but then quickly plastered on what she hoped was a happy smile for the elderly man in an apron behind the counter. "Sam, good to see you. How have you been?"

"Can't complain. My granddaughter just started college, and here you are all graduated from law school. Can you believe it?"

"Not even." The first time West met Sam, she'd been a surly teenager. Hank had brought her to watch a trial, and at the lunch break, he'd taken her to the Cafe and told her she could order anything she wanted. Sam had made a show of telling her all about his special of the day, but she'd turned up her nose at everything and insisted on a grilled cheese sandwich. Every time she'd returned after that, he made her a grilled cheese without her even asking until it became a joke between them.

"I put your sandwich on the grill when I spotted you come in the door. What are your friends having?"

West avoided making eye contact with Camille, but she could sense her intense focus. Unable to put it off any longer, she looked directly into her eyes. "I'm betting the judge here would like a salad, but she might be convinced to have the special if you want to tell her all about it." Her plan worked, and Camille was forced to refocus her attention on Sam as he rattled off details about the chicken fried chicken with mashed potatoes and green beans.

"Did you intern here during school?"

West turned to face Lloyd who was staring at her with a curious expression. "What?"

"I just wondered if you worked here before since this guy seems to know you so well."

West started to answer, but Camille had finished ordering and had tuned in to their conversation. She settled on a flip reply. "Best grilled cheese in Dallas. Can you blame me for being a regular? What are you having?"

Lloyd squinted like he was trying to figure out her angle, but then he ordered a burger and dropped the questioning. Camille insisted on paying, and a few minutes later they were all settled at a table in the corner of the lunchroom. They were about halfway through their food, when Camille started asking questions. "West, Lloyd applied for this job because he has family here in Dallas. How about you?"

She chewed slower while she pondered an answer. Her first impulse was to ask if Camille was curious if she had family here in Dallas, but Camille was really trying to figure out her motivation for clerking. Personal obligation seemed too flip of an answer and too personal considering the circumstances. The bite of grilled cheese was long gone when she settled on a simple, "Just fulfilling a promise."

Camille nodded like she understood, but her eyes reflected curiosity. Her questions would go unanswered, especially now that their roles were defined. Employer, employee. Judge, clerk. West couldn't deny the simmer of attraction between them, but what had been a mild flirtation at their first couple of encounters would never have a chance to flourish. No personal conversation, no sharing of any kind beyond what was necessary to get through the work.

Too bad because Camille looked like she could use a fun time. From what West had read online, she'd been pilloried in the press for a poor, in retrospect, sentencing decision last year, and it had cost her the state bench she'd worked hard to win. She'd suffered a crushing loss in conservative Collin County, and it was actually pretty amazing she'd managed to get this appointment within a year of such a huge professional setback. West wanted to ask Camille about her roller coaster career ride, but feared doing so would leave her open to personal questions she had no desire to answer. Besides, what was the point? Nothing about their relationship had any chance of being anything other than professional, and it was best to keep their exchanges limited to conversations about case facts and the law.

She tuned back in to Lloyd using Camille's reference to his family to tell her how important they were.

"Dad's firm represented the CEO of Tasum Pharmaceuticals in their product liability case this past summer, you may have heard about the case. Judge Avery, I think your parents might have represented one of the parties. It was very complex litigation."

West looked over at Camille, and she swore she rolled her eyes for just a second. She stifled a laugh and took another bite of her sandwich.

"It's possible, Lloyd," Camille said. "I don't keep up with all of my parents' clients, but they're often involved in headline cases." She reached into her bag and pulled out a notebook. "So, tell me about this afternoon's docket."

Lloyd sucked in a breath. "I didn't realize you were going to want to talk about the docket right now. I left my memos upstairs."

Camille shot another look at West, and West caught the sparkle in her eyes. "I'm not looking for a treatise. Just give me a quick rundown."

Lloyd scrambled until she couldn't bear to witness his discomfort any longer and stepped in. "Nothing too hairy. Out of the seven cases, only two are substantive motion hearings, both motions to suppress, and the issues are well briefed. I imagine each side will probably call no more than a witness each. The rest of the cases are procedural matters, bond issues, change of plea, etc."

Camille steepled her fingers. "I'll take the procedural stuff first, so those folks don't have to sit through the rest. West, do you mind ordering the docket for me? Simplest case first, etc. There's one more case to add. The file's on my desk. I'll hear it last."

"Sure. You're going to be popular."

"Not my goal, but I don't mind doing what I can to make sure everyone has a good day."

Smart, charming, and thoughtful. Damn, why did Camille have to be so likable? West shoved her now empty plate aside and stood. "Thanks. I'll let the bailiff know the order. Lloyd, let's head back up and order the cases." She didn't wait for him to answer before moving toward the door. Distance was the only way she was going to survive this gig.

❖

Halfway through the docket, Camille wished she'd had the foresight to load up on caffeine. Several sets of lawyers arguing over procedural details like juror questionnaires and discovery requests made for a total snoozefest, made worse by their insistent and whiny voices in an oppressively quiet room unlike in state court where most hearings were conducted with the lawyers standing at the bench while the regular docket activity—negotiations, arguments, and routine scheduling—rolled on throughout the rest of the courtroom. Unable to bear the endless stream of one-upmanship, Camille finally asked counsel to step outside and work out an agreement or she would impose a compromise likely to make neither side happy.

The truth was she was eager to get to the last case, the one Stroud had angled to steal from her this morning. She'd skimmed through the entire file after he left this morning, fascinated with the issues. What she found even more interesting was that in the time between lunch and docket call, West had distilled a summary of the case worthy of someone with five times her experience.

Camille had heard of the case. Everyone in the Metroplex had. College co-ed goes missing. After a week of frantic searching, the worst scenario comes true when she's found dead at a construction site two hours away. Cause of death: drug overdose. The local police, working with a federal task force, connected the girl to a known drug dealer in Dallas who had a reputation for selling to the local, affluent college crowd, and they determined he was the last person to see her alive. The indictment charged him with distributing drugs that resulted in her death, and Camille was interested in seeing exactly how the government planned to prove that at trial. Today's hearing was a pretrial check-in that had been set by Stroud, presumably to see if there were looming issues before the final pretrial hearing set for a couple of weeks out.

Camille looked at the last attorneys in the courtroom and back at the names on the docket. She recognized the defense attorney. Sylvia Naylor hailed from a well-known firm in town that handled both state and federal cases, and she was accompanied by a young male associate from her firm. Seated next to them was a forty-something-year-old black male dressed in the orange jumpsuit that was standard pretrial attire for federal prisoners. The three young male AUSAs were strangers to her, an unusual role for them since AUSAs often became quite chummy with the judges whose courts they appeared in regularly. With a glance at West and Lloyd who were seated in the jury box, Camille called the case styled *United States vs. Darryl Wilson.*

"Counsel, I see we have a trial date set two weeks from today and a pretrial hearing the week before. Are you all on track to proceed as scheduled?"

One of the three AUSAs stood. "Your Honor, I'm Kyle Merrin and I'm appearing with co-counsel, Andrew Wallen and Noah Frankel." He waved a hand at the two other attorneys seated at his table. "It's a pleasure to meet you." Niceties out of the way, he shuffled from one foot to the other before finally spitting out his question. "Are you planning on keeping this case?"

Camille admired his bluntness, but she couldn't help but wonder if he had some ulterior motive for asking. "I believe I've been hired to handle all the cases that have been or will be assigned to this court. Is there any particular reason I shouldn't start with this one?"

Merrin exchanged glances with his colleagues and then raised his shoulders slightly as if to say "oh well." He pulled a sheaf of papers from the folder in front of him. "Absolutely not, Your Honor." He held up the papers. "May I approach to submit some material to the court?"

Camille started to say yes, but had the distinct feeling she was being ambushed. She settled on an alternative. "I'd prefer if you just told me whatever it is you have to say. I don't see any pending motions in the file, but if you have something you'd like me to review, you can give it to one of my clerks and they'll be happy to provide me with a summary. West?"

West stood and walked over to Merrin and held out her hand. Camille watched, amused, as Merrin seemed to have difficulty releasing his precious documents to someone other than her. It was a hoop and she was making him jump through it for a reason. This guy would probably appear in her courtroom hundreds of times during their tenure here, and she needed to set the tone from the start. Respect for the bench, respect for opposing counsel, respect for the law. "I assume you also made a copy of whatever this is for Ms. Naylor?"

"I did." Merrin took two steps to the side and set a stack of papers on the defense table. "We are in the process of compiling a motion, but because of the complexity of the issues, we wanted to go ahead and make the court aware of the nature of our request, and provide some initial research generated by our appellate division, represented here today by Mr. Frankel." He gestured at the guy seated farthest from him. "We plan to have the motion filed by the end of the week, but since its disposition will affect several evidentiary matters, we didn't want to surprise anyone with the substance."

Camille looked over at the defense table where both attorneys had their heads down, poring over the stack of documents Merrin had presented, and then she looked at West who was doing the same. At that moment, West looked up and met her glance. For a second, it was like no one else was present and she was back at the first time they'd met, transfixed by this cocky, self-sure young woman who knew her way around the courthouse better than she did, but then West frowned slightly and shook her head. Taking the look as a caution about seeming too familiar with her clerk, Camille started to jerk her attention back to the attorneys before she realized West was sending her a message about what she'd read. "Let's take five minutes. I'll be right back." She stepped down from the bench before the bailiff finished shouting "All rise," and started back to her chambers, stopping only briefly to signal for West to join her.

Back in her office, she shrugged out of her robe while making a mental note to ask the bailiff if it was possible to adjust the temperature in the courtroom. She hung the robe on the hook by the door and walked toward her desk, spotting a tan interoffice mail envelope centered on her blotter. She sat down and unwound the string fastening the envelope and shook out the contents. One piece of white paper glided gently onto her desk, but the bold, black, block letters were glaring. QUIT NOW WHILE YOU CAN.

The deceptively simple phrase confused her, and she turned over the envelope searching for any clue about the identity of the sender. Nothing. These types of envelopes were usually filled with to/from entries until there was no space left and were retired, but this one was devoid of information. She would've expected Ester would go through her mail before she received it, but they hadn't had a chance to go over procedures. For all she knew this message wasn't even meant for her. Except it had been left in the center of her desk sometime in the last thirty minutes since she'd taken the bench.

She started to pick up the phone and call Ester but was interrupted by a rap on the partially open door. West, her eyes still scanning the documents, stood framed in the doorway with Lloyd towering behind her. Chiding herself for not specifically asking for just West, she set the envelope on top of the mysterious message, and invited them both in, determined not to raise alarms until she had more information.

"Any ideas what the government's up to?" she asked.

West looked up from the papers in her hand. "Yes. They're planning to try a rape case under the guise of a drug case."

"What the hell?" Lloyd had the good sense to look sheepish. "Sorry, Judge."

"It's okay," Camille said, although she couldn't help but wonder what Stroud saw in this guy. "West, you mind explaining?"

West flipped to the middle of the stack of papers, walked over, and shoved them into her hand. For a second, Camille paused to enjoy the quick, light contact before pulling the papers closer. If Lloyd was out of the room, she was certain she'd try to prolong the touch. "What am I looking at?"

West's hand appeared in her sightline, tracing a path along the words on the page until she settled on a paragraph in the middle of the page. "They've charged the defendant with distributing drugs that resulted in Silver's death, but they want to establish that Wilson got close to Silver by introducing evidence he had sex with her, and they're saying it was against her will by using testimony from other women who claimed he raped them. Here, read this."

Camille stared at the words on the page, but they blurred in the face of her distraction. West hovered over her shoulder, making it difficult to focus on anything other than her solid, steady presence, especially in the face of the odd missive she'd just received. But West wasn't here to give her peace of mind; she was here to offer advice. Summoning all her will, Camille forced her focus back to the page and scanned the paragraphs West had pointed out. As she read, her gut churned with the knowledge this case was about to morph into much more than a straightforward drug case. She flipped through the remaining pages, thankful for a well-honed ability to quickly digest information. "If I read this correctly, the government wants a preliminary ruling on the admissibility of evidence?"

"Yes," West said. "I guess their only redeeming grace is they didn't try to surprise the defense with this evidence at trial. Although I suppose the defense had some notice. There's a motion in the file from last spring about the admissibility of some videotapes, but it doesn't go into the content, and the motion was never ruled on before..." She looked toward the ceiling like she was trying to recall a thought, and her face settled into a pained expression. "They were having the hearing the day that H—Judge Blair collapsed. Those videos might be some of the evidence the government's talking about here."

"What's this evidence?" Lloyd asked.

Camille looked over at him, having almost forgotten he was still in the room. "Tell him."

"In addition to the government having at least half a dozen women who will testify they believe they were raped by Mr. Wilson. They also have video of Wilson having sex with some of these women."

"You're kidding."

"About which part?" West asked. "Basically, they want the jury to hear all of this because they think it'll make it more likely they'll believe he murdered her, you know, because he's a big, black rapist." She didn't try to hide the sarcasm from her tone. "I'm willing to bet every one of these so-called witnesses is a rich, white college student."

Camille had the exact same thought, but she was trying to keep an open mind. The defendant's manner had seemed more gregarious than menacing, but it wouldn't be the first time the government tried to play on jurors' fears. While she wanted to echo West's worry, she was walking a very fine line here, and it was crucial that she appear neutral, even when she wasn't. She made a snap decision. "We're going to go back out and set this for a hearing. I'll want the defense response by the end of the week. In the meantime, I want a thorough memo from you on the applicable law. Plus, go ahead and pull anything you can find on the defendant's history. Are charges pending related to any of these allegations or is this the first time they've come to light? Pull the pretrial officer's report. Finally, what's going on in the press? I'd be surprised if none of these allegations had seen the light of day."

Lloyd looked at West and then back at her. "Who do you want to write the memo?"

Camille started to say West. She was already impressed with her work and it was only the first day, but she wasn't certain her motivation was solely work-related. Guarding against any impulse that could tank her reputation before she'd had a chance to form one, she waved a hand in the air like it made no difference to her. "Toss a coin. Write it together. Whatever. Just have it on my desk by Wednesday morning."

She barely had the words out of her mouth before they started to leave, but she stopped them before they reached the door. "Did either of you leave this for me?" She held up the envelope but kept the message beneath covered with her hand. Both of them shook their heads, and she saw nothing in their eyes that gave her pause. When she finished in court, she'd notify the marshal's service about the note, but it was probably nothing. Hell, it might not have even been meant for her.

Back in the courtroom, she listened patiently to defense counsel's heated objections to the government's motion, and then announced her decision to schedule the matter for a full hearing to hear both sides. Things were about to get messy, and for a brief moment, she wondered if she'd made the right decision by insisting on keeping this case.

CHAPTER FIVE

"Where's Lloyd?"

West looked up to see Camille framed in the doorway. She hadn't realized Camille was still in the office since everyone else had gone home a couple of hours ago. "Home probably."

"And he doesn't care that you're showing him up by working late?"

West laughed. "I doubt he knows. I walked downstairs with him and then pretended I forgot my car keys."

"Trying to impress me?"

"Is that a trick question?" West leaned back in her chair. It felt odd to be the one sitting comfortably while Camille stood. "Come in and sit down. You're freaking me out with the whole towering over me thing." She watched as Camille strode into the room and slipped into the chair Lloyd had occupied all afternoon, happy she'd chosen to stay.

"You're staring."

Damn. Caught. But Camille didn't sound displeased. "You're much more fun to look at than Lloyd."

"West."

Camille's tone was quiet and held a touch of reproach, but West wasn't buying it. "Is there some reason we can't be honest when no one else is around?"

"Honest?"

"Don't pretend like there isn't something going on here." West waved a finger between them.

"If only it were that easy."

"It's as easy as you make it."

Camille shook her head. "That's a nice thought, but not very realistic." She started to get up. "I'll leave you to what you're doing."

West reached over and placed a hand on her shoulder, and was pleased when Camille didn't pull away. "Wait. Don't go. We can talk about the case if you want. I could use someone to bounce ideas off of."

"Any particular reason you didn't want to do that with Lloyd?"

"I think he views me more as competition than a colleague. Either that or he just doesn't like me. Doesn't really matter to me either way." West instantly felt she'd over-shared. "Anyway, he does his thing, and I do mine."

Camille sat back down. "Tell me what you've got so far."

West moved the file so it was situated between them. "This case would make the perfect hypothetical for a law school exam in Criminal Procedure." She turned to the first tab in the notebook she'd started putting together, conscious of Camille's steady gaze and determined not to let the heavy portent between them interfere with her analysis of the case. "Mr. Wilson has quite the past. He's forty-eight years old, but when he was twenty, he went to the state pen for murder."

"Really? How much time did he serve?"

"Twenty-five years. He was paroled a week before his forty-sixth birthday."

"Some parole officer hasn't been doing a very good job of watching Mr. Wilson."

"That's for sure. Apparently, he reported like a trouper until he was arrested on this case, but he lied about his employment, even showed fake pay stubs. The PO never verified his job situation, never did a home visit. If he had, he would have figured out there was a problem long before Leslie Silver went missing."

Camille pushed the file away. "I'm not sure I want to get too heavily into the facts. That's for the jury."

"I hear you, but you're probably going to have to make more evidentiary rulings in this case than most, and a lot of the issues are fact dependent."

"You think the government is going to try to get in evidence of his prior conviction? I don't see how they can unless he takes the stand, and he'd be a fool if he did."

"True, but I do think they are going to try to get in evidence of a bunch of bad acts, and not just the rape allegations."

"What else is there?"

"Years ago, just before he was involved in the shooting that led to his arrest for murder in Texas, he was charged with murder in Michigan. Nasty case, but he wasn't arrested until the Texas case, so Michigan opted to let him be tried here first."

"What happened with the Michigan case?"

"Flood at police headquarters. They lost a bunch of evidence including the DNA that tied Wilson to the murder. The loss pretty much decimated their case."

"So he served his time here and Michigan let it go?"

"Exactly."

"So, tell me why I need to know all this?"

"Context." West pushed back from the table, stood, and began pacing the room. "The government is out for blood on this guy. He murdered someone and walked out of prison with half a life ahead of him. They allege he murdered someone else and the evidence was destroyed. Now they think he's a rapist, but they can't make the charges stick, and a young, rich co-ed who was last seen alive at his house shows up dead. They know deep in their sincere little law-abiding hearts that he had something to do with her death, but they also know they don't have enough evidence to charge him with murder again, so they'll do everything they can to stick him with the most time they can. If he's found guilty in this case, the max is life and you'll be the one deciding punishment, not a jury. So if nothing else, they are trying to sway you, early and often, to convince you to throw the book at him."

West stopped talking, certain she'd probably overstepped. Camille didn't say anything at first, instead she reached over and started flipping through the file.

"You've gotten a lot done on your first day."

"I guess so," West said, feeling a little silly about grandstanding.

"I might be a little impressed. Did you really take all this in today or did you already know about this case?"

West flashed back to the day she'd met Camille. The day Hank had collapsed. "I was here watching the last time Wilson was in court." She paused. "It was the day we first met."

Camille's eyes lit up. "I remember. I was here to interview for the magistrate court position. Were you here interviewing too?"

"Not exactly. I've had this job since before I went to law school, whether I wanted it or not."

"I remember what you told me the day we met when I asked if you worked in the building. 'Not if I can help it.' Yet here you are. Care to elaborate?"

West started to do what she always did when the conversation turned personal—change the subject, but the earnest expression on Camille's face drew her in. Camille was here, sitting down with her, treating her like an equal. They had nothing in common other than dedication to the law and a strong pull of attraction, but West wanted to bridge the gap of age, class, and position that loomed between them.

But not here. Not with files spread out between them and a print of the presidential portrait on the wall. "Actually, I'd be happy to answer, but I'm hungry. I know a place that serves great burgers and beer, if you're game."

She braced the moment the words left her lips, ready to draw back and run if her advance was rejected. She wasn't sure why she felt so vulnerable. After all, Camille was the one seeking answers, but she held her breath. One, two, three beats passed.

"I'm game."

The minute she walked into the bar, Camille felt out of place, and wished she'd stopped at home to change clothes. Of course, if she had, she probably would've decided against this little adventure as the bad idea it was. West, on the other hand, dressed in her funky mix of modern casual and vintage style, fit right in with the millennials thronging the bar.

Deep Ellum wasn't seedy, but it was eclectic. Warehouses gentrified into lofts lined the streets alongside hip restaurants and clubs trying not to be too trendy to scare off the beatnik nightlife that had made the neighborhood the go-to spot it was today. Camille came down here once in a while, but usually during the day for a visit to the

Mozzarella Company to pick up artisanal cheeses or lunch at Cane Rosso Pizzeria.

"You come here often?" she asked, cringing at the cheesy phrase that evoked a sly grin from West.

"Used to," West said, "Haven't been here for a while, but I know the bartender and he'll take care of us." West took off toward the bar, and Camille had no choice but to follow or be crushed by the crowd. By the time she caught up to West, she was leaning over the bar, talking to a ginger-haired guy with a ruddy complexion and full beard.

"Joe, can we get two…hang on a minute." West turned to Camille. "Stout okay?"

"Actually," Camille demurred for a moment, looking around at the drinks in the hands of the people around them. She didn't usually drink beer, but she seemed to be surrounded by it now. Deciding it wouldn't hurt to branch out from her usual wine or martini, she put her fate in West's hands. "Stout sounds great."

West leaned over the bar. "Two Temptresses." She shot a wicked grin Camille's way. "Is your table open?"

"It is, but you better hurry. Go on and I'll bring these."

Camille felt a firm clutch and looked down at West's hand in hers. "Come on," West said. She didn't wait for an answer, and Camille was being tugged into the crowd, while a dozen different thoughts swirled around in her brain. The top two were: I shouldn't be holding hands with my clerk, and I shouldn't be at a bar with her either.

Get a grip. She'd gone out for drinks with her staff many times when she'd been a judge before, enjoying several cocktails with her court reporter, coordinator, bailiff, and clerks, particularly after an arduous case. But being alone with West was decidedly different than decompressing with a group of co-workers, none of whom she'd been attracted to. Deciding that acting like a lovesick teenager wasn't going to improve matters, she started acting like this little outing was a normal occurrence. The first thing she did was let go of West's hand.

If West registered the disconnection, she didn't show it. She continued to move through the crowd like she owned the place until they were across the room. West pushed through the steel door that clearly said No Exit, and suddenly they were looking out over a patio lined with a few clustered tables. She pointed to a table in the far right corner and motioned for Camille to lead the way.

Camille climbed onto the high stool and pulled it closer to the table. A glance around the patio told her this was a different crowd than the young, loud gathering inside. She even spied a bottle of champagne in a bucket of ice on a table nearby and started to mention it to West when the bartender appeared with two pint glasses full of dark liquid.

"Two Bourbon Barrel Temptresses."

Camille reached for her purse, but West placed her hand on hers. "Your money's no good here, Judge." Camille resisted the urge to curl her fingers into West's palm to prolong the heat of their connection, but she was acutely conscious the bartender was standing over them, so she nodded her assent and pushed her purse away.

West took both the drinks and set one in front of Camille. "Camille, meet my favorite bartender in all of Dallas, Joe Duncan."

"Just Dallas?" Joe said. "I thought I was your favorite bartender in the world."

"The world's a big place Joe."

"Whatever," he said, feigning a frown. "Camille, it's nice to meet you. Any friend of West's is a friend of mine."

"Thanks." Camille took a sip from the glass, letting the silky notes of the creamy brew caress her taste buds. "Oh, wow, this is fantastic."

"Local brew. Wish I could hook you up with a growler, but the alcohol content's too high. Drink enough and I can hook you up with an Uber." He cried out when West punched him in the side. "What?"

"Thanks for the beer, Joe."

He did a mock bow. "That's my cue. Enjoy. Text me if you need anything."

Camille took another drink until he was out of sight. "Nice guy. Do you have many bartenders on speed dial?"

"Just the one." West looked in the direction Joe had gone, her expression melancholy.

"Old friend?"

West appeared to snap out of her reverie. "Yes. One of the best."

"Good friends are important." Camille raised her glass. "To friends?"

West raised her glass. "You don't need to keep saying it. I promised I wouldn't make a pass at you again and I meant it. My word is my bond and all that."

The attorney oath being used to make a promise about romance struck Camille as oddly hilarious, and she let loose a light laugh that quickly turned into an uncontrollable mirth. West started laughing too, and Camille was certain the people at the other tables thought they'd lost their minds.

When they finally ran out of steam, West was the first who managed to speak. "I have no idea what that was about, but I think I needed a good laugh."

"Me too," Camille echoed. "Is it really only Monday?"

"That's not really a good attitude since you signed up to do this for the rest of your life."

"I suppose. And you only have a year. Speaking of which, I think you promised me beer, burgers, and a story about why you're working this job." She raised her glass. "One out of three isn't going to cut it."

"Fair enough." West sent a text to Joe about the burgers and held it up for Camille to see before she slipped her phone back in her pocket. "The short story about the job is that I promised Judge Blair I would do a one-year clerkship for him the year after law school."

"Okay, so you do keep your promises. How do you know Judge Blair? Family friend?" The minute the word family fell from her lips, West's eyes narrowed. "Did I say something wrong?"

"I don't really have a family." West took a deep draught from her glass and then rushed her next words. "I grew up in the foster care system. Judge Blair—I call him Hank—was appointed by the court to be my guardian ad litem when I was eleven."

Camille slowly digested the information and focused on keeping her expression neutral, concerned West was a bit like a deer in the forest, likely to run at the sound of a twig cracking beneath her feet. Meanwhile her mind was whirring through facts. A guardian ad litem was an attorney appointed by the court to represent the interests of a child, usually one that had been removed from her parents or was in the process of being removed. Before Blair had taken the bench, he'd been in private practice at one of the large, venerable firms in Dallas, handling mostly corporate litigation. Many of these firms had requirements that their attorneys do a certain amount of pro bono work. Had West been one of Blair's community service projects?

No matter how many questions she had, and there were definitely more now than there were before West's revelation, Camille knew it was none of her business. "You don't have to tell me any of this."

West cracked a half-smile. "I know, but I want to. I don't know why you agreed to keep me on instead of handpicking a clerk for yourself, but you should at least know why you got stuck with me."

"I hardly consider myself stuck with you."

"I know you promised Hank you would keep me on."

Camille heard a note of dissonance in West's voice, and it took her a minute to figure out what she was trying to tell her. It wasn't the obvious, thanks for letting me keep my job. No, West sounded wistful, which was strange, unless… "You didn't want this job, did you?"

"Not really."

"You're kidding." The idea West wouldn't have wanted what was considered to be one of the most coveted positions a new lawyer could land was completely foreign to Camille. "Do you know how many law school graduates would kill to be in your position?"

"I do." West sighed. "I get it and I'd gladly hand this job over, but I promised Hank I would do it. Remember what I said about keeping my promises."

"Okay." Camille fished around for something to say besides pointing out West was taking the place of someone who might really enjoy the position, not to mention how lucky she was to have it herself. When it came to promises, she'd made one of her own to Blair, and West's revelation shouldn't affect her keeping her word. "What would you rather be doing?"

"Railing against the system instead of being a part of it," West said. "I spent the summer interning at the Southern Poverty Law Center. There's still a lot of work to do especially after so much hatred was exposed during the last election. I'd like to work for the Center full-time, but they didn't have a position open right now. But there are other places I could apply. ACLU, Lambda Legal—I have a long list of potential employers."

"None of which happens to be the federal court system."

"No offense, but I feel more like a bystander than a game changer in this job. Don't you feel the same? I mean, you'll get to make decisions on cases, but if either side appeals, your decision—your legacy—is determined by someone else, someone who probably doesn't know you at all and didn't hear what you heard."

"I'm not entirely sure, but I think you just called me ineffectual."

"Maybe." West grinned. "Seriously, you were on the bench before. Don't you feel like you're having a short-term impact?"

"The decisions have to start somewhere. Besides, I might not always be just a district judge." Camille was instantly sorry she'd shared the info since West's eyes lit up.

"Ah, you have your eyes on an appellate court. Good plan. Then you can make a real difference."

"You assume we have the same ideologies."

"I've read up on you. Besides, you wouldn't have gotten this appointment from this president if you weren't on Team Left."

"True," Camille said. "I probably also wouldn't have gotten it without a little help from my parents and their well-placed friends after I got tossed out of state court last year. I guess we're kind of alike that way." She stared at West who looked stunned. "What?"

"It's not the same thing at all," West said, her tone rising. "You having well-heeled parents buy you a federal bench versus me keeping a promise to one of the only adults who ever gave a damn about me."

Camille set her glass on the table, hard. "'Buy me a federal bench?' I never said that, and you certainly have no right to make that assumption. If anyone had something handed to her, it's you. Maybe there's more to it, but all I have to go on is a vague story about how Judge Blair made you take this job, a job many people in your position would be happy to have. I don't know anything about your relationship with Blair or why you felt you had to keep this promise when you so clearly would rather be doing anything else, but I do know it doesn't give you the right to sit in judgment of me." She stopped just short of pointing out it probably wasn't a good idea to talk to her boss the way she had.

West pushed back from the table and stood. "This was a bad idea."

"You're right," Camille answered, not entirely sure what "this" was that West referred to, but knowing she should never have agreed to this rendezvous. She didn't need to know anything personal about West for them to have a boss-employee relationship, and she'd been kidding herself to think they could have a harmless after work dinner. All she cared about now was getting the hell out of this situation with minimal damage. West looked ready to walk out, but she should be the one to go. The quicker the better. She reached in her purse and tossed some bills on the table. "I'll see you tomorrow. Or not. It's your decision."

Camille walked away from the table before she could reconsider. She wasn't going to break her promise to Blair, but if West decided to quit, she had to admit she'd be relieved. But what if she didn't quit? What if she showed up tomorrow morning ready to work?

She had until tomorrow to get her game face on, and she would need every minute.

CHAPTER SIX

Saturday morning, West flipped a pancake onto the stack already leaning precariously on the plate and handed it to Bill who had been hovering since he discovered her in the kitchen. "Put butter on these before they get cold."

Bill made a show of sniffing the plate. "These smell amazing. You should've been a short order cook."

"I still might. I have a feeling I'm not long for this clerk gig."

"Right." Bill's one-word response was slightly muffled by the mouthful of pancakes.

"Seriously. I should've stayed in Montgomery."

"I thought you said they weren't hiring."

"Not right now, but I could've flipped pancakes for a living and volunteered until something else opened up." She poured some more batter into the skillet and checked the temperature. "I don't suppose your place is hiring, are they?" Bill worked for the local office of Lambda Legal.

"You're crazy. I love my job, but I'd give my left nut for the job you have. Do it for a year and you can write your own ticket."

"Do what for a year? Write memos for a judge that lucked into the job?"

Bill cocked his head, and gave her a knowing smile before tucking another huge bite of pancakes into his mouth. "Oh, I get it."

"What?"

"Did someone get rejected by the hot new federal judge?"

"No, smartass, it wasn't like that." West started to say what it was like, but she had trouble putting together a thought that didn't make her sound like she was being irrational. She had kind of flown off the handle when Camille compared their lives, but had she been justified or was her response an overreaction? She'd spent the balance of the week working on the memo about the Wilson case and preparing others for the rest of the cases left over from Hank's tenure, conveniently managing to avoid interaction with Camille who hadn't sought her out either. Their mini cold war left her clueless about where things stood between them personally and professionally. "I mean, yeah, she's attractive and she seems pretty smart, but we occupy two completely different worlds."

"So do we, but that never stopped us from getting along."

Bill had a point. The only thing they'd had in common when they met in law school was they were both from Dallas and both gay. Bill hailed from a wealthy Dallas oil family. He could afford to work for a non-profit since his trust fund held more coin than he could possibly spend in a lifetime. Their differences hadn't prevented them from becoming fast friends and study partners.

"It's different," she offered, knowing it was a weak response. "Don't ask me why, it just is."

"Fine, but if the job's as boring as you say, start looking for something else. No one says you have to give up the income until you're ready to quit."

West tried to imagine how successful she would be, trying to find some other job with the daily distraction of Camille, but the state of her bank account dictated she should give it a go. "Maybe you're right. We did get a case this week that's kind of interesting. You remember the girl who went missing last year and then turned up dead at a construction site near Baylor?"

"Absolutely. Leslie Silver. Her parents are friends of my folks. She disappeared about a week before graduation. So, is this a murder case?"

"Not exactly. It's one of those weird federal laws—distributing drugs that result in death. Treated a lot like murder, but the statute doesn't require intent to kill."

"How is that even constitutional?"

"I know, right? Anyway, there are a ton of other legal issues. The goody-goody AUSAs filed a crazy-ass motion this week. Stuff I can't tell you about, but trust me, tracing through the issues is like navigating the bar exam."

"That sounds pretty cool."

"I guess," West said reluctantly. If she were working as an advocate on either side of the case, it'd be a helluva lot more interesting.

Bill shoved the last bite of pancakes into his mouth, but didn't let it slow down the conversation. "Sounds as interesting as anything you'd get at the Center. Maybe you should quit fighting this gift and take advantage of it."

West piled another stack of pancakes onto his plate and sat down to join him. "Maybe you're right. And maybe I'm being a baby about the whole attraction thing. I just need to get laid, and not with another lawyer."

"I'm all for getting laid. Speaking of which, Gabe's planning on coming over later."

"Is that your way of asking me not to be here?"

"No, I'm trying to be nice. I know he's over here a lot."

"It's your place."

"It's our place until you ditch me for greener pastures, and I'm trying not to be a douche."

"As if. He's your boyfriend. Have him over whenever you want. As long as you two remember to put the toilet seat down, I'm cool with it. Besides, if I meet someone late one night, I don't plan on knocking on your door to make sure it's okay to bring her in. Cool?"

"Cool."

West dug into her plate of pancakes. She actually liked being in a house with someone she knew instead of on her own in Montgomery. Except for Hank, Bill was the closest thing to family she had, and the job wasn't as bad as she'd thought it would be. All she had to do was get past the persistent attraction to her boss and everything would be fine.

❖

Camille handed her barely touched plate of food to the waiter and assured him the leftovers were due to her own lack of appetite, not the taste of the food. As he walked away shaking his head, she attempted to tune in to the conversation. Her very best friend, Jaylyn Renner, was holding court and had the others in stitches. Camille was too distracted to participate in the lively conversation, but Jaylyn seemed determined to single her out. "Hey, Avery, don't you have some clout now that you're a federal judge? Next time don't let them make us wait an hour for a table, okay?"

"I'll get right on that." Camille resisted the urge to excuse herself to the restroom and ditch her friends, but she did say a silent prayer that the powers that be would strike Jaylyn mute. She usually looked forward to these monthly brunches, but today everyone was rubbing her the wrong way and the last thing she wanted was to be the center of attention.

Her agitation had started the minute she'd walked away from West at the bar Monday night. Leaving had been the right thing to do, but she couldn't deny the slow burn of frustration that came from ending the evening on such a sour note when it had had such promise at the beginning. And that was the source of the problem. She should've never been at a bar with West in the first place. Especially not alone. West was edgy and dangerous. She spoke her mind, not caring who she offended. Of course West could afford to say whatever she wanted. She likely never planned to run for office or get caught up in politics of any kind other than to rail against the system. It was easy to buy into the rebellion when you didn't have to pay the price.

But what rankled most was West's implication she achieved her success because of her privileged upbringing. She might have been fortunate enough to never want for money, but there were plenty of things she missed out on. Her parents' deep coffers meant they were rarely home and they'd almost never attended milestone moments in her life. Camille scanned her group of friends. Certainly, to the outside looking in, they all appeared to have charmed lives. Jaylyn sported a vintage Chanel suit and a handbag that cost more than most people's mortgage payments, but her wealth had grown from the seed of a wrongful death settlement after she'd lost her parents in a gruesome plane crash. None of their group had been in foster care, but it looked like West was no worse the wear for her experience. She'd graduated top of her class both as an undergrad and at Berkeley Law.

If she wasn't so unconventional, West probably could've landed the federal clerkship without Blair's help.

The bigger question was why she cared so much what West thought of her. West's opinion had no effect on her ability to perform her job or her likelihood of advancement. In fact, quite the opposite was true. West didn't seem the least bit concerned about garnering favor with her, which might be one of the reasons she couldn't let this attraction go. Was she so used to people sucking up to her that West's obvious nonchalance about pleasing her posed a challenge?

After the bill was settled and the group started to disband, Jaylyn grabbed Camille's arm as they walked out of the restaurant. "I'm headed to Northpark to do a little retail therapy. You in?"

"You'll have to break the bank without me today. I'm going by the office to see if I can get ahead before I get too buried."

"All work and no play…Don't make me finish that phrase."

"Don't tempt me. I just started this job and I already feel like I'm going to need a year to catch up."

"Come on," Jaylyn said. "I'll walk you as far as Neiman's."

They strolled the mostly empty street. This part of downtown was pretty quiet on the weekends, relying primarily on office workers to keep the commerce flowing.

"So, do you like it?"

"It?"

"Being a judge?"

"I've been a judge before. Remember?"

"Yes, but this is pretty different, right?"

Camille considered the question. "It is. When I was on the bench in state court, I spent half my term either holding fundraisers to pay back campaign debt or raising money to run again."

"You don't have to worry about any of that now."

"Not the money part. But when it comes to promotion, they always look at your appellate record. Judges who mess up don't get appointments to higher courts."

"Relax and enjoy what you've got before you go wishing away your happiness."

Jay might be right, but Camille wasn't taking any chances. The Wilson case was an appellate lawyer's wet dream, rife with legal issues, and since the case was going to dominate the headlines during the trial, her every move would be scrutinized. Every decision she made had to be carefully calculated and firmly based in the law. She would have to focus all her energy on the case, which meant no time for inappropriate thoughts about her hot new law clerk. Maybe she should assign West to some other work and use Lloyd exclusively on this case.

Jay's elbow to her side nudged her out of her head. "Don't look now, but a cute little hottie is eyeballing you. Ten o'clock."

Camille whipped her head in the direction Jay mentioned and locked eyes with West. She was standing about twenty feet away, next to a parking meter on Commerce Street, talking to what appeared to be a homeless man. West was dressed in low-slung jeans and a short-sleeved plaid shirt that left the tattoos on her arms on full display. Camille gripped Jay's arm, but the chance encounter robbed her of speech.

"I told you not to look," Jay whispered. "Pretty clear she's into you." She leaned in closer. "How long has it been since you got laid? I mean she's not really your type, but there's no denying she's hot."

Camille struggled to stay calm. West raised her eyes in question before turning back to the man beside her. Their easy smiles and close proximity indicated they knew each other, and Camille's curiosity was piqued. She'd gone all week without exchanging more than a few words with West, and every one had been related to work, but now she wanted to walk over, apologize for their misunderstanding, and start over. Just not in front of Jay. Before she could make a move, West shook the man's hand and walked toward them. Camille cast a sideways glance at Jay who wore a big grin. "Don't."

Jay raised her arms in a classic "Who me?" and took a step back.

"Judge Avery." West's voice was cool, calm.

"West." Camille wanted to ask what she was doing downtown, but even that simple question seemed too personal, so she said the first inane thing that came to mind. "Beautiful day for a walk, isn't it?" She heard Jay clear her throat and knew she'd take a ribbing later. "You headed to the park?"

"Actually, I was headed to the office. I thought I'd get a jump on some of the case files for Monday. And you?"

Camille started to answer, but Jay appeared at her side with her hand stuck out toward West. "Hi, I'm Jaylyn Renner, friend of Camille's."

West paused for a moment and then shook Jay's hand. "West Fallon. I'm one of Judge Avery's clerks."

"Is that so?" Jay shot a look at Camille, and she wanted to melt into the sidewalk. "Well, Judge Avery here was headed into the office too. Guess you can both get some work done, you know, without the distraction of everyone else."

Camille wanted to punch her and she would've if West wasn't looking, but the best thing she could do to minimize the destruction was to act like nothing was off. "It's true. I get more done when the phones aren't ringing, but, West, there's no need for you to go in since I'll be there."

West cocked her head. "Are you telling me I can't?"

"Well, of course you can if you want to. I just meant…" She let the words trail off because she really had no good answer. Was the very idea of being alone with West at the office so scary she couldn't handle it? Clearly, West had decided to stick around despite their disastrous dinner, and if they were going to make it through the next year working together, she was going to have to be alone with her on occasion. She made a snap decision to dive in and get used to the temperature. "Actually, since you're headed that way, maybe we can go over the motion in the Wilson case. I've been giving it some thought after reading the memo you prepared, and I have some ideas." Camille turned to Jay. "Okay if I bail on you here?"

Jay looked between them and gave her a knowing smile. "Absolutely. I have shopping to do, but since you've already found what you need, you should go with it." She waved at West. "Very nice to meet you, West Fallon. Have a wonderful afternoon."

Camille watched Jay as she walked up the block, reluctant to face West now that they were alone. It was one thing to act like she was in charge, but quite another to play the part when she was feeling so disconcerted.

"Your friend seems nice."

Camille turned to face West. "She's pushy, overbearing, and opinionated. And I love her for it."

"Friends like that are important." West shifted in place. "If you were just being nice because she was standing there, that's cool. I can come by some other time to work on the case files."

"Nonsense. You're here, you're smart, and I could use the help." Camille waved her forward. "Come on." She started walking before she got an answer, ignoring the voice in her head that said the bounce in her step was because of West.

CHAPTER SEVEN

West followed Camille into the office suite, suddenly unsure about her decision to come in today. She'd planned on a few hours of uninterrupted work in the silence of the quiet office in an effort to get a head start on the week, but with Camille present she was in danger of being too distracted to accomplish anything.

"Want to set up in the conference room?" Camille asked.

West backed toward the door. "Maybe I should go."

"Do you want to go?"

"No, but maybe I should. I can do research at home and that way you can work without being disturbed."

"You won't disturb me."

West studied Camille's face, but her expression was iron, and she read nothing other than impassive indifference. After the last few days of barely speaking, maybe indifference was all that was left of their initial attraction. An afternoon of working together—just working—might be exactly what she needed to get over the distracting attraction between them. "Good to know. Conference room sounds great. I'm going to make some coffee. Be right there."

She walked to the kitchenette before Camille could respond, desperate for a solitary minute to regroup. She took her time, measuring the special blend, half Guatemalan and half Italian, she'd brought from home into the filter and filling the coffeemaker with fresh water from the cooler, drawing composure from the simple motions. When the coffee started to brew, she closed her eyes and leaned against the counter, slipping into one of the few pleasant memories of her youth.

Her first job in high school had been at a local coffee shop. She'd lied about her age to get the work, but the owner hadn't complained since she'd been the hardest working employee he'd ever hired. She'd started cleaning and stocking but had eventually worked her way up to barista. Hank had encouraged her to work as an intern for a law firm, but she'd enjoyed the simple pleasure of blending coffee beans to her will and the eclectic atmosphere of the shop. People used coffee shops like their homes or offices, carrying on all sorts of personal business, seemingly oblivious to the potential for eavesdropping. She'd seen real estate deals, a couple getting marriage counseling, and one time a guy walked in with a twenty-seven-inch iMac under his arm and proceeded to start running his furniture moving business while sipping on a double latte. These people lived out in the open, not caring who heard their business or saw inside their personal matters, and she envied their transparency. She had never felt like she could let her guard down. Very few people knew her story. To most, she was either a punk kid with tattoos or a top legal scholar and which one depended on how she chose to appear, rather than what they actually knew.

"That smells good."

West held two mugs. "I was going to offer you some."

"I figured as much, but I couldn't resist the smell, so I thought I'd make sure."

West poured the fresh brew into one of the mugs asking, "Room for cream?"

"Black's great."

Oddly pleased they shared the same preference, West poured Camille's cup full and handed it over.

"This is incredible. Pretty sure this isn't from the big red canister Ester has stuffed in the cabinet."

West grinned. "Nope. Hank loves that stuff, and I couldn't convince him to try anything else." She caught Camille cocking her head and realized what she'd just said. "I meant Judge Blair, of course."

Camille took another sip of coffee. "I knew who you meant, and you don't need to be formal on my account. Especially not when it's just us."

West heard the words, but Camille was dead wrong. Formal was exactly what she needed to be if they were going to maintain necessary boundaries.

"You two are close."

"Yes."

"I'm sorry you missed the opportunity to clerk for him."

West started to say it was okay, that she hadn't wanted to anyway, but bit back the words. Maybe it was time she quit acting like this job was one of the worst things to happen to her and take advantage of the opportunity. "It's okay. This could be fun." She waved a finger between them. "I mean, how many brand new clerks get to work with a brand new judge. It's like we're carving our way through judicial history."

Camille burst out laughing and she joined in. "That's one way of putting it," Camille said. "Another way is the blind leading the blind." She pointed to the door. "How about we discuss the Wilson motion and see if we can find our way to a solution?"

Once they reached the conference room, West pulled out her notebook and opened the file containing the AUSA's motion and defense counsel's response, along with a copy of the memo she and Lloyd, mostly she, had authored. "Before we get into this motion, the defense filed another motion right before Hank collapsed. The magistrate ruled on it in his absence, but as the district judge, you could take a second look."

"What's the gist?"

"That the statute charging Wilson with the death of Leslie Silver is unconstitutional." West rushed the words, pretty sure she knew what the reaction would be. She wasn't wrong.

"Not going to happen."

"You haven't even heard the arguments."

"Don't have to. I get it. It seems unfair to charge a man with the death of someone who made a conscious choice to do drugs, but Congress enacted these laws for a reason. It's no different than charging prostitutes for offering a service Johns are happy to pay for, but the point is to discourage the activity at the source by exacting punishment for the consequences."

"So much for a free market system."

"Do you really believe it should be okay for the drug trade to operate without consequences?"

"I believe it's more complicated than that. There were consequences. Leslie Silver made a choice to purchase drugs from Darryl

Wilson and she wound up dead because of it. Should he be punished for violating drug laws? Yes, but that's different from what basically amounts to a murder charge."

"You make some good points, but you're not going to sway me. I'm not here to take down the system." Camille smiled. "But feel free to write your representative and ask them to overturn the law. Now, back to the motion that's actually before us."

West hesitated, annoyed with Camille for dismissing her pitch so quickly and annoyed with herself for bothering to make it in the first place. Did she really want a known drug dealer like Darryl Wilson to escape the consequences of his actions or was a simmering anger about the "victim's" role in her own tragedy overriding her legal analysis? Until she figured out her own motivation, she'd probably better abandon the cause.

She pointed at the government's motion. "The arguments are pretty straightforward. The government says they have evidence that Wilson had sex with the victim, Leslie Silver."

"What's the evidence?"

West turned to a section in her notebook, acutely conscious Camille was standing close, the scent of her flowery perfume intoxicating. She drew her finger along the page. "Sperm sample taken from her clothes. DNA match to Wilson."

"Anything else?"

"Not anything they've revealed in the motion. Anyway, their logic for getting in the evidence about alleged prior sexual assaults basically goes like this: Wilson did drugs with Silver and raped her, and they should be able to show he did the same thing to others to show a pattern of behavior."

"Seems like a bit of a stretch to me. Sex isn't rape unless it was nonconsensual."

"They get that."

"So, what's their evidence?"

"A group of young women have come forward who say they woke up after partying with Wilson to find signs they'd had sex. Underwear missing, soreness, etc. They have no recollection of the act itself, just that fuzzy feeling that something happened and it wasn't something they wanted."

"Did they file police reports?"

West listened for, but didn't hear any tone in the question. "Most of them didn't. The two that did, did so much later, presumably after talking to their friends. You know, hey, anyone else feel like something weird went down after doing coke with Darryl Wilson? That kind of conversation."

"Got it. Any other evidence?"

"Kind of. And this is their smoking gun. They have videos of Wilson having sex with some of these girls. I suspect that's what they really want to play for the jury."

"They do, do they? If they turn this into a porn screening, the jury is going to come after Wilson with pitchforks and torches."

"I'm pretty sure that's the goal. The defense brief says the same thing you did. Their argument is that the prosecutors are bootstrapping. They shouldn't get to show evidence of rape of other women to prove he raped the victim, and the evidence of sex with the victim shouldn't be used to allow them to introduce these other cases."

"What's Lloyd's take on all this?"

West pushed back from the table. "I'd rather not speak for him if it's all the same to you."

"You disagree."

"He's more a fan of let it all in and let the jury sort it out."

"Does he have any legal support for his theory?"

"Just the crap that's quoted in the government's brief." West noted Camille's eyes widen with surprise. "Well, some of it is crap. They're citing cases from random district courts back East. Nothing binding."

"But you have law on your side?"

West bristled at the question. "Well, for one thing, it's not my side, it's the right side. Trust me, there isn't anyone who has more reason to see scum like this—" She stopped abruptly, conscious she'd said too much.

Camille's eyes narrowed in question, but all she said was "And the other thing?"

"Quit patronizing me." West saw Camille's look of surprise and knew she was walking a fine line, but she'd already dug in so she kept going. "The other thing is, yes, I do have law to support my conclusions. It's pretty basic, Federal Rule 403 says you, the judge, can exclude evidence if it's probative value is substantially outweighed by a danger of unfair prejudice and confusing the issues, among other things. That should be enough, but if it's not good enough for you, then there's a bunch of case law that says the same thing."

"That may be true," Camille replied. "But there are exceptions to the rule, and I happen to think juries are usually smart enough to sort most things out on their own. If the government is able to present solid evidence that Darryl Wilson had sex with Leslie Silver while she was comatose from drugs he sold her, that would certainly constitute a sexual assault and they'd have a decent argument that they should be allowed to show the defendant has a pattern of this type of behavior."

West wondered if Camille really believed what she was saying or if part of her motivation for the "lay all the cards on the table" approach stemmed from the case that had gotten her voted out of office. In the conservative county where she'd been on the bench, there had been a backlash in the recent election against judges who the voters thought had substituted their own views for those of a jury, and West had no doubt Camille's loss was perceived as a stinging rebuke against that type of behavior. It had to be hard, balancing the law with the facts, but it was the job Camille had signed on for and, in West's view, abdicating wasn't an option.

"The bottom line is this isn't a rape case," West said. "If they want to charge Wilson with rape, nothing's stopping them unless they don't have the evidence. And if they don't have the evidence, well then, they shouldn't be bringing any of this up in the first place."

Camille leaned back and steepled her fingers. "You're very passionate for someone who wasn't really interested in this job in the first place. Is there a particular reason this case has you riled?"

West suffered through the slow burn of the blush she was certain was creeping up her neck. "I might not look like much of a lawyer to you, but I care about getting it right."

Camille's careful gaze was long and lingering, and with each passing second, West grew even more uncomfortable. If Camille didn't think she could do a good job, she could let her go. She couldn't be expected to keep her promise to Hank if Camille broke hers, right?

"I'm sorry if I've done something to make you think I doubt your skills," Camille said, her words dripping with double meaning. "I have no doubt you're an excellent lawyer. I remember having that kind of passion, but sometimes what seems clear in the moment, isn't right when it's examined from all sides."

West's chest tightened at the truism. Was she fighting so hard for the rights of the defendant because she didn't want to admit that Leslie Silver, despite her apparent choice to take Wilson's drugs, might not have been in control of what happened afterward? Her mind whirred with memories of the Leslie Silvers she'd known when she was a child, surrendering to the now only to be swept away by the consequences of their actions and inactions.

Camille gazed at a spot across the room, seemingly lost in thought, and West wondered what memory held her interest and why her passion was in the past. She wanted to ask, but she worried any personal digging on her part would result in a reciprocal unearthing of the life she'd rather leave buried. Better to dive back into the work, trust that Camille would do the right thing, and let be the things she knew she couldn't have.

CHAPTER EIGHT

Monday morning, Camille pushed through the doors of the office suite, hoping she was early enough to avoid having to interact with anyone, but she stopped short when she saw Ester already seated at her desk, typing away on her computer. "If I didn't know better, I'd think you never went home for the weekend."

"I went home all right, but judging by the mess in the conference room, someone put in some extra hours." Ester didn't look up from her work as she spoke. "Don't worry. I cleaned up all the evidence."

Camille's stomach clenched at the words. Evidence. Ester's tone was hard to read, but Camille did a mental inventory of the state of the room when she and West had finally called it a day and gone their separate ways. Coffee cups, a pizza box, and paper plates—all of which she'd intended to clean up this morning before anyone else arrived. That had to be what Ester was referring to, but the fact there might be something else she could get caught with, left her cold. She raised her hands. "Guilty as charged. In my defense, I planned to clean up the mess myself this morning."

"Didn't look like you were working alone."

Ester's comment hung in the air inviting, but not demanding a response. Camille wavered between no comment and the risk of sounding defensive. She settled on a simple. "West was here and we went through the research on the Wilson case."

A veil came down over Ester's eyes. "That's a rough one all around."

"It is." Camille didn't say anything else, hoping Ester would elaborate. Everything about West's reaction to the talk about the case yesterday had set off alarms that the case pushed personal buttons, but she was surprised to see the same reaction reflected in Ester's demeanor. What did Ester know that she didn't? "How long did you work for Judge Blair?"

"Seems like forever. I knew him when he was on the partner track at Goss and Landry. When he made partner, I was assigned to be his secretary, and when he got the appointment here, he brought me along." She shook a finger at Camille. "Before you go getting any ideas, he was able to hire me on because my predecessor was retiring."

Camille laughed. "I have no designs on replacing you." She took a beat to consider her next question. It stood to reason if Ester had known Blair that long, she might have an inside track on Blair's protégé. "Do you know of any particular reason why the Wilson case would bother West?"

Ester averted her eyes as she answered. "Case is pretty gruesome if you ask me. Somebody left that poor girl for dead. She had a bright future ahead, but she became an addict and no one intervened to get her help. Now she's dead, and someone's going to have to pay."

Camille wanted to push the point. Of course the case was disturbing, but she was interested in how it was disturbing to West, not the average person. She told herself she cared because of how it affected West's ability to be objective, but the truth was she wanted the insight into West's psyche.

Well, she wasn't going to get any insights from Ester. As much as she wanted information, she appreciated Ester's discretion. She'd have to find what she wanted to know another way, but in the meantime, there was work to do. "I asked Lloyd to contact counsel on this case. They should be here in about thirty minutes. We'll meet in chambers, but I'll need George there as well."

She didn't wait for a response. Once she was secluded in the small conference room connected to her office where she could wait for Lloyd and the court reporter in peace, she ran through the key points both sides had raised, but second thoughts about which clerk she'd chosen to be part of this morning's conference hearing crept in. She wasn't going to rule the way West wanted, not entirely anyway, and she'd convinced herself that wasn't the reason she'd asked Lloyd to run point. But now that she was on the verge of ruling, she was starting to question her motives. Her rumination was interrupted by a knock at the door, and she pushed her doubt aside. She had two clerks, and it wasn't right to favor one over the other, especially not when her favoritism was based in lust as much as intellect. Before she had a chance to respond, the door opened and Lloyd poked his head in. "Everyone's here."

"Have them come in."

Once everyone crowded into the room, Camille experienced a moment of hesitation. Maybe it hadn't been such a good idea to cram all these people into such a small space. But what she had to say, she didn't want to say in open court since she planned to seal the record for now. "Thank you all for being here on such short notice. I've thoroughly reviewed the government's motion and defense counsel's response. You'll have my written opinion by midweek, but I'm going to give you a preview of my decision because I know both sides are getting ready for trial and I don't want any arguments for a continuance based on my ruling."

She paused and watched while Sylvia squirmed in her seat, apparently believing she'd lost this round. Time to put them out of their misery. "I'm granting and denying portions of the government's motion." She turned to squarely face Kyle Merrin. "I will not allow you to put on a mini rape trial during this case. If you want to try Mr. Wilson for rape, indict him on that charge. However," she turned back to defense counsel. "I will allow the government to call these women to testify about their interactions with Mr. Wilson as it pertains to drug sale, use, etc. That evidence is relevant. The government shall instruct their witnesses that they cannot mention the rape allegations or even consensual sex with the defendant without a proper foundation. If the government establishes the defendant's action were part of a pattern, motive, or other exception to Rule 403, then and only then, will I consider allowing testimony about sexual assault. I will not let this case devolve into a circus. Understood?"

"But, Your Honor, it's going to be pretty hard for these women to distinguish," Merrin said. "They often received drugs for sex. If they are going to testify about their drug use with the defendant, then the next natural subject is the sex they used to pay for it."

"Nonsense. These college girls should be well versed in boundaries. Just tell them I set all the boundaries. If they're in doubt about what they can say, then you can make a proffer to the court. Out of the presence of the jury. Understood?"

They grumbled their assent, but it was clear neither side was entirely pleased, which told Camille she'd probably made exactly the right decision. While the lawyers filed out of the room, she asked Lloyd to hang back. "Here are my notes, and this," she handed him a flash drive, "this is the draft of the opinion. Just needs some cleaning up, and I'd like you to insert the citations and make a full table of the annotations. We can count on some or all of these issues going up on appeal, and I want to make it as easy as possible for the next judge to see how I reached my conclusions."

Lloyd stood still for a moment, a puzzled look on his face. "You know, most judges have their clerks write their opinions and then they review the draft, not the other way around."

And most judges don't lust over their law clerks. "Let's try it my way." Camille's desk phone rang. "Get that to me this afternoon. Thanks." She picked up the line, and Ester let her know Stroud had called to cancel the lunch he'd arranged with the other judges to welcome her to the courthouse. While she was relieved not to have to spend valuable work time socializing with the other judges, she couldn't help but notice Stroud had been acting a bit cooler to her now that she was a colleague. Just as well since she could do without the distraction of office politics. It was eight thirty in the morning, and she'd already accomplished the most dreaded task of her day. She walked into her office and looked longingly at the couch in the corner. Too bad she couldn't curl up in the corner and take a nap until lunch. Instead she slipped on her robe and scanned her desk for any last minute to-dos.

The interoffice envelope was bulging with mail, typical for a Monday morning. She thumbed through the contents, giving each piece a quick scan until her gaze landed on an envelope with the words PERSONAL AND CONFIDENTIAL printed in neat, big block letters across the top. She reached into her drawer and pulled out the message she'd received the week before and compared the handwriting. Identical.

She'd never gotten around to reporting the first note to the marshals. She'd shoved it in her drawer and gone into the courtroom, and after a few days had passed the threat had faded. She was new. She didn't want to make waves. The note could have been intended for anyone, considering it hadn't been addressed to her specifically. Now she cursed her stupidity. This new letter was most certainly for her since the envelope was addressed to the Honorable Camille Avery. She should take it directly to the marshal's office along with the first and let them sort it out, but she couldn't resist the urge to see inside. Hand trembling, she reached into her desk and pulled out a letter opener, slit the envelope, and shook out the contents.

Like the first note, this one was on a plain white sheet of paper and the message was brief. QUIT THE BENCH. YOU HAVE NO BUSINESS HERE. LEAVE NOW OR ELSE.

Or else. Vague, but ominous enough to cause her gut to churn. She picked up the phone and buzzed Ester's phone, speaking before Ester could get out a hello. "I need to check on something. Please let the lawyers know I'll be in court in about fifteen minutes."

Peter Donovan was walking toward the door of the marshal service when she approached and she waved him over. She'd placed both of the messages she'd received in another interoffice envelope and handed it over. "I only have a minute, but I wanted to bring these by. I received the notes inside on two separate occasions, and only one of them appears to have come through the postal service. Both of them urge me to quit the bench, although the first one wasn't actually addressed to me, it just appeared in my office. I seriously doubt there's any real danger, but I wanted to make sure you had these just in case. I included a full statement with the pertinent information, including dates and times. Let me know if you need anything else." She turned to walk away, but he reached out to grab her arm.

"Hang on a minute. We take threats on federal judges pretty damn seriously. How about I come back to your office with you and take a full statement?"

Camille started to edge away. "You know, I've received threats before and these fall pretty low on the danger meter. Do I like getting hate mail? Of course not, but it comes with the job. I really need to get back to court. Just keep me posted if you find out anything, okay?"

She didn't wait for an answer before turning to leave. She knew he was only doing his job, but she'd provided all the information she had along with the letters. The best thing she could do was get back to work and not let the jerk who'd threatened her keep her from her job.

❖

"Good morning, Ester," West called as she walked into the office with a box of donuts in hand.

"Hi, West. Are you holding what I think you're holding?"

West lifted the tall white box up out of reach. "I don't know what you're talking about." She made a show of following Ester's gaze. "Oh, you mean this box? The one that smells like cinnamon and is still warm?" She brought the box down and set it on Ester's desk. "Well, let's take a look."

Ester barely waited for the box to hit the surface of her desk before she dug in. "Best apple fritters in Dallas." She took a bite and moaned. "I can't remember the last time I had these."

West smiled, happy to see the donuts were having their desired effect even if it was really Camille she'd planned to surprise. "Glad you like them, but don't eat them all. I brought enough for everyone to share. Speaking of which, is the judge in yet?"

Ester wiped away a trace of glaze from the corner of her mouth. "Don't worry. I only think I could eat them all, but I'd probably pass out by number three. These are as good as I remember. Judge Blair brought them in for Secretary's Day, or Administrative Professional's day," she finger quoted the last words, "last April, and I haven't had any since."

"Speaking of judges…" West prompted again, cautious about being too direct, but anxious to see Camille. She'd been up half the night contemplating their interaction the day before. She'd definitely had a reaction to the facts of the Wilson case, but that was natural. She could even see why Camille might be concerned about her ability to compartmentalize her feelings, especially since Camille didn't really know anything about her experience and all she'd done to get past it. By now she was the queen of walling off parts of her life from others. She'd had to assume the role or risk self-destruction, but if her circumstances in life so far hadn't brought her down, then this case didn't have a chance. Still, it was probably best she tell Camille what had triggered her reactions so they could have everything out in the open.

"Judge Avery is already in the courtroom, so I'll take her share if that's why you're asking," Ester said, her voice jarring West from her introspection.

"Oh, it's kind of early, isn't it?"

"For donuts?"

"Ester, are you trying to drive me crazy?"

Ester pointed to the double doors of the courtroom. "Judge is on a roll this morning. She's already met with the attorneys on the Wilson case, and she's probably on the second case of the docket. In fact, She…"

West stopped listening because she could barely digest the words she'd heard already. Why had Camille met with counsel on the Wilson case? West was in the process of finalizing a memo based on the information they'd discussed the night before, and she'd fully expected to discuss it with Camille after docket this morning. She muttered an "I'll be right back" to Ester and walked toward the courtroom.

She slipped into a seat in the back, not wanting to draw attention to her entrance, but Camille locked eyes with her within seconds. West raised her eyebrows in question, but Camille's expression was fixed and neutral. What did she expect? Just because they'd shared a day alone at the office, didn't mean Camille would suddenly start confiding in her, checking with her before she made decisions on her cases. West had no right to expect any such things from Camille, especially when she clammed up every time Camille broached any subject that might touch on her past.

Out of the corner of her eye, West saw Lloyd, seated in the jury box, paying more attention to her than the proceedings. She forced her attention away from Camille and onto the hearing. The attorneys in the Wilson case occupied both counsel tables, but instead of a contentious debate over the legal issues in the government's motion, they were engaged in a fairly civil discussion about scheduling, not unlike the one that had been going on right before Judge Blair had his stroke. Both sides were telling the judge how long they anticipated they would need to put on their case at trial, what additional motions might be filed, and other routine housekeeping matters. For anyone not directly involved with the case, it was boring.

Instead of tuning in, West looked around the room, making a game of sorting the people in the gallery into groups. Two guys dressed in boots and blazers she pegged as cops, probably DEA, since FBI agents tended to be a little more buttoned up. She recalled that some of the law enforcement types who'd worked on the Wilson case were Texas Rangers so it was entirely possible they'd been called to court expecting to testify for the motion hearing and were not aware the case had already been decided in chambers.

Over to her left, she spotted a woman seated by herself, in what looked like her Sunday best, a navy blue dress with a white collar and a brooch shaped like a cross. She sat with her hands crossed over a Bible in her lap, staring straight ahead, but she didn't appear to be engaged in what was going on in front of her. West scanned the rest of the room. There weren't any in-custody defendants present for the docket, and if this woman had a family member who wasn't in custody, West would have expected to see him or her seated next to her. Maybe she was a witness. West wasn't sure why she cared, but the more she looked at the woman, the more she thought she looked familiar.

Her musings were interrupted when Lloyd slipped into the seat next to her. "Where did you come from?" she asked, startled that she'd been so absorbed she hadn't noticed him leave his seat in the jury box.

"I cut through the holdover," he whispered, referring to the rooms next to the courtroom where defendants were held before the docket started. "Where were you this morning?"

"What are you talking about? I got here the same time as usual. I even brought donuts, but apparently everyone decided to start work without me."

Lloyd's expression was smug. "I figured you overslept. Judge called me last night and asked me to notify counsel on the Wilson case she wanted to meet with them. When I got here this morning, she told them her decision and said they'd get her full opinion on Wednesday. She practically already wrote the entire thing herself."

West didn't bother trying to hide her surprise. So Camille not only decided how to rule, but wrote up her opinion yesterday after they'd parted ways. No matter how things had shaken out between them, she'd fully expected to have a heads-up about the ruling and even imagined she'd author the opinion for Camille. "Do you have it?"

"What?"

"The opinion. Do you have it with you?"

"It's on my desk. I planned to get back to it right after this. Want to cite check it when I'm done?" he asked, referring to the process of making sure all the supporting decisions in the opinion were properly formatted and still good law. "I know it's not exactly rocket science, but it is the kind of thing a more junior clerk should do."

So that was why Lloyd was suddenly being nice to her—he wanted her help, but a bigger revelation than that was the fact Camille had put Lloyd in charge of the opinion. The realization left West speechless. Lloyd hadn't come in on a Sunday to work. Lloyd was smart, but not inventive. Was Camille's decision to give the opinion to him a sign she was going to take the safe route and keep out the evidence about the defendant's priors? Without even knowing what the opinion said, West was disappointed in Camille and hurt she'd been left out, but her desire to see the finished opinion outweighed her other emotions. "Yeah, I'll do your grunt work."

At that moment, the courtroom came alive with the sound of movement to signal the hearing had ended. The bailiff called the next case while the attorneys on the Wilson case filed out of the courtroom. Anxious to see Camille's draft of the opinion, West decided now was the perfect time to escape back to their office. She nudged Lloyd in the side. "Come on, let's get out of here."

He didn't respond, his gaze transfixed on something across the room. West followed his sightline and honed in on the woman she'd noticed earlier. She was standing now and was way taller than she'd first appeared when she was hunched over her Bible in the gallery. A maroon copy of the Bible was raised high in her right hand, and an angry scowl marred her face.

"What the hell?" Lloyd said in a barely concealed whisper.

"Who is that?" West asked, but before Lloyd had time to respond, the woman's booming voice commanded the attention of everyone in the room.

"Where is the justice?"

"Holy hell," West muttered. She watched as one of the marshals ducked into the holdover, certain he was calling for backup.

"Where is my brother?" the woman shouted. "Why are you keeping him from these proceedings?"

Camille leaned over the bench, gavel in hand, but opted to make a simple request rather than bang out her order. "Ma'am, I'm going to have to ask you to leave. We have important matters going on in here, and your actions are disruptive."

The woman made no move to leave. "Yes, there are important matters." She pointed at the rear doors of the courtroom, where Wilson's attorneys had exited only seconds before. "My brother is Darryl Wilson, and those people are supposed to be representing him. Darryl told me to come and be with him this morning since your decision would change the course of his case. But you haven't made any real decisions. Two weeks for trial, when everyone should exchange witness lists, what the attorneys can and can't say outside of this courtroom. Little details that don't change anything. Where is Darryl and what is going on?"

West looked around the room. The marshals up front would cover Camille in the event this woman whipped out a weapon, but it looked like she was here for information, not vengeance. West could relate. She'd been in court plenty of times with teams of lawyers, wondering what was going on with her life while decisions about her future were made by strangers. She pushed past Lloyd and walked over to the woman, deliberately placing herself between her and the front of the courtroom. "I'm West Fallon. What's your name?" She stuck out her hand.

The woman stared at her hand for a moment and then pulled it into hers. "Gloria Wilson."

West placed her other hand on top of their joined hands and smiled, thankful very few people were able to resist an outstretched hand. "Nice to meet you, Gloria. I'm one of Judge Avery's clerks. If you want to walk outside with me, we can talk about the case, but the judge has another pressing matter right now that she needs to attend to."

Gloria shot a look toward the front of the room. Camille was glaring at both of them, and West caught sight of the marshal who'd returned from the holdover. He gave her a slight nod, and she took it as a sign to keep going. "Gloria?"

Gloria moved like she was in a trance, but all West cared about was getting her out of the courtroom as quickly as possible to avoid a potential physical altercation. Once they were outside the double doors, a team of marshals descended, including Peter Donovan. The marshals escorted Gloria down the hall, and West turned to go back into the courtroom when she heard Peter call her name.

"Hey, West, what was that all about?"

"Good question. Probably nothing. Disgruntled family member. She came to see a show and there wasn't one, so she held her Bible in the air. She was probably about to smite the judge." She shrugged. "Couldn't let that happen, could I?"

"Hell no." He jerked his chin toward the door. "She working out okay?"

The question was loaded, but since only she knew how much, she feigned indifference. "Sure. I mean, what do I know about being on the bench? I'm barely out of law school."

"Thought he'd be here forever," Peter said, a wistful look in his eye.

"Me too, Peter, me too." She started to walk back into court, but Lloyd pushed through the door and motioned for her to follow. "What's up? Docket over already?"

"On a break. Judge wants to see you."

That didn't sound good, and the look reflected in Lloyd's face confirmed it. She pushed past him and strode back into chambers. Ester was into her second, maybe third donut, and she merely pointed back toward Camille's office. Lloyd hung back. "Maybe I'll just meet you in the conference room whenever you're ready to get started."

She studied his pale face and the way his fists were clenched. "Chicken."

"Maybe."

West smiled at the honesty, thinking this moment was the first real connection they'd shared. She strode up to Camille's door and knocked, immediately hearing Camille's voice, sharp and short, calling out for her to come in. West walked in and said, "You wanted to see me?"

"Close the door."

West glanced back and pulled the door shut. She chose not to sit. Camille's tone told her she was in for a dressing down and she'd just as soon take it standing, though she couldn't imagine what Camille had to be mad at her about.

"What were you thinking?" Camille blurted out the question, despite a promise to herself to remain cool. All she could see was a picture of West standing between her and a potential threat. The rest was a blur. Fear pierced her heart, cold and sharp. On some level she knew part of the source of her fear was the second letter she'd received—evidence that danger could come from any direction, but the idea that West might be hurt by a threat intended for her was inconceivable.

"What are you talking about?"

"Gloria Wilson. She could've been armed. There's a protocol to follow. The marshals are in the room for a reason. When you get in the middle of things, you can put everyone's life in jeopardy."

West slid into a chair. "Hey, let's dial this back a bit. First of all, I seriously doubt Gloria Wilson is a danger to anyone. She's feeling a little left out of the loop. She's attended her brother's hearings before, and I'm sure she expected a little more today than a bunch of administrative mumbo jumbo. She's not the only one."

Camille met West's challenging stare. She'd seen West and Lloyd, huddled and whispering in the back of the courtroom. No doubt West was aware by now that she'd already written the opinion and had asked Lloyd to review it. West probably felt slighted, but she could clear that up. "I guess Lloyd told you I've already written the opinion."

"So, I spent last night working on a draft for you which was apparently a total waste of time? To top it off, you called everyone in and handed down your decree, without so much as giving me a chance to at least be around to see it all go down."

Camille felt every push of the buttons. "I don't have to run my decisions by you. I don't even have to ask for your input."

"But you included Lloyd. How do you think that makes me feel?"

Camille started to say it clearly made her mad, but anger wasn't what she saw reflected in West's eyes. What she saw was hurt, and Camille regretted being the cause. "I was trying to spare you."

"Because I got a little zealous about how I thought you should decide the motion? Am I not allowed to have opinions?"

Camille reached for middle ground. "Maybe. Look, I did what I thought was best. We have plenty of cases to work on, and I could use your help on some others. I've made up my mind on this particular issue, and Lloyd can do the cleanup work."

"He's not as smart as I am."

"This is true, but I'm pretty smart myself. I think I can make up for any of his deficits."

West shook her head. "Not fair. I'll quit before I get stuck doing all the boring stuff. I promise not to be a jerk just because we disagree if you promise to let me keep working this case."

Camille wanted to say it wasn't the mere fact they disagreed that colored her decision, but she didn't want to admit, out loud anyway, their undeniable attraction was getting in the way of her focus. Deciding it was easier to give a little, she said. "Okay, work with Lloyd to finalize the opinion and let's get it filed no later than tomorrow. But I have one condition. Promise me you'll quit trying to take on the job of the marshal service."

"I bet you a hundred dollars, they come back and say Gloria Wilson is harmless, but yes, I promise."

"Fine." Camille said the word reluctantly, but the truth was, she was relieved to put West back on the case and not just because she was smart.

CHAPTER NINE

Oh my God, I don't think I'll ever eat again."

"You'll be hungry in an hour." West opened her wallet and threw down a twenty, motioning for Bill to do the same. "Come on. We need to get out of here if we're going to make a matinee. Besides, I bet you'll be the first one in line for popcorn." After a long week balancing a fine line between working with Camille and wondering what it would be like if she didn't work for her, West was ready for a Saturday of escapism at the movies.

"You can have popcorn if you want, but I think I'm going to die," Bill said.

"We'll see." West planned to have popcorn and Milk Duds, the salt and sweet combo a favorite memory from when Hank used to pick her up once a week from whatever foster home she was in at the time and take her to the movies. The other kids had been consumed with jealousy about her outings, so she'd never shared with them the fact she was not only getting to leave the house for the day, but she was having an awesome time too. Hank had been the bright light in her life at the time. His regular visits were the only consistency she had. He would take her to the movie theater, getting all the usual questions out of the way during the drive. Did she need anything? Were the insert-name-here foster parents taking good care of her? Making sure she had hot food, clean clothes, her own bed? The answer was usually yes, but she didn't care about any of that as long as he continued to show up. She knew she was too old to get adopted once she went into the system, so his visits were the closest thing she had to simulating a family.

Once they were at the theater, the questions stopped and the rest of the day was about movies and munchies. She usually got to pick the film, and she could order any food she wanted within a certain budget. On the way home, she would ask Hank questions about his life. How were his real kids? And what was it like to be an attorney? He told her stories about his children and his cases that caused her to long for a sense of belonging and purpose.

Today, the parking lot at the theater was jam-packed, but Bill managed to find a spot on his third turn though the lot. While he squeezed his car into the tiny space, she pulled out her phone to check the movie schedule and saw she had a new text.

Hate to bother you, but I'm looking for the notes on the draft jury instructions in the Wilson case. Any chance you know where they are?

Camille. Damn, even a text about work had her heart racing. She thumbed a quick message back: *Did you check the binder labeled pretrial?* The reply was instantaneous.

First place I looked.

How about the file cabinet by the copier? Bill turned off the car, and West started to shove her phone back in her pocket, but it buzzed in her hand.

Second place I looked.

West considered before typing again. They could go back and forth like this all day, but if she were at the office, she would probably be able to lay her hands on the notes Camille was looking for in a matter of seconds. She looked at the movie schedule. Nothing grabbed her and she was feeling pretty sluggish from the huge lunch. "Hey, Bill, would you be really upset if we skipped the movie? I've got something I need to take care of."

"Are you kidding?" Bill said, rubbing his stomach. "I'm on the edge of a food coma. I was going because you wanted to, but if I can get a nap instead, I'm totally on board. You need me to drop you off somewhere?"

West considered her options. She didn't like being without wheels, but they were close to downtown and she didn't want to take the time to go all the way back home.

Within fifteen minutes, she was standing in front of the court building. She'd texted Camille to let her know she was still thinking about where the documents could be, but she hadn't mentioned she was coming by. Partly she didn't want to risk Camille telling her not to come and partly she just wanted to surprise her. But now that she was here, she felt kinda silly for dropping her plans to run to the office for the chance to spend a few minutes alone with Camille. *You're a lost cause, Fallon.*

When she poked her head in the office, she heard Camille's voice. "Who's there?"

"It's West," she called, biting back anything else since, for the first time, it occurred to her Camille might not be alone. "A little bird told me you might be having trouble finding some documents?"

"The bird was correct." Camille appeared in the doorway of her office. "But I certainly didn't mean for you to ditch your plans and come in on a weekend to help supplement my lousy investigational skills."

"I know, but I wanted to."

"Then you're crazier than I thought." Camille waved her in. "Don't just stand there looking handsome, start searching for the lost scrolls of case notes."

"Sure. Right." West dove into the box Camille had pointed to, happy to have a task that would distract her from Camille's words. Did Camille really think she was handsome? *Could you be more like a ten-year-old school girl?* "I was thinking Ester might have it. She was going to type up the notes and put them in the binders. It's possible she didn't get to it yet. I bet they're in her desk."

West walked over to Ester's desk and fished around behind the computer monitor until she located a small key. She unlocked the top drawer and pulled out a stack of papers. "Here you go," she said, handing the document to Camille, whose face was scrunched up in a weird, questioning expression. "What?"

"I don't know where to start. First, apparently, Ester likes you way better than me since I had no idea that's where she kept her desk key. Second, you could have told me all this over the phone."

But then I wouldn't have gotten to see you. West chose not to speak the words for fear they would break the mood. "You know, I bet the typed up version is on the computer network."

Camille's face scrunched into a pained smile. "Yeah, I seem to have locked myself out of the system. I can only access documents on my local drive."

"I bet I can help you with that."

"It's the weekend. Don't you have plans?"

"You're working, I'm working. That's kinda how it's done. Although, I bet most judges would make their clerks work while they took the weekend off."

"I'm not most judges."

"I noticed."

Camille cleared her throat. "I mean I need to put in the extra time. I have a feeling this trial is going to be very different from any I presided over in state court."

West decided to let the flirtatious moment pass since Camille clearly had some reservations about the trial. "Piece of cake. Besides, you've seen all this from the other side. Weren't you an AUSA?"

"I was, but we did a lot less litigating than state court prosecutors. Most people faced with federal charges opt to plea. Besides, that was a long time ago. You were probably in high school back then."

The remark hung in the air between them. West was already conscious of their age difference and it didn't bother her, but it seemed Camille felt the need to point it out. Time to steer this conversation in a different direction. "Do you want to talk about the jury charge?"

"Yes, that would be great."

"I'll go make a copy and meet you in the conference room."

West flicked the power button on the copy machine and used the time waiting for it to warm up to clear her head. She was here to work and nothing more. Playful banter wasn't an invitation for more, and as attracted as she was to Camille, it was better for both of them to stay professional or this year was going to seem like two.

The smell of freshly brewed coffee greeted her when she walked into the conference room to find Camille arranging her papers on the table, two steaming mugs in front of her. "You made coffee."

"You say that like it's a modern miracle. I may not be so handy with the computer network, but coffee is my life blood." She raised one of the mugs. "Black, right?"

West reached for the cup, lingering as their fingers touched. "Exactly." This year was going to be hard. Very hard.

"Okay, so I made some more notes last night and I want to sort through what will likely be some of the major issues before we start the trial so we can stay on track with evidentiary rulings." Camille shoved a legal pad her way. "Here are my notes."

"Pen and paper. Old school." West pulled the legal pad toward her.

"Sometimes I can't tell if you're making fun of me or…"

"Or?"

"Never mind." Camille pointed to a spot on the page and West followed her lead. If Camille wanted to keep things professional, she could deal even though what she really wanted was to reach over and pull Camille into a kiss to find out if they had undeniable steamy chemistry or if the attraction would fizzle and fade away.

She resisted the urge and instead spent the next few hours engaged in spirited discussion about the jury instructions in front of them. When she returned from a trip to the bathroom, Camille had packed up her paperwork and was sitting on the edge of the conference room table. "I think we should call it a day. It is Saturday after all."

"Not to mention I've searched every drawer in this place and the only food on hand are a few stale granola bars."

"You should talk to the boss about that."

"Oh, I plan to. I'd write a memo, you know, if I weren't so busy writing other kinds of memos."

"Oh my, sounds like you're overworked."

"And underfed."

"Let me buy you dinner."

West did a double take, unsure if the invitation was a natural extension of their playful banter or a genuine invite. Camille's expression was part hopeful, part bracing. West wanted to accept—anything to keep this connection alive, but it was probably a good idea to be extra clear where they were headed. "Dinner would be great. Two conditions."

"Conditions," Camille said, nodding her head. "Sounds serious."

"I pay my own way."

"Okay. And the other condition?"

West started to say what she'd planned to. That whatever dinner was, it was just a meal between friends, but something—the hope in Camille's eyes, the undercurrent of push and pull that had pulsed between them all day—kept her from cutting off the possibilities that might exist. It might be silly to think anything could happen between them, but she wasn't ready to write it off just yet. "The other condition is pizza. I've been craving it all day," she lied, unwilling to admit out loud that she'd been craving something else entirely.

Cane Russo, the popular pizza spot in Deep Ellum, was starting to get crowded, but they managed to snag one of the last tables. Camille watched West look around like she was unfamiliar with the place. "I take it you haven't been here before."

"No. I've heard great things, though."

Camille had chosen the spot not just because it had great pizza, but also because it wasn't far from the place West had taken her on their first date. Date? That hadn't really been a date, and this wasn't either even if both occasions had felt exactly like that. "If you don't like it, I'll owe you another pizza dinner, and you can choose the place."

A waitress walked by with a steaming pizza, and the amazing scent wafted through the air. West closed her eyes and smiled. "Wow. I think I'm going to like it here just fine."

They ordered and the wood-fired pizza came quickly. In between bites, Camille struggled to find something to talk about that didn't seem too personal. "What were you doing when I texted you today?"

"I was on a date."

"Really?" Camille braced for whatever she was about to say.

"Really," West said. "Lunch and a movie. I ditched the movie to help out a certain judge, but lunch was good."

"I'm sorry you missed your movie."

"No worries. I didn't pick the flick. Bill did."

"Bill?"

"He's my roommate."

"Date, huh?"

"I didn't say it was a romantic date."

Camille tossed a piece of crust at West who feigned injury. Roommate. Camille wasn't sure why the idea of West having a roommate bothered her. Perhaps because it was a marker of youth, starting out. Young college kids had roommates. West was still at the very beginning of her career while Camille had already experienced several professional successes. But the only reason to be bothered about the difference in their respective places in life was if there was going to be something more to their relationship than judge and clerk. And there wasn't. Camille tried to imagine showing up at an event with West on her arm. Even if West was perfectly polite, people would talk, and she couldn't blame them. She'd already noticed the glances West received from some of the more conservative judges and attorneys at the courthouse, certain they disapproved of her edgy appearance, not to mention the hint of a tattoo snaking up the side of her neck. Even her liberal parents would probably be appalled if she showed up at a function with West by her side.

"Tell me about your tattoo." She blurted the words without thinking, and West's look of surprise told her she'd crossed a line. "Sorry, none of my business."

West laughed. "Don't be silly. I was just wondering which one you were asking about."

"There's more than one?"

"Uh-huh."

"But you're not going to tell me how many?"

"It's more of a show than tell kind of thing."

Acutely conscious she was walking a thin line, Camille gingerly stepped further into the conversation. "Why don't you tell me about the one I can see?"

"Fair enough." West rolled up the rest of her sleeve to reveal an intricate drawing of a dragon. "Dragons are ubiquitous, I know, but that doesn't make them any less cool, right?"

Camille reached over, traced the tail, and then drew quickly back as if the act had been unconscious. "What makes this one particularly cool to you?"

"Well, I was born in the year of the dragon, you know, Chinese zodiac." West's eyes took on a faraway look, and Camille suddenly felt like she was intruding on a private memory.

"You don't have to tell me."

"It's okay. There's really not a lot to it. Symbolizes strength, passion, you know, things you need to overcome adversity."

Camille wanted to acknowledge without prying even though she was dying to know more about the exact adversities West had overcome. "We could all use a dose of dragon. That one's pretty intricate. Did it hurt?"

"Yes. And no amount of alcohol makes it hurt less, no matter what anyone tells you." She leaned back in her chair. "You're wondering why anyone would put something so permanent on their body."

"A little."

"Sometimes you need something permanent. A constant reminder. Especially when everything else about your life has been in flux." She pointed to the tattoo. "This kept me grounded when I needed it most."

Camille took a moment to let West's words penetrate. She could think of plenty of times she could've used something to ground her. After last November's election, she'd felt like she'd lost her way, unable to reconcile her career choice with the choice of the voters who'd turned on her at the first mistake. In the end, she'd clung to the tenacity that had saved her time and time again and forged a new career path. She tried to imagine what a tattoo representing that would look like.

"And the others," Camille asked. "Do they all have special meaning?"

"Yes, but like I said, you'd have to see them to really get it."

Camille sucked in a breath at the thought of West slowly undressing to reveal one story after another. A truly personal telling she'd never witness. Suddenly, the restaurant was claustrophobic and the air crackled with anticipation, threatening to consume her. They'd demolished the pizza and there was no practical reason for them to stay. She looked at her watch. "This was fun, but I need to go."

"Have another date?"

Camille resisted saying this wasn't a date, but she didn't bother examining why. Instead she settled on a vague "kind of," and was immediately sorry to see the disappointment flash in West's eyes. Better to disappoint her now than let things get too heated between them. She pulled out her wallet. "Let me get this. We spent half of dinner talking about work."

West looked like she was about to protest and then changed course. "Sure, whatever."

Camille paid the bill and they walked out to the parking lot together. The warm night air only served to magnify the chill between them, and when West insisted on getting an Uber instead of a lift from her, Camille told herself it was best they go their separate ways. She waited until West was in the car, and then reached into her purse for her keys.

"Judge Avery?"

The familiar voice came from behind her, and Camille's first thought was to wonder how long Lloyd had been standing there. Had he seen her with West? Had he read anything telling in their body language? She was being silly. Lloyd Garber wasn't the kind of guy who noticed anything that didn't revolve around him. She plastered on a fake smile and turned his way. "Hi, Lloyd." She nodded at the woman wrapped around his arm. "Are you two having a nice evening?"

"Absolutely," Lloyd said, although his date's expression remained sour. "You out by yourself tonight?"

"Just grabbing a bite to eat." She held up her keys and feigned a yawn. "You kids have fun." She walked briskly away, anxious to escape his questions, only half caring that her failure to introduce herself to Lloyd's date might be perceived as rude. Of course, he'd seemed more interested in what she was up to than introductions, so she wasn't sure why she felt bad at all.

The truth was nothing had happened between her and West, so any guilt or anxiety she felt about the possibility of getting caught socializing with her outside of work was misplaced. She should be more worried about the way West made her feel both on and off the job.

❖

Camille was halfway home when her phone rang. She glanced at the display on her dash. Jay. She pressed the answer button on the steering wheel. "Hey, Jay."

"What are you doing right now?"

"Driving."

"Wherever you're headed, abandon the destination. I'm at Luxe. Meet me there."

"It's late, Jay."

"Don't give me that BS. It's not even eight o'clock on a Saturday night."

"Can it wait until another time? I still have work to do."

"No. It can't wait. I promise I wouldn't ask you if it weren't important."

Jay rarely asked for favors, and after the way her evening with West ended, she was feeling restless. "One hour and then I'm heading home before I turn into a pumpkin. Understood?"

"Completely. I'll leave your name with the doorman."

Luxe was a new club in town, trendy and exclusive, and Camille hated it. Jay professed she had joined only to have a place to impress some of her most important clients, but Camille suspected she might actually enjoy the VIP treatment she received as a premier member. Camille found the whole place, from personnel to price, stifling.

Once she made it past the gatekeeper at the door who'd spelled her name wrong, she walked back to the special members section roped off from the rest of the well-heeled crowd with tall blue velvet curtains.

"Camille!"

She turned and Jay drew her into a hug. "I was by the door, but I didn't see you come in."

"Probably because Mr. Hulk, aka gatekeeper, was blocking the view. If this place does such a good job of screening out the undesirables for membership, you'd think you wouldn't need a bouncer at the door."

"Someone's grumpy. No worries. I have something that's going to cheer you right up. Come with me."

Camille didn't have time to protest before Jay grabbed her by the arm and pulled her toward one of the curtained off sections. "What's the surprise?"

"Make that who's the surprise. I'm here with Liz, and she brought a friend who just happens to be on assignment in Dallas for the next six months. And what a friend she is."

Camille pulled back. "Oh no you don't. If you'd told me this was a setup, I could have saved you the trouble and me the trip."

"Don't be a killjoy, Avery. The best remedy for a stressful job is a carefree personal life. Besides, I checked her out already. She has the perfect pedigree and she's smart and gorgeous. Would I ever steer you wrong?"

"Yes, but you wouldn't mean to."

"One drink. If you aren't interested after that, I'll tip the valet and send you on your way. Deal?"

Camille weighed her options. She was already here. If she went home, chances are she would try to work, and West would distract her thoughts. Maybe a drink with a pretty stranger was exactly what she needed to take her mind off of everything else. "One drink." She held up a finger as Jay's face glowed with victory. "I reserve the right to bug out before my drink is done if she's a dud."

"She's not, and you won't." Jay looped their arms. "Trust me."

Camille followed Jay into the curtained-off private room, prepared for anything. Liz, Jay's on-again, off-again, girlfriend, was seated on a cushioned sofa with a bottle of Cristal and four glasses on the table in front of her. "Hey, Camille, come on in. Allow me to introduce you to my dear friend, Sadie Jackson."

As if on cue, a tall, leggy brunette appeared from Camille's right. Jay had not been wrong. Sadie was beautiful. Honey brown waves of hair framed her classically beautiful face, and her deep brown eyes seemed to read Camille's hesitation. "Nice to meet you in person. Don't worry, I hate setups and blind dates. They're the worst."

"So instead of lying in wait, plotting ways to win me over, you've been planning your escape?"

"Something like that." Sadie pointed to the table. "But the champagne is top-notch, so there's that."

Witty, pretty. Camille made two mental marks in the plus column. "Looks like you've had a little more time to prepare for this. How about you pour me a glass and we can commiserate."

While Sadie poured her drink, Camille looked over at Jay who mouthed "told you so" and then grabbed Liz's hand. "You kids can bitch about us in private. We're going to dance." They vanished past the curtain before Camille could say a word.

"Those two don't play nice," Sadie said, handing over a glass of bubbly.

"True." Camille took a sip. "Please tell me you made them buy."

"Absolutely. This stuff is special occasion only for me. Although, tonight is turning out to be way more of a special occasion than I thought."

"You did not just give me a line, did you?"

"I guess I did. Pretty lame, huh?"

Camille started to say yes, but she'd already started to relax. This fun banter came with no strings attached, unlike the flirtatious conversations she'd had with West that were loaded with risk. She surrendered to the moment. "Are you going to invite me to sit down?"

"You don't strike me as the kind of woman that waits to be invited, but please, have a seat. Tell me all about your day. Liz tells me you're a federal judge."

"True. I spent the day working, I'm afraid. Big trial coming up."

"Civil, criminal?"

Not the type of question a layperson usually asked. "Criminal. Are you a lawyer?"

"Doctor, but I've testified in plenty of court cases."

"Specialty?"

"Trauma surgeon."

"Ah, adrenaline junkie."

"I do like a good rush."

"Jay said you're here on assignment. Where from?"

"Chicago. I'm here to help train some of the fellows at a partner hospital."

Smart, stable. Two more checks in the plus column. Add to that the fact that unlike all the other eligible women in town, Sadie didn't know anything about her and probably hadn't seen any of the headlines crucifying her in the press. For all Sadie knew, Camille had been a federal judge for years.

They made small talk for a while, and eventually Liz and Jay reappeared, but when Jay suggested a second bottle, Camille begged off. "I still have a lot of work to do tomorrow. Enjoy your champagne."

"I'll walk you out," Sadie said. Camille started to protest, but Sadie was by her side in record time. She slipped her arm through

Camille's, and they strolled through the crowded bar to the front door where Sadie stopped and turned to face Camille. "This was one of the best non dates I've had in a while."

"You know, it was for me too," Camille replied. She stared into Sadie's questioning eyes, unable to tell exactly what she was asking and uncertain she'd have an answer even if she could.

"You sound surprised. How about this? Let's have another non date soon and see if this was just a fluke?"

Camille paused. Sadie was perfect. Funny, smart, good-looking. She should be crushing hard right now, but all she felt was the pull of what she should be feeling instead of actual emotion. Maybe she wasn't trying hard enough. Jay always said she gave up too easy. What harm could it do to go on another date? "That sounds like a perfect idea."

Chapter Ten

West ran until she could no longer feel her feet, but the brutal exercise didn't improve her mood. Endorphins, my ass. Now she had one more reason to hate this Monday morning.

She kicked off her shoes just inside the door and padded her way to the kitchen. Bill was lounging at the table with a cup of coffee and a box of donuts that made her want to punch him in the face.

"You look like shit," he said before biting into an enormous powdered pastry.

West waved a hand in the air. "And you're a slob. Who's going to wipe up all this sugar? And you think Gabe's going to want to marry someone who's carrying around twenty extra pounds of donut weight?"

"Uh, who said anything about marriage? Besides, Gabe brought the donuts and loves me just the way I am." Bill patted his stomach and then waved. "Hey, honey, West thinks I'm getting fat."

West turned to see Gabe standing behind her. "That's not exactly what I said."

"Close enough."

"I heard everything," Gabe said. "You girls need to quit fighting." He pointed at West. "Sit. Eat a donut. Lord knows you could use one."

She slid into a chair and stared at the pink box while Gabe fixed her a cup of coffee and set it down in front of her. "Now," he said. "Do you want to tell us what's on your mind?"

"Nothing."

"She's been in a foul mood since she ditched me for work on Saturday," Bill said. "They're overworking you, kid. You want me to give the judge a call and tell her you're taking a mental health day?"

"Don't even think about it." West instantly regretted her snapped reaction, because Bill's eyes opened wide and he went into teasing mode.

"What's up, darling?" he asked. "Trouble in paradise?"

She reached for a donut, more as a distraction than because she was hungry. She hadn't eaten much since Camille had left for her date Saturday night, and her appetite wasn't the only thing that was off. She'd canceled lunch with Hank and Diane yesterday, certain Hank would be able to tell something was wrong, and not wanting to have to dissect her feelings or hide the truth. She shouldn't have gone running this morning on an empty stomach, but pounding out her frustrations seemed like the only reasonable way to deal with the irritating image of Camille on a date.

"There's no such thing as paradise," she said. "Well, unless you count this donut." She tore off a chunk of the maple iced long john and shoved it in her mouth.

"Stop teasing her," Gabe said. He picked up the paper and started reading. "Hey, isn't this the name of the judge you're working for?" He folded the paper and handed it over.

West scanned the page until she spotted the small article under the fold. The headline read *Jury Selection to Begin Next Week in Overdose Death of Richards University Student*, followed by a three-paragraph mention of the trial that was starting in a week. The reporter mentioned Camille as the newly appointed federal judge and provided a thumbnail sketch of the charges, along with a brief "no comment" from the government and a "he's not guilty" from the defense. "Yes, that's her. Trial starts next Monday. It's a pretty interesting case."

"I remember when that girl went missing. Didn't they think the boyfriend did it?"

"The cops thought a lot of people were suspects from what I hear. I don't know if anyone will ever know what really happened, but the government charged Wilson with selling her the drugs she overdosed on. He's looking at a potential life sentence."

"Sad."

West nodded. Everything about the case was sad, from the wealthy co-ed with a bright future who'd become a drug addict, left for dead in the woods, to the convicted murderer left unsupervised so he could resume his criminal ways. She'd spent the summers advocating for the oppressed, many of the cases focused on overturning decades-old criminal convictions, long past the time when the presumption of innocence had passed. Those cases often involved the same kind of overreaching from prosecutors that this one did, but never had she felt such a personal connection to the victim. From the moment she'd read the indictment, she'd been torn between sorrow at the indignity Leslie Silver had suffered and anger that she'd willingly put herself in danger by using. The vivid description of how construction workers had stumbled across her naked body, wrapped in a rug, stirred memories of the day she'd come home from school to find her mother, naked on the bathroom floor, a needle still hanging from her arm and her body battered from the man who'd raped her and left her for dead. The comparison left West cold.

She shook her head. She had no business letting her personal aversion get in the way of this case, or any cases for that matter, but it wasn't easy. Still, she didn't believe someone should be facing life in prison for selling a commodity in such high demand. Wilson should go to prison for violating drug laws, but punishing him also because the willing drug user had overdosed? Total overreaching.

But it didn't matter what she thought. Camille had already made it clear she wasn't about to declare a well-settled federal law unconstitutional and the issue wasn't hers to raise anyway.

"West?"

She tuned back in to see Bill waving a napkin in front of her face. "What?"

"Don't you need to get to work? It's almost eight o'clock."

"Shit." She'd fallen into a post-run, donut sugar coma, and now she had negative minutes to shower and drive downtown. Balancing how she felt about this case and her growing feelings for Camille was going to be the death of her.

❖

Camille poked her head into the office Lloyd and West shared. Lloyd was combing through a binder, but West was nowhere in sight. She'd already looked in the kitchenette and the conference room, and there was no sign of her in either place. In a minute, she was going to have to resort to asking someone if she wanted to know where West was.

And she did. The realization surprised her a little. She'd gotten used to West being around, and when she wasn't, everything felt a bit off. Plus, she wanted to smooth over how they'd parted Saturday night, but she wasn't going to be able to tackle that uncomfortable subject unless she could catch her alone.

"Hi, Judge, you need me?" Lloyd asked, his expression hopeful.

"Actually, I was hoping you and West could come to my office. Is she around?"

"Haven't seen her yet this morning, but I can tell she worked over the weekend." He pointed to her desk. "She left it all neat and clean on Friday, but now it looks like a frat house on Sunday morning. Guess she didn't go out over the weekend like the rest of us."

He smiled at his own joke, and she returned the smile to cover her concern, ignoring his reference to seeing her over the weekend. West was usually early, never late. "Okay, I was hoping to go over the cases for the morning docket."

Lloyd stood with a fistful of files. "I've got them right here and I'm ready to go over them if you want."

She didn't, but she couldn't very well tell him that without looking foolish. "That's great, but sit down, we can do it here." She settled into West's chair, happy she'd figured out a way to see her the minute she walked in.

Half an hour passed, and she spent the time half-listening to Lloyd while casting surreptitious glances between her watch and the door. To her surprise, Lloyd had done a decent job of summarizing the case issues, and if she'd had the wherewithal to fully focus on what he was saying, she'd probably be very well prepared for the morning docket. As it was, she'd be lucky to make it through the day.

"And that's it," Lloyd said. "Do you want the files or do you want me to have Ester put them on the bench?"

She reached for the stack. "I'll take care of it." In her struggle to focus, she started with him. He looked eager and pleased to have been singled out to brief her this morning. She'd been so fixed on West, Lloyd had seemed like an afterthought. "I'm going to grab a quick cup of coffee and then get started." She held up one of the files. "I have a feeling counsel on the Johnson case are going to need to speak to me in chambers. If you're not busy, why don't you sit in?"

"That would be great. Thanks."

She strode through the door to the kitchen, desperate for more caffeine, but what she saw jolted her awake. West was leaning against the counter, carefully tending to a French press while Ester looked on. They were laughing and talking like old friends, and West seemed entirely unconcerned that she was late and certainly not in any hurry to start doing actual work.

"Good morning." Camille injected all the authority she could muster into her tone. "Looks like you're having a good time."

"Thanks, Judge. We sure are," Ester said. "West was showing me how to improve my coffee-making skills." Ester held up the French press before pouring a cup. "Thanks, West." She looked at Camille. "I'll be at my desk if you need me."

So much for authority. Camille started to follow Ester out of the kitchen, but West's voice held her back. "No coffee for you?"

"I've already had coffee this morning. It's almost time for docket call. I don't like to be late."

West's eyes blazed. "You mean you don't like me to be late. We never really discussed coming and going requirements."

"I guess we didn't. I guess I didn't think we had to."

"You're mad at me," West said, sounding defensive.

"Mad? No. I'm…" Camille sorted through her feelings, searching for the precise emotion, but nothing she came up with was anything she wanted to say out loud. Disappointed? Sad? Out of sorts? She'd shown up expecting West to be at the office, available and ready for whatever she had planned, and she'd been agitated when that hadn't been the case. Now West was here and instead of their friendly back-and-forth, there was a distinct edge between them and she sensed it might be partly her fault. But she couldn't say any of this because if she did there was no telling what else might come tumbling out.

Jay was right. She needed to get out more. If she'd come to rely on her law clerk for social interaction, it was time for an intervention, and she knew exactly how to self-help. "I'm not mad at you. Not at all. Why don't you and Lloyd meet me in my office? I'll be right there."

She waited until West left the kitchen and then she pulled out her cell. She'd looked at Sadie's number a few times since Saturday night, but she hadn't been motivated to actually punch the buttons that would put them in contact. She wasn't sure if she was ready now, but she didn't let that stop her, typing the message as fast as her thumbs could fly across the keyboard.

I'm game for another non date if you are.

She hit send before she could change her mind, the whooshing sound of the text winging its way toward the unknown oddly comforting, like the whole thing was out of her hands.

Despite what she'd told West, she could use a cup of coffee, so she poured a cup of West's special blend and took a much needed sip. Time to get her game face on because not only did she have to pretend she had no attraction to West, she also needed to start acting like she was in charge and not like they were equal members on the same team. Camille was two steps toward the kitchen door when her phone chimed.

Sounds perfect. Let's non date Friday night. Meet you at Cafe Izmir on Greenville. 8 p.m.?

Camille typed a quick yes and shut her phone down, happy to have her personal life settled. Too bad she felt anything but.

Chapter Eleven

West leaned back in her chair and yawned. "Time to make more coffee."

"No, it's time to go home," Lloyd said. "It's finally Friday, and we've worked our asses off this week."

West considered her options. This week had both dragged on and spun past. With the trial starting Monday, there had been a flurry of last-minute filings from both the defense and government. Witness and exhibit lists, jury questionnaires and proposed voir dire questions had all come in at a fast clip. Lloyd was right. They had worked their asses off and they deserved to head home at a decent time. Once the trial started, they'd be working double-time.

The week had been made harder by all the energy she'd had to expend pretending there was nothing going on between her and Camille. Camille had done her part by keeping her distance, and it wasn't lost on West that Camille avoided being alone with her at every turn. Meetings in Camille's office always included Lloyd or Ester, and every time she encountered her alone, Camille had been on her way to a meeting or waiting for an important call.

Bill and Gabe had both pointed out that she was pining for something she couldn't have, and they'd tried to convince her to go out with them tonight. She couldn't remember the last time she'd been out dancing, and she wasn't in the mood. Besides, she could barely stay awake as it was. "I think I'll grab a coffee. I've got one more thing I want to do before I head out."

"You're welcome to it. If I don't get home soon, my fiancée is going to give back the ring."

Fiancée. Lloyd never referred to her by name, only by the relationship moniker, which kind of drove West crazy. Like the nameless chick had no more importance than the role she would fill. West didn't relate to the need for a personal life. Not having one allowed her to keep her options open. She could move to Montgomery or anywhere else at a moment's notice once this year's obligation was fulfilled, maybe earlier. With the current tension between her and Camille, maybe she could convince Hank to absolve her of her promise. She planned to talk to him about it over Sunday brunch.

In the meantime, she wanted to put the final touches on the draft of the juror questionnaire, and she wouldn't be able to without some java. The office was pretty quiet, and she figured it was safe to roam around without a chance of running into Camille. She picked up her coffee cup, walked to the kitchen, and methodically measured coffee into her French press while she waited for the electric kettle to heat the water. The coffee supply was running low and she'd have to make another trip to White Rock Coffee soon to pick up more. When she'd started bringing the special blend to the office, she hadn't intended to get the entire office hooked on it, but now that they were, she took pride in elevating their standards. Once upon a time, she'd never imagined she'd be drinking fancy coffee, being a lawyer—any of the accomplishments she currently enjoyed. Times had certainly changed.

"I knew it was you when I heard the kettle."

Camille's voice was soft and low, and West's body responded immediately to the sexy tone. She didn't turn around at first, taking time to assume a neutral expression. When she finally did turn, she almost lost her cool. Camille wasn't wearing the tailored suit she'd had on earlier. She was dressed in a curve-hugging little black dress and tall, tall heels. West wished she'd taken more time to gain her composure. "Am I that obvious?"

"I wouldn't call it obvious. Consistent, reliable maybe."

"Yeah, 'cause those adjectives are so much better."

"I've come to count on you."

Had she heard a hint of suggestion or was she imagining it? Her only hope to get out of this situation unscathed was to ignore the undercurrent. "Do you want coffee?"

"No, thanks."

"You look like you're going out." West hated that she'd spoken the words aloud, but curiosity got the best of her. What she really wanted to say was Camille looked crazy gorgeous, but drawing attention to the specifics would only stoke the fire burning her inside out. Did Camille have another date? Was it the same woman she'd rushed off to see last weekend? Was that some new perfume she smelled? Citrus and woods this time instead of flowers. What had happened to her that she was this obsessed over her boss?

"I am," Camille said. "Dinner plans. You?"

"Sure. I'll probably have dinner." West gestured at her own outfit. Like Camille, she'd changed clothes after work too, but her jeans and Converse spoke a night at home with pizza, not a night on the town.

Camille stepped closer. "You look good in casual. It suits you."

"Better than a tie and blazer?" West asked, caring way too intently what Camille thought about her appearance and hating that she did.

"Of course not." Camille ran a hand across West's shoulder, tracing her fingers along the seam of her sleeve. "I guess I just like this look best. It's more like what you were wearing when we first met."

"Right. Bet when you first met me you thought I worked in the Cafe on Six."

"Crossed my mind."

"You elitist, you."

"Hardly, but maybe I am too quick to judge."

"Clever." West's back was against the counter. She should feel trapped, but all she felt was deliciously captured. Every cell in her body cried out for Camille to come closer. She settled on a simple question. "And what do you think of me now?"

Camille leaned in close and whispered, "I don't know what to think."

Camille was inches away, her eyes dark, her lips slightly parted. "Maybe you think too much." West didn't wait for a response before she closed the few inches between them and claimed Camille's lips between her own.

Soft, firm, warm, and tender. She'd imagined this kiss many more times than she cared to admit, but never had she let herself think Camille would taste this good, feel so right. When Camille ran her tongue along her lips, she groaned, her knees weak with the shudder of intense heat between them. Whatever awkwardness had developed over the last week ebbed away, and the pull between them was undeniable.

A buzzing phone broke the spell. "Let it go," West gasped.

Camille pulled back, her hand already digging through the purse she'd tossed on the counter. "I'm sorry." The words were rote, but she had to say something. What had she just done? She'd kissed West. Or West had kissed her. Either way, she needed a second to process. She stared at her phone, relieved that the alarm telling her she was due to meet Sadie had saved her from… She had no idea what was going to happen next, but whatever it was, she knew it was dangerous.

"Don't be sorry."

Camille looked into West's eyes, burning with questions, shining with desire. She didn't have answers, and she couldn't afford to return the emotion reflected there. Sadie would be waiting at the restaurant. Beautiful, accomplished, safe, and appropriate. Camille had one choice, only one right one anyway, and she dug deep for the strength to make it. "I have to go." The low echo of soft footfalls drew her attention to the door. "What was that?"

West followed her gaze. "Nothing."

"Is someone here?"

"No one's here. Maybe it was the janitor." West reached for her hand. "Don't leave. Not yet."

Camille looked down at West's hand. She wanted to fold into her grasp, kiss her delicious lips again, and forget everything else. But she couldn't do it. She wouldn't do it. And she told herself it was for West's sake as much as her own. "Good night."

Too many steps to the elevator. Too many floors to the exit. Too many miles to meet the date she no longer wanted. Every inch of the distance away from West gripped her with regret, but she couldn't face the alternative. By the time she reached the restaurant, she'd managed to cage her emotions and was able to fake a convincing smile in the rearview mirror. What she wanted was back at the courthouse, but what she needed was waiting inside. She didn't really have a choice.

❖

West walked into the house and slumped onto the couch. The kiss. The kiss had been everything and nothing all at once. Camille had melted against her. She hadn't imagined that, but she also hadn't imagined how Camille had dashed away at the first opportunity, the haunted look in her eyes telling West she regretted the moment they'd shared. West knew she should be used to being second choice, but she kept making the mistake of hoping for more.

Maybe she shouldn't have kissed her. But she'd been so close, so beautiful, so inviting. Maybe Camille shouldn't walk around the office wearing sexy cocktail dresses if she didn't want to be kissed. West laughed at her own insanity.

"The first sign of demise is when she starts giggling and she's all alone."

Bill was standing across the room eating ice cream directly from a pint container. "I don't giggle," West said.

He waved his spoon in the air. "I beg to differ."

"You can beg all you want." She squinted at the ice cream. "Hey, isn't that the salted caramel I bought yesterday? And why are you here? I thought you and Gabe had a date."

"He got called in to work. Some emergency. Lots of broken limbs and blood. He was more excited about it than going dancing with me, so here I am." His eyes got wide and his lips curved into a knowing smile. "Hey, I have an idea!"

West recognized the look, and she acted quickly to ward off the idea engine chugging through Bill's brain. "Oh, no, not going to happen." West slouched down further into the sofa. "I'm staying right here and binging on episodes of *Orphan Black*."

"Right. Why drool over real hotties when you can watch them on TV?" He set the ice cream down and tugged on her arms. "Please come out with me. I can't remember the last time my weekend didn't get interrupted by surgeries galore, and if I don't go out dancing soon, I'll forget how. You can make sure I don't get into any trouble."

"Sounds like a blast for me," West said, but her resolve was crumbling.

"I'll be your wingman. I'm a great wingman."

"You'll be a lousy wingman because you'll be trolling for someone to keep you company while your boyfriend plays doctor."

"Boyfriend is a strong word for someone who I rarely see. And he's not playing doctor, he is one."

West looked from the ice cream in Bill's hand, to the TV, and back to the pretty please expression on Bill's face. Going out might be exactly what she needed to shake this malaise. Why should she sit home pining away over what might have happened if Camille hadn't dashed off after the best kiss ever?

"Okay, but—"

"Yes!" Bill punched the air.

"Wait," West said. "There are conditions."

"Sure. Whatever. Let's get dressed." He started to dash out of the room, but she grabbed his arm. "Three things. One, you don't get to ditch me for some shiny object you see in the bar. Two, you're driving. Three, I need to go shopping for a few new suits for work tomorrow and you're going with me. Agree to these terms and I'll go with you."

Bill cocked his head. "Hmm, I never figured you for stereotyping." He pointed his thumb toward his chest. "Me no like to shop."

"Great, we can be miserable together. Look, I hate it too and I don't want to go alone. Besides, you're the only person I can count on to make sure the salesclerk doesn't try to stick me with some femme 'career girl' clothes." She assumed what she hoped was a fierce look. "It's a deal breaker."

"Fine. I accept your terms. Now go get dressed. You're going to have the time of your life."

West laughed at his cliché. A night at the club dancing with strangers would hardly qualify as the time of her life, but the kiss she'd shared with Camille? Definitely in contention.

The club was starting to get really crowded by the time they arrived. She sent Bill to get beers, then took up a spot on the edge of the dance floor. Dancing wasn't really her thing, but it was the best people watching on the planet and she desperately needed the distraction.

"Here's your beer," Bill said, handing her the bottle. "See any prospects?"

"I'm not here for that."

"Well, you should be. Getting laid might make you a happier person. Remember, I'm dating a doctor, so I know all about these things."

"Yes, Bill, of course I'm going to take mental health advice from you since you're dating a doctor and all. Besides, if you were Mr. Happy, you wouldn't be here, you'd be home waiting for your doctor man to get home."

"Wait not for happiness. You must seek it out." Bill pointed a hand in the air like he was making a profound declaration. "Besides, we don't have that kind of relationship yet. Not even sure if I want it."

West took a healthy swallow from her beer. She got where Bill was coming from. She'd never gone for more than a semi-steady relationship, but she liked to think she was open to more, which was kinda crazy since she had little reference for how committed relationships even worked. Her mother had never been married, and men drifted in and out of her life like fickle shoppers. Hank had been married to Diane forever, but West had always considered them the exception, not the rule. Bill and Gabe seemed perfect for each other, but neither one seemed committed to ruling out others. Who was she to think she could be in a committed relationship? Crazy. "I hear you."

"Then let's have some fun tonight."

"Is that code for I've just spotted some guy I want to check out and so I'm ditching you now?"

"Not yet, but I'm keeping my options open." He wagged a finger in her face. "And so should you."

"Fine." She touched her bottle to his. "Options open. And you have permission to ditch me, but don't leave without saying anything. Deal?"

"Deal."

They drank their beers while scanning the room. One of the things she liked about Bill was they could be quiet with each other, neither one of them feeling like they had to fill the silence with constant chatter, but tonight the quiet cloaked her in loneliness. Bill didn't seem to notice, his eyes sweeping the room intently. "Tell me what you see."

"For you or me?" he asked.

"You. I'm not looking."

"Whatever." He jerked his chin to the left. "By the bar. Jet-black hair, piercing blue eyes."

West squinted in the direction Bill had indicated. "I spy jet-black, but no way can you see eye color from here. If we're making stuff up, then I see an Emma Watson look-alike standing by the DJ booth and she wants me. Bad."

"I thought you promised not to be a killjoy."

"I promised I would come with you, but my mood wasn't part of the negotiation."

"Spoken like a true litigator."

"Got to get practice somehow. Won't get to do any litigating until next year."

"How's it going or should I not ask?"

West studied his face, but saw no signs he was asking for any reason other than friendly curiosity. Part of her wanted to tell him what had happened with Camille after work, but the rest of her screamed no. Besides, she was probably making too big a deal out of it. They'd kissed and Camille had run away, leaving a pretty clear message in her wake.

But the kiss… The kiss had left West wanting more, and she was certain Camille had too before her phone rang and broke the trance, leaving West to wonder what would have happened next if they hadn't been interrupted.

It didn't matter. Camille was off somewhere, in her sexy black dress, dating someone else. Another judge, a veteran lawyer? A socialite? She shook her head. Whoever it was, it wasn't her, and she had no claim on Camille. She should borrow a page from Bill's book and seize the moment. She was in a crowded bar, surrounded by pretty people. Maybe getting laid was exactly what she needed to get past the angst of whatever wasn't happening between her and Camille.

"Tell you what," she said to Bill, "If the next song is slow, you go ask jet-black piercing blues to dance, and I'll take Emma Watson for a spin."

Bill grinned wide. "You've got yourself a deal."

She kept an eye on the woman by the booth, sizing her up. She was youngish, probably mid-twenties, and she was here with three other women West pegged as friends based on the way they each gazed more at the rest of the room than each other. She wasn't keen on asking her to dance in front of her friends, but it was clear none of them were going away anytime soon. When the music switched and Beiber's "Company" came on, she took a deep breath and walked over.

"Hey," she managed as they all turned to greet her.

"Hey," the Emma Watson look-alike answered. Bar shadows were playing tricks because up close she didn't really look like Watson. She was pretty, just not striking. Not like Camille. Hell, one word in and West was ready to abandon this plan. She scrambled to find some way to retreat, but the woman grabbed her hand.

"You're not leaving are you? You just got here."

"Sorry, I'm here with a friend."

"That one?" The woman pointed a few feet away where Bill was deep in conversation with the guy with the jet-black hair. "He looks like he might be staying for a while."

"You might be right."

"My name's Kelsey."

West looked down at Kelsey's hand, feeling like if she shook it she'd be all in—not a signal she wanted to send. Which was silly. When she finally reached out, Kelsey's grip was firm and sure and followed by a question. "You wanna dance?"

She didn't really, but there were only two other alternatives: carry on a conversation or walk away. Talking was at the complete bottom of her list, and surprisingly, she wasn't quite ready to walk away. "Yeah, sure."

Kelsey took her arm and they walked out onto the dance floor. The song was still playing, and Kelsey moved into West's arms and placed her hands behind her head. West closed her eyes and focused on the rhythm. When Kelsey drew closer, she pretended she was Camille and shivered against her touch. This night might have been about forgetting, but maybe she wasn't ready to shelve her feelings even if she should.

She'd figure it out later. For now, she'd enjoy being touched by this stranger until she couldn't pretend anymore.

❖

"Confess, you don't like Mediterranean food."

Camille looked up from pushing food around her plate into Sadie's questioning eyes. Truth was she loved Cafe Izmir with its cozy dining rooms, attentive service, and incredible selection of Middle Eastern tapas, but tonight her mind was too tangled up with thoughts about the kiss she'd shared with West. Every time she took a bite of food, her stomach pitched and swayed. It wasn't the food, it was her mood, torn between being relieved to be anywhere West wasn't and disappointed that she wasn't sharing this intimate dinner with her.

"I'm sorry. I've been a horrible date."

Sadie put down her fork and reached for Camille's hand. "No, you're not, but I can tell you have something on your mind. Want to talk about it?"

"Not really." Camille looked down at their intertwined fingers, the pseudo intimate touch. She should feel something, shouldn't she? Sadie checked off so many boxes on the perfect date list. Determined to try harder, Camille said. "Work stuff. You know…"

"I do," Sadie said. "It sucks to have jobs where the things that bother you the most are the things you can't really share with anyone else. Confidentiality blows."

Camille laughed at the blunt remark. She liked this woman, she really did, and she made a resolution to try harder. She picked up her fork. "And for the record, I adore Mediterranean food, especially this place. It's one of my favorites."

"Excellent. Then you better dig in before I claim dibs on that last dolma."

The rest of the meal was spent swapping stories about their careers, and Camille shared a glossed over synopsis of her work history. "And now here I am with a lifetime appointment to a federal bench."

"That's some kind of tenure. Is it everything you imagined?"

Camille started to say yes, but the truth was this experience was nothing she could have ever imagined. If someone had told her she'd develop a crush on a law clerk she'd been pushed to keep, she would've said they were crazy. But now she was locked in for the next year and she was going to have to figure out a way to make it work without crossing the line she'd plowed through early this evening. "It's a bit more challenging than I would have thought, but nothing I can't handle."

"I have no doubt." Sadie raised her wine glass. "To challenges."

"To challenges." Camille tipped her glass against Sadie's and drank to the toast.

"My personal challenge now that dinner is over is to convince you to help me work this food off. I hear there's an excellent dance bar on Cedar Springs."

Camille's gut told her to beg off. She'd barely been able to do justice to the date so far—bright lights and disco balls would hardly help. But after moping her way through dinner, she owed Sadie some fun to round out the evening. She liked that Sadie hadn't suggested they return to Luxe, instead selecting one of the more down-to-earth places in the gayborhood. A big bass beat and a wide-open dance floor might be exactly what she needed to clear her head. "Consider me convinced."

Sadie drove, insisting it was silly to take two cars, so Camille acted as navigator, pointing out some of her favorite Dallas spots to Sadie along the way. Playing tour guide was a perfect task to keep her mind from wandering to thoughts about West and what she was doing tonight. By the time they reached the club, Camille managed to shove the memory of the kiss to the back of her mind and shift her entire focus to her date. As they walked through the door of S4, Sadie took her arm and Camille didn't move away. Progress.

"Is it always this packed?" Sadie asked, her mouth close to Camille's ear, her voice warm and inviting.

"I haven't been here in a while." Camille scrunched her face. "Actually, I can't remember the last time I was here." She'd been a political animal for the last five years, and although she'd never kept her sexuality a secret, there was a big difference between being a lesbian and being a lesbian running for judge who frequented bars where go-go dancers wiggled their butts for cash and the upstairs room featured a drag show every night. She cared just as much about her reputation now as she had then, but the security of a lifetime appointment meant she should be able to indulge every once in a while. She cast a long look out over the crowd, but there wasn't a sign of any stuffy lawyers or judges in the place. "Let's get a drink." She grabbed Sadie's hand and tugged her through the crowd.

They ordered extra dirty martinis from the buff bartender, and then climbed the stairs to the second floor balcony, scoring a table by the railing from a couple of guys who, judging by the smoldering looks passing between them, were headed home early for a little privacy.

"Dallas is much more fun than I thought it would be." Sadie raised her glass.

"I was just about to say the same thing."

"Let me guess. You're all work and no fun."

"Ouch. That makes me sound like a bore."

"I didn't mean anything by it. I know how hard it can be to find time to indulge when you have a high pressure career, but I also know it's absolutely essential."

"Spoken like a true doctor." Camille sipped her martini, enjoying the briny olive juice against the earthy juniper flavor. "Is this the perfect medicine?"

"It's a good start." Sadie clinked their glasses together. "When you're finished with this dose, we'll head downstairs and add a little exercise to the de-stressing program."

Camille pressed against the railing and watched the writhing crowd below, letting thoughts of the upcoming trial and West Fallon recede against the rhythm of the music and the mellow course of gin through her veins. She couldn't remember the last time she'd let everything go and just enjoyed life without questioning the consequence of every action, however small. Everyone on the dance floor seemed to have already found the secret to having fun—moving in time to the music, hands in the air, hands on each other. She took another sip of her martini determined to relax enough to join them.

When she reached the bottom of her glass, she started to turn back to Sadie and tell her she was ready for phase two of the program when a familiar face caught her eye. West, moving through the crowd. Camille leaned further over the railing, but West was gone, lost in a sea of bodies. If she'd really been there in the first place. Camille felt a hand on her back and looked over her shoulder at Sadie who wore a quizzical expression.

"Do you want another drink or are you ready to dance?"

Camille wavered. If she said she wanted another drink, she could use the time while Sadie was getting it to scour the crowd again, but if they went down to the dance floor, maybe she'd run into West. Either prospect both excited and horrified her. She had no business thinking about West at all, especially not when she was out on a date with another woman. After their kiss, she'd rejected West's advances, and that had been the absolute right thing to do, but apparently, it hadn't been enough to kill the desire. This obsession was making her crazy, paralyzed, and distracted. She was here with a smart, beautiful woman. Someone her own age who understood professionalism and didn't challenge her every move. The right choice was clear. "I think I'm ready—"

Words fell away when she spotted West again. She was in the farthest corner of the room, half on, half off the dance floor. Her body swayed in time with the beat, but her movements weren't about the music since she appeared to be moving in response to the woman whose hands were running down her body. Camille stared, transfixed, as West's head titled back, eyes closed, as her dance partner's hands moved down to cup her ass. Was she groaning against this woman's touch? Was it the same husky, sexy sound she'd made when they kissed at the office?

Camille gripped the railing as her stomach roiled, but she couldn't look away. She was locked onto West, her mind crawling with questions, all of which added to her growing ache.

"Camille, are you okay?"

Damn. In the span of seconds, she'd completely forgotten about Sadie. They'd been talking. Sadie had asked her something. Asked her to dance. And she'd almost said yes. Now the idea of being in such close proximity to West and the woman clawing her was unthinkable. "Actually, I'm feeling ill."

Sadie eased an arm around her, and Camille resisted the urge to pull away. "Sit down," Sadie said. "You look a little pale."

Camille fanned her face with her hand. "I'll be okay. Really." She pulled away gently. "But I think I need to go. Probably a bit too much work this week, but there's more to come so I better not overdo it."

Sadie stood. "I'll drive you home."

"No, don't be silly. Stay here. Have fun. I'll get a car."

"You're the one who's silly now. I came here to have fun with you, not be by myself. At least let me take you back to the restaurant. Maybe the fresh air will help you feel better."

Camille gave in, even allowing Sadie to hold her close as they walked down the stairs and out of the bar. They barely exchanged two words on the ride back to the restaurant, but she didn't think Sadie knew the true source of her discomfort. When they arrived back at Izmir, she couldn't get out of the car fast enough.

"You're sure you're okay to drive?"

Camille nodded. "You were right. Fresh air was exactly what I needed."

"Text me when you get home?"

Camille agreed, but only to hasten her departure. She knew she should've apologized for the abrupt end to their date, but she couldn't manage even the simplest nicety. The drive home seemed to take forever, and more than once she considered pulling over at one of the bars along the way to get something to take the edge off, but kept driving. When she finally pulled into the garage of her townhome, she yanked the keys out of the ignition and tossed them on the seat beside her, letting her head fall onto the steering wheel. She was hurt, angry, and sad, and the whirl of emotions left her drained. Hours later she woke, still in the car, stiff and sore, but firmly resolved to never let West Fallon get under her skin again.

CHAPTER TWELVE

West stood in front of the mirror wishing she'd become a barista instead of a litigator. Despite the hard lighting and the funhouse mirrors, the suit didn't look too bad, but claustrophobia was already setting in, which didn't bode well for the long couple of weeks ahead.

"Stop fidgeting. You look great. Well, except for the bags under your eyes. Maybe you shouldn't have stayed out all night with Emma Watson."

She didn't have to turn around to see Bill standing in the doorway of her dressing room. "I didn't stay out all night with anyone. One dance. That's it. You'd know that if you hadn't ditched me at the bar." She'd danced the one song with Kelsey and then, forced to open her eyes and face the fact Kelsey wasn't Camille and never would be, West had mumbled some vague excuse and gone outside to get some air. Later, when she went looking for Bill, he was deep under the spell of Mr. Piercing Blue Eyes and told her she could take the car, he'd catch an Uber home. That was the last time she'd seen him until he met her today at Northpark for this shopping debacle.

"Let's not get into who ditched who and return to the subject of your clothes. You do look great."

"Great is not the word I would use."

"You're acting like it's the first time you've worn a suit."

"I can count on two hands the number of times, and most of those were for moot court competitions in law school. So far for this job I've managed to get away with blazers and chinos. Not the same thing at all." She ran her hands down the crisp lines of the navy blue jacket. "I feel like I'm going to work at a bank."

"It's perfect. You think I'd let you buy anything that made you look bad?"

"Maybe."

"Shut up and try the other one on."

Bill pulled the curtain and wandered off. West peeled off the suit and jammed it back on the hanger. One down. Regular work days were one thing, but everyone dressed up during a trial, and she didn't want to stick out. She could make do with three new suits and a few extra shirts so she could rotate. The suits would come in handy later when she was interviewing for permanent jobs, if the Southern Poverty Law Center didn't have a position open by the time she fulfilled this commitment.

But all her equivocating was just that. The real reason she wanted new clothes was because of how much face time she'd be having with Camille when the trial started. She and Lloyd would be in the courtroom for most of the trial, as they'd be expected to prepare any legal memos Camille would need to rule on issues that might arise. She wanted to look good if only to let Camille know what she was missing.

Bill insisted on buying lunch to make up for breaking his promise to stick with her at the bar. Over mimosas and migas at La Duni, he struck up the conversation about the night before. "You're judging me for leaving the bar with Trent."

"I'm not. Although I am proud of you for knowing his name."

"You are, a little."

"Not hardly. Like I know anything about relationships."

"Do you like that girl you were dancing with?"

"Kelsey? I don't know her well enough to like her or not. Seriously, it was just the one dance."

"You seemed kind of into her."

"I may have been thinking about someone else at the time."

"And you're accusing me of two-timing?"

"I'm not accusing you of anything. I swear. I don't really get what you and Gabe have going on, but if you're both cool with it, then I am too. But we were talking about me, and it's complicated."

"That's what people say when they don't want to commit to something."

"*You're* lecturing me about commitment?"

"No, I'm just saying that the hard part is making a decision. The commitment I have with Gabe is simple. When we're together, it's just us. When we're apart we can do what we want. It would only be complicated if we didn't agree."

"If only it were that easy."

"It is."

West drank down half of her mimosa. "It's Camille." When Bill responded with a dumb look, she cleared her throat and tried again. "Judge Avery. You know, my boss."

"You're going to need to speak in complete sentences."

"I have a thing for Camille Avery." West spoke slowly and over-enunciated her words.

"Oh," Bill said and then realization dawned. "Oh, yeah, that's a little complicated. What the hell, West? There's like dozens of available women you could fall for and you pick the one you work for?"

"I didn't pick her. It just happened. Besides, I met her before she was my boss."

"This is so not a good idea. Maybe you're just having a schoolgirl crush. Trust me, it will go away."

West considered the idea that what she felt for Camille was only a crush, but quickly rejected it. She'd had plenty of crushes before, but this was different. The memory of their kiss gripped her still. It was hot and steamy and she'd felt the connection in every cell of her body. Crushes were fleeting and surface, but what she felt for Camille burned at her core. This was no crush, but it was very complicated. If only Bill was right and it would just go away.

❖

"What do you mean you're skipping brunch?"

"Get in here." Camille wished she hadn't opened the door, but now Jay was standing on the threshold and she had no choice but to invite her in because she wasn't having this conversation in view of her next-door neighbor, Mr. Dimitri, who was pretending to trim his rosebushes.

She led the way to the kitchen. "Coffee, juice?"

"Uh, they'll have plenty of that where we're headed." Jay checked her watch. "Get dressed and let's go."

Camille looked down at her sweats. She planned to change clothes, but for the office, not for brunch with the girls. "Jay, I've got to work today."

"All work and no play…"

"Not fair. I play."

"Not what I hear." Jay poured herself a cup of coffee and settled at the bar counter in the kitchen. "Tell me about your date with Sadie."

"We had a nice time. She's very nice."

"You're using the word nice a little too much."

"What do you want me to say?"

"I want you to tell me why you bailed on such a nice date." She punctuated nice with finger quotes.

"Did she call you?"

"Yes, but I want to hear your version."

"I don't have a version. We had a nice," she winced at the word, but kept going, "dinner, but then I started not to feel good and called it early."

"Really?"

"Seriously, Jay. That's it." Camille hoped she would buy the lie, but she could tell by the dubious look on Jay's face, it wasn't happening. She sank into a chair. "I don't need to be dating right now. This job, it's more than I thought it would be, and I need to focus my attention on getting it right."

Jay took a sip of her coffee. "This is good stuff. Much better than the lies you're telling. What's really going on?"

Camille wavered. Part of her wanted to tell Jay everything. How she spent her days simultaneously trying to avoid her law clerk while at the same time inventing excuses to be alone with her. But another part of her was scared if she said the words out loud, it would be too real. And then what? What's the worst thing that could happen? She took a deep breath and plunged in. "I kissed West."

Jay scrunched her eyes and furrowed her brow. "You did what to who?"

"Don't make me say it again."

"Isn't West the girl we saw on the street a couple of weeks ago? The young one who was striking up conversations with homeless people?"

"Woman, but yes, that was her."

"And she's your law clerk?"

"See, this is why I didn't want to tell you. You've got that something doesn't smell right look on your face."

"Give me a minute to process." Jay slowly began nodding her head. "Makes perfect sense now."

"What?"

"You acted all giddy when we ran into her downtown. I haven't seen you act that way since…Hell, I don't remember. And then you pass on the hot, no strings attached surgeon. But seriously, Camille, how serious can this thing be? I mean she's your law clerk."

"Quit saying that. It was just a kiss. Once. It won't happen again." Camille nearly flinched at the lie, but she was dead set on convincing them both it was true.

"How old is she?"

Camille shifted in her seat. "Late twenties."

"You don't know?"

"I didn't hire her. Judge Blair did. I just agreed to keep her on."

"I guess you went the extra mile to make her feel welcome," Jay said with a wry smile.

"Shut up. She kissed me, not the other way around." The memory of the kiss came back full force. West standing close, the sweet taste of her soft lips pressing hard into hers. Camille had kissed back, her desire so strong she'd barely struggled against the impulse, and she'd been thinking about the kiss ever since. Rather than admit the lie, she settled on a half-truth. "I didn't stop her. And I haven't been able to stop thinking about it since."

"I guess that explains why you tanked your date with Sadie."

"It wasn't planned. Sadie insisted on going to S4 after dinner and West was there." At Jay's panicked look, she rushed to say, "I didn't do anything. I just told Sadie I wasn't feeling well, and we left."

"You haven't told anyone else yet, have you?"

"You're the only one."

"I know you know this, but as the former chair of your reelection committee, I have to say it. I'm into having as much fun as the next person, but you cannot sleep with your law clerk. Bad karma, bad politics, bad everything. Nothing good can come of it."

Camille nodded. Jay was right, and she knew it, which was exactly why she'd dashed away from West's warm touch when every ounce of her had been screaming to stay and indulge the fantasy. But fantasy was all it was. In the real world, good bosses didn't sleep with their employees, and judges who'd been burned by controversy didn't tempt fate.

"You sure I can't convince you to join us for brunch?"

"Sorry, but with this trial starting tomorrow, I need to work." At Jay's stare, she added, "By myself."

Camille spent the hour after Jay left in a distracted daze before deciding working at home was proving completely unproductive. She changed out of her sweats into jeans, an oxford cloth shirt, and a blazer and drove downtown. Like the weekends before, the court building was eerily quiet, but more so because she was there alone. Or so she thought. As she made her way down the hall toward her office, she heard footfalls behind her, and she looked back, hating herself for hoping it was West. It wasn't.

"I was hoping I would find you here," Judge Stroud said. "May I come in?"

"Certainly." Camille unlocked the door to the suite and walked straight to her office. She motioned to the couch and chair by her desk, but he remained standing. "Big day tomorrow," she said, willing him to get the hint and leave her alone.

"I won't keep you long." He walked over to her bookshelf and picked up a picture of her with her father. "I remember the first time I tried a case. Your dad and I were trial partners. I threw up at least three times before jury selection started. By the time I accepted the appointment to this bench, I'd tried dozens of cases and I didn't think anything could faze me, but there's something about presiding over a big case…I only threw up once before the first trial in my court, and it was a simple felon in possession of a firearm."

Camille cleared her throat. "Is this supposed to be some kind of pep talk?"

Stroud laughed. "Sorry about that. But I actually have a point. I realize how important this case is in terms of launching your new career. You'll make some errors, everyone does, but if you eliminate any distractions before it starts, you'll have a much better chance of getting through it unscathed. I assume you'll have one of the clerks in the courtroom with you during the trial. Have you decided which one?"

He knew something. Camille's gut churned at the word distraction, and by the time he said the word clerks, she was in full on panic. Breathe, breathe. "I was thinking I'd have both of them watch. Seems like it would be a good learning experience."

"Maybe. But maybe a better experience would be that you don't always get to do the fun stuff. Sometimes you have to stay behind the scenes."

"Makes sense," she said, but it didn't make any sense at all. She wasn't at all sure what he was talking about, but he didn't seem inclined to explain, and trepidation kept her from asking.

"I knew you'd agree," he said, walking toward the door. "I'm heading out, but I wish you the best of luck tomorrow. I'll stop in during the trial just to see how it's going."

He left, waving his hand over his shoulder and saying good-bye. Camille stared after him, doing her best to discern some meaning out of the odd visit, but she eventually gave up in favor of getting some work done.

The Wilson file was arranged neatly in the center of her desk. Since she'd last seen most of it spread around on the conference room table, she knew West had to have been the one to place it there. A note on top, in West's neat and precise handwriting said simply, *Let me know if you need anything else.*

Such a simple yet loaded statement. The list of things Camille needed was long, but at the top of the list was her wish that the circumstances between her and West were different. And what then? Would she have introduced West to her friends, her parents, and her colleagues? Everyone who knew her would think she was having a midlife crisis if she showed up with a much younger girlfriend.

Girlfriend. The word shocked her back to reality. West, thoughtful, intelligent, rebellious West, would probably make an excellent girlfriend, but not for her. She needed someone stable, steady, and accomplished. Someone who would enjoy being on her arm for formal functions, someone focused on career, someone who didn't challenge her every idea, her every preconception. Someone like Sadie. West was a distraction, and she would not allow her focus to waver.

She picked up her phone to call Sadie and apologize about their aborted date, but stopped when she spotted a large brown envelope tucked under her desk phone. Under normal circumstances, an envelope on her desk could mean any number of things, but she recognized the familiar big block letters on the outside stating simply PRIVATE: JUDGE AVERY.

Camille hunched forward, staring at the envelope like it was a coiled snake. She'd come to the office to work, but she had a strong feeling whatever was in this envelope was going to derail her plans. She should call the marshal's office, let them process it for evidence, but curiosity spurred her to grasp it by the corner, pull it toward her, and twist open the clasp. When she shook out the contents, a photograph and a clipped stack of paper landed on her desk.

She examined the photo first, intimately familiar with the subject, but completely stymied as to who had captured the picture of her kissing West in the kitchen not ten yards away from where she was sitting right now. She turned the photo over and read the ugly, puzzling words several times: QUIT OR EVERYTHING WILL BE REVEALED.

The memory of how the searing kiss had consumed her was now tainted by the knowledge someone had violated their private moment and was using it as a threat. She'd been certain she'd heard someone that night, but it had never crossed her mind that whoever it was had been documenting her indiscretion. She shoved the photo back in the envelope and examined the stack of papers that had accompanied it. The first page blared the words PERSONAL AND CONFIDENTIAL in large, bold letters, but it was the name below the warning that caught her eye. West Fallon.

Certain she shouldn't be digging deeper, but consumed with curiosity, Camille flipped the page and started reading. An hour later, she shoved the papers aside, wishing she could unsee every word.

❖

West stood on the sidewalk outside of Judge Blair's house wearing a new shirt and carrying a bouquet of flowers, but her thoughts were firmly fixed on the memory of the day she'd run into Camille in this very spot. Camille had been as polite as possible while turning her down, and she hadn't known at the time the woman pressing her for a date was going to wind up being her employee. *She turned me down then, so why am I surprised she's rejecting me now?*

The answer was the rush of want they both felt when they were close. It consumed West, and she could see it consumed Camille too. The way her eyes darkened, the hitch in her breath, her hungry lips begging for more, left no doubt that in the moment, Camille was right there with her, ready and willing. But no matter what, Camille was somehow able to break the current and walk away. Every. Single. Time.

West didn't get it. If she were smart, she would stop trying to stoke the flames. Maybe when the Wilson trial was over, she'd quit. Maybe then Camille would see her for something other than just her law clerk. She'd explain to Hank this job just wasn't working out, that it was getting in the way of the full, rich life he'd always said he wanted her to have. She imagined explaining to him the full, rich life involved Camille. She knew he'd disapprove, and she had to admit, she still cared about his approval.

Like the last time she'd visited, Diane greeted her at the door. "These are for you," West said, shoving the flowers at her, feeling silly all at once for the overly chivalrous gesture.

"Thank you, West. They're beautiful." Diane smelled the bouquet. "I love tulips. How thoughtful."

West shrugged. She picked them for the pretty colors, and the attention made her uncomfortable. "Is Hank upstairs?"

"He is. Go on up. Dinner will be ready in about thirty minutes."

"Got it."

Hank was napping in his wheelchair behind the desk, and West paused in the doorway. He looked like he'd aged several years in the past few weeks. Impossible, but she couldn't deny something had changed. She considered ducking back downstairs and telling Diane she didn't have the heart to wake him when his eyes fluttered open.

"West," he said, his voice sluggish. "Have you been here long?"

"Just got here, but I can go back downstairs if you want to keep napping. I'm told we have thirty minutes until dinner."

"You're hilarious. Have a seat. Let's catch up."

West sank into the couch. Catching up wasn't on her agenda since telling him about the last few weeks would necessarily involve talking about Camille. "How are you feeling?"

"I'm starting to regain some of the muscle memory in my left side, but I still sound like I'm trying to talk around marbles."

"It's cool. I can understand you just fine. You look tired."

"Physical therapist is a slave driver."

"Ester says hello," West said. "She misses you, but not your penchant for getting to the office in the middle of the night."

"Seven a.m. is not the middle of the night," Hank said. "Besides I'm sure Judge Avery has a pretty tight schedule having taken over a docket that's been sitting idle for way too long."

"We'll all be working pretty long hours with the Wilson trial starting tomorrow. It's supposed to last three weeks."

"I've seen the articles in the paper. I was surprised to hear Stroud hadn't reassigned the case or at the very least granted a continuance."

West read the worry in his eyes. "Why?"

"First off, it's a pretty complex case, at least in terms of the various legal issues that are likely to be raised."

"You think Cam—I mean, Judge Avery isn't up to handling the legal issues?"

"I didn't say that." He smiled like an indulgent parent. "Besides, she has you, right?"

"Nice save, but seriously, what did you mean?"

"I'm sure she can handle anything that comes her way, but it's her first trial on this bench. A federal trial is very different from one in state court. The formality alone takes some getting used to, but having to make decisions on the fly about statutes she hasn't parsed through in a while, especially in a high profile case like this one, is a big deal. The press is going to write about this case every day, and whatever they say about her will either be the building block for her future career or the hole she'll spend years digging out of."

West's mind started spinning. Camille, bright new, young federal judge, would be in the spotlight, more than anyone else on this case, and it probably didn't help that a year ago she'd been the center of attention for how that other case had gone down. She'd be understandably anxious about perceptions, and West's advances probably hadn't helped matters. Camille didn't need an office sex scandal to add to the weight on her shoulders. "You said first of all. Is there another reason you're concerned about her having this case?"

Hank frowned. "I'm not sure how much I should say considering it's an ongoing investigation."

"Hey, you can't leave me hanging like that. Is there something I should know?"

He studied her for a minute before answering. "I suppose you have a right to know. Apparently, Judge Avery's gotten a couple of vaguely threatening notes. The marshal's service contacted me to find out if I knew of anyone who might have something against her or if I'd received similar notes."

"Vaguely threatening? What did they say?"

"I don't know. Judges get a lot of hate mail. People in prison figure they don't have a lot to lose by violating another federal statute and threatening a judge. Usually they're about a specific case. I got one the month before I left that something like the Lord is the only one fit to sit in judgment of Darryl Wilson. There's a place in hell for those who try to usurp the role of the Lord. Stuff like that."

"That sounds pretty specific." West shifted in her seat, wondering if Camille had received notes like that. Surely, she'd know if she had.

"Those were actually tame considering some of the letters I've received over the years, but I handed it over to the marshal's office and they said they'd look into them. Of course, I never heard anything else about it since, well…" He pointed to his chair. "But I'm not sure the notes Judge Avery has received were about the case."

"Okay." The minute West spoke the words the memory of Darryl Wilson's sister standing up in court yelling about injustice raced through her mind. But the marshal's office already knew about that outburst, so there was no point in worrying Hank by recounting the episode. Besides there was a big difference between a crazy letter writer and a concerned relative. "Judge Avery's pretty tough. I don't think threatening letters would deter her from the case."

"You like her."

It was an observation, not a question. West wanted to tell him everything. How she'd felt a spark with Camille the second they'd met and what a weird coincidence it was that she'd first met Camille at the courthouse on the day of his stroke. How she admired Camille's level-headed intellect even while engaged in a duel of opinions. She wanted to say all the things she imagined a child would say to a parent when reporting on having met someone special, someone about whom they would want to share relationship details. But Hank wasn't her parent, and Camille wasn't her girlfriend, which meant the mental exercise was pointless, so she simply said. "Yes, I like her okay." Lame, but true.

"And the job?"

"It's okay too." West noted the look of satisfaction on his face and resisted the urge to qualify her answer. Setting aside any angst about Camille, she was enjoying the work. It was one thing to work as an adversary, but as much as she hated to admit it, getting a look behind the robed curtain was a valuable tool she'd be able to use later whether she wound up at the Center or some other nonprofit. "If you promise not to say I told you so, I'll even admit I actually like it, and I'm looking forward to the trial. Can you give me some idea of what to expect?"

"Sure. There'll be a lot of evidentiary decisions that have to be made during this trial, and the debating will start during jury selection. You'll have to be ready to research issues, review motions, and draft bench opinions on the fly, so it's likely Judge Avery will want one or both of you in the courtroom for most of the trial."

"Got it. Any tips?"

"Both sides are going to try to cozy up to you. They know you'll be the one doing the judge's research and whispering in her ear, and they'll make their best pitches to you, hoping to have greater influence. Nod politely, listen to what they have to say, and stay neutral."

West nodded.

"Are you okay?" he asked. "This case has got to bring up a lot of issues for you."

"You mean about people who get so hooked on drugs they no longer give a shit about anything or anyone, including staying alive?" She looked down at her crossed arms and realized she'd reverted to a petulant child, mourning the loss of what her life could've been, and she mentally chastised herself. She had no business focusing on her loss when she'd gained so much in the process. Not for the first time, she wondered what would have happened had her mother lived. More likely than not, West would have struggled right along with her, watching her decline, but unable to dig her way out of it. Food stamps, public housing, and clothes from the local Goodwill would have been her only lifelines, and opportunities like Richards College and Berkeley Law would have been distant and unattainable goals. She'd probably have wound up some smartass barista who acted like she knew everything while never actually applying her smarts to some greater good. Her mother's overdose and Hank's intervention had saved her life, or saved her from that life anyway. "I'm sorry. That was uncalled for. I'm good. It's been a long time."

He stared at her for a long moment, and she struggled not to fidget under the appraisal. Whatever he saw seemed to satisfy him. "I think our thirty minutes is up," he said. "Shall we go downstairs?"

At the table, Diane entertained them both with stories about their first grandchild. West listened and laughed in all the right places, but her mind was stewing over Camille, the Wilson case, and the way she'd sidestepped Hank's questions about both. Everything about the next few weeks was going to be rough, from the facts of the case that so closely mirrored her own life to the chore of pretending Camille wasn't more than her employer. She'd have to rely on the memory of their kiss to get her through.

Chapter Thirteen

Camille stared into the mirror. She'd picked the perfect power suit for the first day of trial even though nobody would see. The sleek lines of the crisp black gabardine wool usually infused her with confidence, but not today. The bout of nerves took her off guard. She'd presided over dozens of trials while on the bench, but she was as anxious as her first time.

She'd been fine until she read the front page of the paper at breakfast. The over-the-fold headline blared news of the case. She'd expected the premium coverage, but it was the subject of the story that caught her off guard. When she'd gotten to the office this morning, she'd told Ester the minute the attorneys arrived they were to report to her in chambers. Someone had some explaining to do. Camille took one last look in the mirror, practicing her stern jurist expression, and then made her way to the conference room.

The room was packed. Three attorneys for the government and two attorneys and one intern for the defendant. In the corner of the room, tucked out of the way, Lloyd was huddled with West, and they were engaged in an animated, whispered conversation. Camille cleared her throat to draw everyone's attention, but when Lloyd turned around and she got a full view of her other law clerk, she was completely unprepared for trial-ready West.

West, normally pretty casual around the office, was dressed in a power suit of her own. Black, like hers, but with decidedly more masculine lines, and instead of a boring white shirt like the one she was wearing, West shined in royal blue with a vintage Oscar de la Renta tie. Even though West was seated, Camille had no trouble imagining she'd be even more striking when she stood and the trim cut hugged her slim body.

After a few seconds of drinking the image of West in, Camille tossed a copy of the newspaper onto the table. "Before we get started," she said. "I'd like to know who's talking to the press about issues I have already ruled were not coming into evidence without additional hearings during trial."

She looked around the table to see who would squirm first. At some point she needed to apologize to West, tell her she was right. The story in the paper was long and editorial, detailing all of the allegations that had ever been made against Darryl Wilson, giving special attention to the rape allegations of the witnesses listed in the government's motion. While she'd said she would issue final rulings as the evidence developed during the course of the trial, the spirit of her ruling should have made it clear neither side should be trying this case in the press and possibly tainting the jury pool.

When no one answered her question, she launched in. "You all know this is my first trial in this court so you may be laboring under the impression that the new judge, fresh from state court where things tend to be a bit more casual, will let you get away with trying your case outside the courtroom instead of in it. You would be wrong. As an AUSA, I've tried many cases in federal court, and I never stooped to this level. The evidence will be presented in the courtroom, not the press and," she paused for effect, "only after I've had an opportunity to hear proffers and make rulings on each and every matter. Since someone at this table doesn't seem to understand the prudence of that, I'm imposing a gag rule, effective immediately."

"But, Your Honor, the information about the defendant's prior convictions is public," said Merrin. "We don't have control over every single person who has knowledge."

"Well, we sure don't have any motivation to spread libelous lies about our client on the eve of trial," said Sylvia Naylor.

"It's not libel if it's true," Merrin snapped.

Camille shook her head. If she'd had a gavel, she would have thrown it at the AUSA. "That's enough. I'm inclined to rule right now there will be absolutely no mention of the sexual assault allegations.

If I see one more story in the paper, I may do just that." She looked around the room, daring anyone to challenge her. Merrin and his co-counsel looked sullen, but didn't speak.

"Okay. I've arranged for a pretty large venire this morning. They are already in the central jury room completing their questionnaires. I'll begin the voir dire, and each side will have thirty minutes to question the panel. We should have our jury before lunch, and opening statements will begin this afternoon. How long do you anticipate for your opening?"

"Judge, do you plan to include asking the venire about whether they've seen the story in the paper?" Sylvia asked.

"She didn't plant the story," Merrin said, "but she wants to make sure the jury knows about it."

"Not true," Sylvia shot back. "I'm only trying to clean up the mess one of your agents has made by leaking all this info to the press."

Camille stood. "I will ask the usual questions about whether or not the potential jurors have heard about this case, but I'm not getting into specifics about today's article because it will only draw attention to the allegations, which I presume you do not want to happen." She pushed her chair under the table. "Be in the courtroom in thirty minutes. I want you all ready the second the jurors are finished with the questionnaires. Have an answer about your opening statements and report to Lloyd."

She moved toward the door, but not before she saw West's eyes flash with questions. She motioned to her and kept walking toward her office. When West showed up at the door, she invited her in and shut the door. "Have a seat."

"I'll stand if it's okay with you. I figure it's going to be a long day of sitting."

Camille winced. West was under the impression she'd be in the courtroom for the span of the trial, but after what she'd read in West's CPS file, it would be irresponsible to let West continue to be involved in this case. She'd spent the last twenty-four hours trying to come up with a way to handle dismissing her delicately, but now that she was down to the last thirty minutes, she couldn't find the words. "Is that a new suit?"

West's smile was tentative. "Yes. Thought it might be time to buy some grown-up clothes. My pal Bill helped me pick it out, so if you hate it, blame him."

She didn't hate it. She loved it, everything about it from the slim cut to the way the color of the shirt brought out the blue in West's eyes. But compliments seemed shallow considering West had bought new clothes for trial, and she was about to ban her from the proceeding. She settled for a simple. "It looks good on you."

"Thanks."

"West, I need to ask you something. Something personal."

"You can ask me anything."

West's voice was husky, her expression equal parts earnest and hopeful, and Camille quickly realized her error. Images of the pages detailing West's troubled upbringing buzzed in her mind. Her mother, a drug addict, dying of an overdose, the needle still in her arm and her naked body bruised and violated when West came home from school to find her lying in her own vomit. The dealer had eventually been arrested and charged with sexual assault in addition to drug charges, but with the only witness dead, he'd worked out a plea that amounted to a slap on the wrist. Meanwhile, West began an endless progression in and out of foster homes until she aged out of the system. That West had risen above these circumstances was a miracle, but now her prior experience was about to crash into her present success.

West's situation was too close to that of the victim in this case to allow her to brief opinions, and no way was she going to let West sit in on the trial, if for no reason other than the toll it would take on her mentally. Again, she wondered how and why the copy of West's file had shown up on her desk. That the same person who had seen them kissing had left the file made the violation sting worse.

She looked West in the eye and made a split decision. She would remove her from the case, but she didn't have to share the reason why. Not when doing so would unnecessarily hurt her and lay bare the invasion of her privacy. "I only need one of you in the courtroom during the trial. There's a lot of work that needs to be done to catch us up on the other pending cases. I need you to work on those and when this trial is over, we can do a full review." Once she realized she was rambling to stave off West's response, she stopped abruptly.

"If you want me to say I'm sorry I kissed you, I won't do it."

"What?" Camille shook her head. "No, this isn't about that."

"Right." West spat the word.

Camille wanted to pull West into her arms and assure her that wasn't the case, but every step toward intimacy was a step closer to the edge. She was West's boss and she had every right to make the call about her clerk's assignments. She crossed her arms to signal the conversation was over but tried one more time to smooth things over. "I kissed you back."

"Yes, you did."

"I shouldn't have."

West stepped closer. "You should do what makes you happy."

If only I knew what that was. Camille resisted the urge to step back. She didn't want to encourage West, but she didn't want to reject her either. The memory of West's lips on hers seared her brain, and she couldn't process the difference between her happiness and doing the right thing. "I have to go. The courtroom. They're waiting." She reached for her robe on the hook by the door, but she didn't stop to put it on before she pushed past West and rushed out of the room. A cowardly, but necessary exit.

Chapter Fourteen

West stood alone in Camille's office stunned by the rebuke. She shouldn't be. Camille had been clear from the moment they started working together that nothing could happen between them, and West had been a fool for thinking Camille's decision wouldn't affect how she treated her on the job. But she hadn't expected Camille to rip away the opportunity to work on this case.

She looked down at her suit, feeling like a rube. She'd spent too much money to dress for this part, and she didn't even want the role. She pulled off her jacket and stalked out of Camille's office, intent on reaching her own office without talking to anyone, but Lloyd met her at the door.

"What's up?"

She pushed past him. "You better get in the courtroom."

He followed her into their office. "About that. I would've expected her to pick you if she was only going to have one clerk in court. She seems to like you a whole lot better than she likes me."

West wanted to say she should be in the courtroom not because she was better liked but because she was a helluva lot smarter than he was, but she held back for fear she'd look like she was protesting too much. Besides it didn't matter what she thought since she wasn't in court and she wasn't going to be. "Guess you would've been wrong."

"Did she say why?"

West turned to Lloyd, trying to read his tone, but his genuinely curious facial expression told her he wasn't being a jerk. "I don't know. Maybe she just thinks you're the best person for the job." She pointed at the door. "Seriously, you should go."

He shrugged and sauntered off, and she opened a file on her computer and pretended to read a brief while she stared into space. What was she doing here? She'd be better off volunteering at a nonprofit and working nights at some restaurant or bar to make ends meet. Acting purely on impulse, she pulled out her phone and called Bill.

"Hey, you," he said. "Guess where I am right now?"

"Any chance Lambda is hiring?"

"Uh-oh. Did they not like your suit?"

"Seriously, Bill, focus." She glanced at the door Lloyd had left cracked slightly open and lowered her voice. "I'm not cut out for this. Sitting in an office all day, poring over briefs, listening to arguments—watching what other people are doing, but not actually doing anything myself. I didn't go to school for this. I want to be doing what you're doing."

"Be careful what you wish for. I spent last night talking a bunch of people off a cliff about going all ninja protestor, and now I'm headed to court to file an emergency motion to stay against the Garland School District for trying to check IDs in the school bathroom. Matter of fact, I'm outside your building right now. Want to grab a coffee with me after I take care of this?"

"Absolutely. I'll meet you in the clerk's office."

West stopped by Ester's desk on her way out. "I'm headed to the clerk's office and then to meet a friend for coffee. I have my cell if you need me."

Ester barely looked up from the computer. "Nice suit, West. New?"

She vowed never to buy new clothes again. "Thanks and yes."

"Makes you look smart."

Ester's tone was teasing, but West couldn't help a retort. "I am smart."

"Of course you are, but it doesn't hurt to look the part." She glanced up from her computer screen. "I know you didn't want this job, but he had his reasons for making you keep this promise."

West began to wonder if she'd been too loud on the phone with Bill, and regretted the indiscretion. "I don't know what you heard, but I—"

Ester held up a hand. "Don't. I'm not in the habit of sharing people's personal business or butting in. I only wanted you to know I had a first row seat to see how much he cared about you all those years. You can do what you want to do and I imagine you will, but sometimes it doesn't hurt to trust that the people who care about you have your best interests at heart." She waved her hands. "Now go, get out of my hair. I'm busy here."

West started to ask her what she meant, but Ester's stern look told her she was done talking. On the way to the clerk's office, she mulled over Ester's words. Hank did care about her, and she was certain he made her promise to take this job to beef up her résumé since she didn't have much of a pedigree without it. When she'd agreed to it, she'd been midway through law school, and graduation seemed like forever away. The concrete consequences of the promise had been illusory.

Bill was finishing up at the clerk's office when she walked in. He flashed her a grin and shoved a sheaf of paper in her hand.

"You know," she said, "Most people file pleadings electronically."

"I did, but I wanted to deliver a copy to the judge in person. Read it."

She scanned the first few pages. "Wow. This is pretty in your face. You're really taking them on?"

He grinned. "Yes, we are." He looked at his watch. "I give it an hour before the press gets wind. Do I look okay for my close-up?"

"Whatever. Come on, you're buying coffee, Mr. Big Shot."

Going back to the office was out of the question, so they walked down the street to the coffee spot at the Joule Hotel. When they had their orders and settled in at a table, she jabbed the stack of papers in Bill's hand. "This. This is what I want to be doing."

"You're crazy. I was up all night in case you didn't notice. My boss got the call from the kid's parents yesterday afternoon and decided not one more school day would go by without legal action." He took a sip of coffee. "Besides, I was one of a team of five people who worked on this brief. If anyone gets a close-up in primetime, it'll be the director, not me."

"Still, at least what you're doing matters. I don't even get to sit in on this trial. She picked that jerk Lloyd to assist her during the case."

"Lloyd Garber?"

"That's the one."

"He was in my class at Saint Marks," Bill said, referring to an elite Dallas prep school. "That guy's as dumb as they come."

"See!" West said, jabbing the air with her fist. "I just don't get it."

"Maybe it's time you quit your bellyaching and admit the real reason you hate your job." He bobbed his head and said the rest in a singsong. "Someone's hot for teacher, someone's hot for teacher."

"She's not my teacher, douche."

"Whatever. I've been thinking about this because, you know, your love life is way more interesting than mine."

She rolled her hand. "Get to the point."

"Despite my previous warnings, I've decided there's no reason you can't date her. I mean you're both consenting adults. The whole boss thing doesn't really count because it's not like you want the job anyway, so you wouldn't be trading sex for work favors. And I Googled her—she's kind of hot."

"I'm with you, but that's not how things are done and I can tell she really means it. Oh, and kind of hot doesn't even begin to describe her."

"What do I know?" He shrugged. "Anyway, I don't think it's such a big deal."

"Great. I'll count you in the Team Camille camp."

"Camille, huh? You've got it bad."

She tossed a balled up napkin at him. "Shut up."

"So, tell me about this case you're cut out of. I read a pretty salacious article in the paper this morning."

"Don't believe everything you read."

"So it's not true?"

"Truth is an interesting concept."

"Your sidestepping tells me all I need to know. Sounds like this defendant is a major dirtbag. Selling drugs to co-eds and then raping them once they're high."

"*If* that's what he did. And even if he did, that doesn't mean he's guilty in this case. Hell, that's not even what he's accused of."

"Spoken like a true defense lawyer. But hey, I thought you were a law clerk."

She jabbed him in the side. "Shut up. I'm just trying to keep an open mind. Besides, those girls may not even get to testify about any of that stuff."

"You think she'll keep the evidence out?"

"I don't pretend to know anything about what she thinks at this point," West said. "If it were me, I'd keep it out or tell them to charge him with rape. Seems pretty cut-and-dried."

"Well, however it goes down, it's pretty interesting stuff."

"It would be if I was getting to be part of it. Camille, I mean Judge Avery, has benched me for this case."

"You screw something up?"

West grunted at the loaded question. "Not that I know of, but I guess kissing the boss is enough."

He downed his coffee, stood up, and tossed a couple of dollar bills on the table. "This has been fun, but I better get going. My public awaits. My advice? Don't wallow. Get in there and show her she needs you. And as for the other stuff? It'll work itself out."

West stayed put for a few minutes after he was gone. Nice advice, but easier said than done.

Camille felt like she'd worked an entire day, but the jury panel was just filing in. She'd spent last night thinking about West and reviewing the standard federal voir dire questions along with the specific questions each side had submitted. One big difference between this case and her time on the state court bench was that the defendant didn't have the option of going to the jury for the punishment phase of the trial, so she wouldn't be questioning any of them about whether they could impose both the minimum and maximum range of punishment. What would the jurors think if they knew the defendant could potentially be sentenced to life without the possibility of parole if they found him guilty of a single act of selling the drugs that had caused Leslie Silver's death? Would they balk like West had or would they chalk it up to the price Wilson had to pay for conducting an illegal business? A big part of her was glad she wouldn't have to have that particular conversation with them.

When the potential jurors filed in, all of the courtroom personnel and the attorneys for both sides stood out of respect. She'd called up a hundred people, hoping no matter how hard each side tried to eliminate some for cause, twelve would be left when they were done. The jurors were dressed better than the average state court juror, and she remembered from her time as an AUSA, federal jurors were usually better educated and of better means than their state court counterparts. And they were predominantly white. She silently counted eight Asians and only six blacks, a factor that could come into play with an African-American defendant. Oh, well, she hadn't expected this to be easy.

"Ladies and gentlemen, thank you for being here this morning, although I expect the big bold letters on your summons that mentioned something about jail time motivated you to appear." She paused for the sound of nervous laughter. "This service is both a duty and a privilege of your citizenship, and the system wouldn't work without you." She started by introducing the attorneys and asking if anyone on the panel knew any of them. Each side had a set number of preemptory strikes they could exercise for any reason, as long as it was race and gender neutral, but since the strikes would be made after all the questioning was over and without knowing which jurors the other side would strike, the attorneys would all try to get her to cut any jurors they didn't like for cause, thereby saving their strikes for whoever was left over.

There were a couple of very loose associations—one man said he'd volunteered at the local food bank with Sylvia Naylor, the lead defense attorney, but that would have no impact on his ability to weigh the evidence in this case. Another woman said she'd seen one of the prosecutors eating at her restaurant, but neither situation merited a strike for cause.

Having dispensed with the preliminary questions, she launched into an introduction of the case, followed by the question, "Have any of you read about this case in the paper?" About a dozen jurors raised their hands, and she noticed defense counsel scribbling furiously, no doubt poised to make an argument these jurors should be stricken for cause. She made her own notes, thinking if it came to it, she'd question them separately from the rest of the panel to determine what exactly they'd read in the paper. She wasn't about to let either side ask those kinds of questions in front of everyone. Jurors had a keen ability to hone in on what was likely to get them out of duty. If they sensed answering a certain way meant freedom from the courtroom, they'd be like sharks on a bleeding carcass, and this panel would bust within the hour. Once she'd noted the names, she motioned for the jurors to put their hands down, but a woman in the second row kept hers up, actually vibrating with the need to speak. Camille consulted the chart. "Yes, Mrs. Lansing? Do you have something you would like to say?"

Mrs. Lansing stood and smoothed out the lines of her Sunday best dress. "Yes, Your Honor. Well, I didn't read anything about the case in the paper, but I raised my hand because…" She paused and looked around at the rest of the venire. "You see there's a TV in the room downstairs, and the news was on this morning. I'm pretty sure they mentioned this case, you know, based on your description just now. I can't be entirely positive, but—"

"Thank you, Mrs. Lansing." Camille rushed to shut her down before she could say more. Sylvia Naylor was already out of her seat, and the prospect of a completely tainted venire sent Camille's day plummeting into disaster. She motioned for Lloyd to come over to the bench and hit the switch for the white noise machine before she leaned down and whispered, "I'm calling a break. Get down to the central jury room and tell them to shut the TV off right now, but before you do, find out what channel it was on and find out whatever you can about the news coverage on that channel this morning."

He nodded nervously and practically tripped over himself rushing from the room. As she watched him go, Camille said, "Ladies and gentlemen, we're going to take a fifteen-minute break to take care of a few housekeeping matters before we go any further. If you have any questions about where the restrooms are located, the bailiff will be happy to help you." She stood and kept a smile on her face until the last juror filed out of the room.

"Your Honor," Naylor started to walk toward the bench and Kyle Merrin wasn't far behind.

She cut them both off. "Chambers now."

She glanced around, but she didn't see any sign of West. She'd prefer to have a clerk in the room if any issues came up that needed research, but since she'd sent Lloyd downstairs, she'd have to do without. She was more than capable of doing her own research, but presiding over a trial wasn't conducive to searching for applicable cases on Westlaw.

"We'd like to strike this entire panel for cause," Sylvia said.

"Of course you would," Kyle replied, rolling his eyes.

"It's clear Mr. Wilson can't get a fair trial."

"If by fair you mean one where the jurors suspend belief, you're probably right about that."

Camille slammed a hand on the table. "Enough. Do you act this disrespectfully to all judges or just ones that are newly appointed to the bench?"

"I'm sorry, Your Honor," Naylor said. "I think we all were a little caught off guard by this striking news."

Camille allowed a smile to sneak out at her attempt to act surprised. "I'm pretty sure the article in the paper this morning signaled we are going to have an ongoing press problem in this case. The question is not whether the jurors have been exposed to information, it's whether the information has tainted their ability to fairly judge the facts of this case."

"Your Honor is right, of course, but I'm not sure there is precedent for this particular situation where an entire panel was sitting together watching coverage about this case within an hour of voir dire." Naylor plowed on. "We have no idea if they've already discussed the case with each other, whether they've formed opinions, whether they've been exposed to information that might not even be admitted at this trial. We need to be able to question them at length about this issue."

"Right, so you can poison the well," Merrin said. "If they haven't already formed opinions about the case, they'll figure out pretty quickly how to answer to get stricken for cause." He turned to Camille. "They are trying to bust the panel."

Camille steepled her fingers, tuning them both out. If jurors said they couldn't be fair because of their exposure to the news coverage, she should dismiss them for cause, which might not leave enough people left on the panel to compose a jury, after allowing for each side's preemptory strikes. If they busted this panel, they'd have to start this process over again. Federal jury summons were sent out weeks in advance, and she had no idea if there were additional jurors available in the central jury room today or if they could pull from other jurors scheduled to appear later in the week for other matters. They might have to reset the trial for weeks, which would probably only heat up the press coverage and throw her docket into disarray. The docket she could manage, but more press coverage would only make it less likely Wilson would ever get a fair trial from a group of impartial jurors.

"Judge?"

Lloyd was standing at the door, squirming in place. She excused herself from the group and followed him to the office he shared with West, but West wasn't there. She resisted the urge to ask Lloyd if he knew where she was. She had every right to know, but asking seemed like a blaring signal she was way too interested in West's coming and goings. Instead, she settled into West's chair and waited to hear what Lloyd had to say.

"The TV was supposed to be showing preliminary instructions about jury duty, but apparently the guy who switched it on didn't check to make sure it was on the right channel."

"Okay, so what were they watching?"

"Channel five, *Good Morning America*."

Camille gasped. "You're not saying the case had national attention, are you?"

"No, but they have a local news break every half hour. It's about five minutes, including local weather. Not a lot of time to get into anything much. I watched the last one while I was down there. They mentioned the trial was starting this morning, but the whole report consisted of about two lines." He looked down at the paper in his hand. "'Trial is scheduled to begin this morning in the case of Darryl Wilson, the man accused of being responsible for the death of Richards College student, Leslie Silver. Sources say the trial should last two to three weeks and many prominent Dallasites are listed on the witness list.'" He set the paper aside. "I talked to several of the marshals and the clerk in the jury room. They all confirmed the report was the same each time the local news segment aired."

Camille breathed a sigh of relief. It wasn't as bad as she'd feared, but it was still a big deal and likely to create its own bit of news. The reporters in the courtroom were probably phoning in now. This ruling would be the first story about the start of the trial, and she had to get it right. Cursing her decision to pull West off the case, she said, "Pull up Westlaw and find me some analogous cases. Run every search you can think of. I doubt you're going to find any fact pattern exactly like this one, so you'll need to get creative. Get me your research in thirty minutes."

Lloyd rushed out of the room, and Camille sank back into her chair. She'd use the time to do some digging of her own, but it was better to have two sets of eyes. She took a moment to imagine West sitting next to her, brainstorming search terms and dissecting case law. Hell, if she was working with West, she might even enjoy the adrenaline rush of doing research on the fly instead of feeling like every decision she made might send her career spiraling out of control.

❖

"Hey, West, you have a minute?"

West looked up from the file she'd been buried in all morning. Lloyd was standing in the doorway to their office. "Sure. Not like I'm doing anything important."

She regretted her petty tone. She might not like him, but it wasn't Lloyd's fault she'd been kicked off the Wilson case. She had only her poor judgment to blame for being stuck doing grunt work while the big show was happening in the courtroom next door. She'd spent the morning mulling over Bill's advice and trying to figure out what she really wanted when it came to Camille and this job. The problem was she wanted both, and no matter what Bill said, it just wasn't that easy. The only thing she was clear about so far was sitting around while everyone else was in trial totally blew, but not as much as knowing Camille wanted to keep her distance. Maybe whatever Lloyd wanted would distract her from the dissonance. "What's up?"

"We're on a break. It's been a rocky start."

"I heard. In case you haven't figured it out already, Ester knows everything that goes on, and if you supply her with donuts, she will tell all."

Lloyd looked surprised at the nugget of intel. She didn't blame him. She'd kept him and everyone else at arm's length since she'd started, not interested in becoming too attached to the work or the people. She'd failed miserably at the last item on the list, and when Camille tossed her off the Wilson case, she realized how attached she'd become to the work.

"Donuts, got it."

She hated to ask, but she had to know. "Any ideas on who's leaking to the press?"

"Not a clue," he said, not meeting her gaze. "The courtroom is packed with cops for opening statements, and I've seen a few of them huddled with the AUSAs, but it's not like anyone's raising their hands. You know, I have a friend whose father works at the paper. Maybe I should give him a—"

"Stop, right there. Don't even finish what you're about to say."

"What?"

"You call the paper, or your friend talks to his father, and the next story won't be about Wilson, it'll be about how officials in the judge's office were looking to undermine the objectivity of the free press. They'll have a field day with it."

"You know, I didn't even think about that."

West smiled to ease the harshness of her warning. She was pretty sure this was the closest Lloyd had come to admitting he might be wrong about something. "It'll work itself out."

"Well, it may not. Did Ester tell you about the TV in the jury room?"

"She mentioned it." West had only heard a snippet of what she imagined was the bigger story, and she was dying to know more. "Were they seriously all just sitting there watching the news?"

"If they were, the judge's decision would probably be pretty easy." He told her what he'd just relayed to Camille. "Judge Avery wants research notes in thirty minutes."

West shook her head. "Then you better stop talking to me and get online." She turned back to her computer, but Lloyd's only move was to shuffle in place. "You need something?"

"Help a guy out? She always likes your research memos better than mine. If you help me out, I'll make sure she knows."

West looked at the pile of files on her desk and the notes on the computer that she'd lost interest in typing up about five minutes in. If she helped Lloyd, at least she'd be doing something interesting, and with that realization came another. She didn't need the spotlight. In fact, she might be able to use working in the shadows to her advantage.

"Okay, I'll help you," she said, "but on one condition."

"Name it."

"Your name and your name only on the notes. If anyone finds out I helped you, you're cut off. Deal?"

Lloyd narrowed his eyes at her like he was trying to figure out her angle, but only for a second. "Deal."

West shoved aside the files on her desk and motioned for him to take a seat and sign on to Westlaw. If she played her cards right, Camille would never know she'd done the work, and with a little professional distance, she might have a better shot at convincing Camille to do some very personal and decidedly unprofessional things.

CHAPTER FIFTEEN

Camille stretched her arms over her head and yawned. In thirty minutes they'd start the fourth day of trial for the week, and she was grabbing a few solitary moments in her office before the bickering began anew. Every day so far had started with either a fight about evidence or a come-to-Jesus meeting with counsel about the pervasive press leaks. Today was no different, and the newspaper on her desk boasted another story about the defendant's past—part fact, part speculation—but full of references to the allegations from sexual assault victims who seemed eager to talk to reporters under the guise of anonymity.

She thumbed through the folder on her desk that contained another set of memos about various evidentiary topics that were likely to come up based on the witnesses the government planned to call to testify today. The heading of each one was the same. To: Judge Avery, From: Lloyd Garber, but if his name hadn't been on them, she would've sworn West had written every word based on the nuanced detail of the analysis. Leave it to Lloyd to take all the credit.

West had done an excellent job of avoiding her since Monday morning when she'd yanked her from the case. With every objection raised by counsel, Camille regretted her decision, although she knew it was the right one. But the distraction she'd plotted to avoid had only gotten worse in West's absence, and too many times during the preceding days, her thoughts had wandered to wondering what West was doing, where she was. Totally unacceptable. She needed every ounce of focus she could muster to handle the nonstop barrage of decisions during trial. Maybe she should find West now and try to shake this obsession, get it out of her system once and for all.

"Judge?"

Camille looked at her phone and registered Ester's voice coming through the intercom. "Yes?"

"I know you said not to disturb you, but your mother is on line one. She said it's urgent."

"Put her through." Camille waited anxiously for the line to ring. She hadn't spoken with either of her parents since the pseudo-celebratory breakfast they'd shared the day she'd started this job. For her mother to call out of the blue, especially to contact her at work, meant something must be really wrong.

When the line rang, she grabbed it quickly. "Mom, is everything okay?"

"Well, it will be if I can get the hotel banquet manager to quit being such an ass. I mean how hard is it to set up a few cash bars and serve passed hors d'oeuvres? You'd think we were planning a state dinner at the White House."

"What are you talking about?"

A sharp intake of breath. "You've forgotten, haven't you? Your father said you'd forget, but I didn't think you would. I know I started planning a long time ago, but it never occurred to me you would forget."

Camille rubbed her head and tried to digest the nonsense. "Mom, did you need something? I have a lot going on right now."

"You did forget. Camille, this event's been on the books for months."

Event. Shit. Camille reached for her cell and punched open the calendar app. There it was. Tomorrow night at the Adolphus, a mixer to benefit MADD. Last year, her mother had met the director at a networking event and had latched on to the organization like a lifeline, telling anyone who would listen how her dead son, Carl, had succumbed to the evils of substance abuse and lost his life because of it. To hear her talk, she was the one who'd nearly died, but had clawed her way back to the land of the living by railing against the perils of driving under the influence. When she'd agreed last year to sponsor and help plan a fundraising mixer for the organization, she'd insisted Camille attend in her capacity as state judge, but she hadn't mentioned it after Camille lost her bench. Now, apparently with her reputation restored, Camille was back on the slate of dignitaries and couldn't think of anything she'd rather do less. "I'm not sure I can make it. I don't know if you've read the papers lately, but I'm in the middle of a pretty big trial."

"I'm doing this for your brother. He would want you to be there. Everyone has something. I had to cut my trip short to make it back in time to help. All I'm asking is for you to be there. Well, and you should bring some people. I really want to pack the place."

Of course you do, so you can look more important than you told them you were, as if that were possible. "I'll come, but by myself."

"Bring some people from your office. Don't you have other lawyers, judges that work with you? Judge Stroud is coming. It's just down the street."

Camille stopped looking for excuses. If Stroud was going to be there, he would think it strange if she didn't show up, especially since her mother was likely to mention her brother if she made any kind of remarks. But she couldn't imagine dragging any of the other judges along, and other lawyers were out of the question. Like she was supposed to pressure attorneys appearing before her to go to a benefit. Plenty of judges did that kind of thing, but she wasn't going to be one of them.

But there were other lawyers that didn't appear before her. Two were right here in this office, and one of them would probably jump at the chance to hobnob with the Dallas elite, while the other would likely rather do anything but be subjected to a night of networking. But maybe if she asked really nicely.

"Mom, I have to go. I'll be there and I'll bring people. See you then." Camille clicked off the line, determined to act before she lost her nerve. She buzzed Ester. "Will you ask Lloyd and West to come in here please?"

"Only because you said please."

When they appeared at the door, Camille invited them in. Lloyd handed her the mail, and she tossed it on her desk, more interested in West's reaction to being called to her office. West met her eyes, but her expression was devoid of affect. What had she expected? Jubilant excitement? If she were West, she'd probably still be stewing over the fact she'd been pulled from one of the more interesting cases any clerk would work.

"Thanks for coming in. I'll be quick." Camille picked up the folder of memos on her desk. "First, I want to say this is some amazing work. Top-notch research and writing, and I'm lucky to have you on my team." She looked at Lloyd as she spoke the words and watched him shuffle a bit at the praise.

"Thanks," he said, shooting a glance at West. "Lots of interesting issues."

"Yes, there are. And there will probably be more, but enough about work. I have to go to an event at the Adolphus tomorrow evening and I'd like you both to be my guests. We can walk down after we finish for the day. It's a benefit for MADD, but don't worry, you won't be asked to donate. Just eat, mingle, and make the place look packed, so the deep pockets can show off their donations." She shut up, wishing she hadn't run on and shown her true feelings. "Anyway, I would appreciate you being there, but if you have other plans, I completely understand."

"Sounds great. I'll be there," Lloyd said.

Camille didn't wait to hear West's answer. "Thanks. Lloyd, I'll see you in the courtroom. West, can you stay for a minute so I can talk to you about another matter I'd like you to work on?"

West eyed Lloyd as he left. "Have a seat," Camille said.

"I'm good."

"Are you mad at me?"

"Should I be?"

Camille pointed at the folder on her desk. "Lloyd does great work, doesn't he?"

"I'm sure I wouldn't know."

"Oh really? I spot your fingerprints all over those memos. I don't know what I would've done without you this week."

West shrugged. "You seem to have done just fine without me."

"Will you come Friday?"

"Who else is coming?"

Camille frowned. "I don't know everyone on the guest list, but I'm sure there will be a lot of lawyers who know my parents."

"If I don't go, will it be just you and Lloyd?"

"Oh." It suddenly hit Camille what West was asking. "A bunch of strangers, many of them lawyers who will want a minute or two alone with me because I'm a judge. I could use the buffer. Are you in?"

West held her gaze for a minute, her eyes piercing. "I guess. Should I wear a suit?"

If you want to look better than everyone in the room. Camille let her mind wander to the image of dressed up West. "If you want. I bet a lot of people will come directly from work, so there's likely to be a lot of suits, but it's not necessary. It's definitely not required that you be there. I mean if you really don't want to, I understand." She shut up to keep from rambling more.

"I'll be your buffer. It's probably as challenging a job as what you've had me doing."

Camille heard the sarcasm, but chose to ignore it. What would she say, anyway? Secretly, she was glad to know West was doing most of the work.

"Do you need anything else?" West was edging toward the door.

"Hang on just a second." Camille pulled the inner office envelope toward her, hoping it contained the pleadings she'd requested from the clerk's office. "I was reviewing the Santiago file, and there were a few old pleadings not scanned into PACER yet. I bet they're in here." She twisted the string loose and reached into the envelope. "I'd like you to…" Her voice trailed off as she pulled the contents free and recognized the same block letters she'd seen before.

"What is it?" West asked, her hand on the door.

"Nothing." Camille forced her gaze from the desk to the door. "Nothing. I'll talk to you about it later."

West strode back toward her. "You're pale." She reached for the envelope. "And your hands are shaking." Camille put up a hand to stop her, but West was too fast. She yanked the paper up and read the note out loud.

IT'S NOT TOO LATE TO QUIT. DO IT NOW OR EVERYTHING WILL BE REVEALED. FINAL WARNING.

"Who sent this?"

Camille summoned the strength to answer. "I don't know."

"But it's not the first one you've received, is it? What does it mean—'all will be revealed'?"

"It's nothing, West. Judges get crazy things in the mail all the time. I received hate mail once a week from a guy I sent to the pen for life. He's probably still writing to me, completely unaware that I no longer work for Collin County."

"Camille," West said, her voice low and quiet, "How many of these letters have you gotten?"

West was standing close. Close enough that Camille could smell her spicy cologne. Close enough to touch. In that moment Camille wanted nothing more than to confide in West about the other notes, about how the prospect of attending the benefit for her brother stressed her out, about how she missed their conversations about the law, about everything. But instead she slipped the note back into the envelope. "It's nothing."

Before West could respond, Camille was on the move, envelope in hand. She pulled her robe from the hook by the door, and turned back before she left her office. "West?"

"Yes?" West answered, her expression hopeful.

"Wear the suit. It's the perfect look."

West lingered in Camille's office after she left, replaying Camille's words in her head. The perfect look for what? Camille hadn't spoken to her in days and now she'd invited her to a party? She tried not to read too much into it, but the exchange left her feeling aroused and cautiously optimistic. After a few minutes of driving herself crazy with speculation, she headed for Ester's desk.

"I'm busy," Ester said, without looking up. "And I can tell you don't have any donuts, so I have no use for you this morning."

West laughed. "You'd think I'd be paid ahead by now."

"Takes a lot of donuts to sway me." Ester pushed back from her desk and faced her. "Tell me what you need."

"The judge received an interoffice envelope with her mail this morning. Do you know where it came from?"

She placed a finger to her temple and closed her eyes. “No, not a clue. Judge had a bunch of mail this morning. I didn’t have a chance to go through it before your sidekick swiped it off my desk. Guess he wanted to impress the judge with another of his many skills.”

Ester’s voice dripped sarcasm, and West wanted to hug her for her keen assessment of Lloyd, but she wanted information more. “Do you know how long the mail was on your desk before he got it?”

“And here I thought you were a lawyer, but it turns out you’re a detective instead.”

Okay, so it wasn’t as much fun when the sarcasm was directed at her. “Come on, Ester, it’s important.”

Ester stared hard, like she was trying to decide if this was serious, but she finally said, “Ben from the mailroom brought it first thing and handed it directly to me. I set it on my desk and went to get a cup of coffee. Wasn’t gone more than five minutes, and when I came back, you two were in there with the judge. When Lloyd came out, he told me he’d taken the mail in to her.” She raised her hands in the air. “That’s all I know. Now, may I get back to work?”

“Thanks, Ester.” West delivered the words on the fly, while she jogged back to her office. When she crossed the doorway, she was surprised to see Lloyd sitting in her chair, typing on her computer keyboard. “Hey, dude, any particular reason you can’t use your own space?” She kept her voice even, but she was pissed. Did he have to horn in on everything?

He closed the browser and stood up. “Sorry. I forgot my Westlaw password, and since you’ve been signing on as me, I figured you might have it saved in your system.”

Something about his tone didn’t ring true. “You need me to help with something?”

“No, it’s all good. I got it. Thanks for the offer.” He edged toward the door as he rambled, his face growing redder. She watched his back until he was out of sight, and then she slid into her chair and pulled up her browser to check the history. There was a sign-in on Westlaw about ten minutes prior that matched his story, but there were also visits to the website for the local paper and TV news outlets, and Yahoo. None of the activity was hers, and it had all happened while she was with Camille. Consulting the news was no big deal.

Lloyd had probably been doing that every day to see what they were reporting so he could be ready for any objections raised in trial. Still, West felt there was something off, like someone had been sleeping in her bed when she wasn't there. And Lloyd had brought the mail into Camille's office. The mail that contained the threatening note.

Whatever she'd been about to work on could wait. West signed out of her computer and strode out of the office, calling out to Ester that she'd be back soon. She recognized the deputy at the security entrance, but didn't know him very well, so she kept walking until she was at the marshal's office and asked to speak to Peter. A few minutes later, he appeared and ushered her back to his office.

"What's up?" he asked.

"Has Judge Avery been getting threatening notes?" She watched him carefully and saw the curtain fall. "She has, hasn't she? What steps are being taken to provide security? I haven't seen any and she works at night and on the weekends quite a bit."

"Whoa, girl, slow down." He motioned to a chair by his desk, and she sat down ready to listen, but ready for answers. "I can't talk to you about an ongoing investigation, no matter how much I like you."

"So there's an investigation."

"That's as much as you're going to get out of me."

"Hank told me about the notes." West hoped he'd misunderstand the extent of her knowledge and tell her more. "I think he wanted me to be on the lookout."

It didn't work. "If Judge Blair told you something that's his business. Judges can do that sort of thing. If you want to pay my pension when I retire, then I'll tell you whatever you want to know. In the meantime, I work for the US government and I'm not spilling a word. Clear?"

"Clear." She remained seated, intent on making sure this little interaction wasn't entirely in vain. "How about I tell you something?"

"Okay," he said, his voice wary.

She started to tell him that Lloyd had made a point of picking up the mail from Ester's desk and she'd seen him searching the Internet on her computer instead of his own for no apparent reason, but as she heard the words in her head, they sounded silly. Every marshal in the building had stopped in during this trial to watch the show, and they were likely all aware she wasn't working on the case. Ratting out Lloyd for a couple of easily explainable actions would make her look petulant and wasn't going to lead to anything productive. She'd be better off convincing Camille to confide in her about the investigation into the notes, but only if she was sure Camille had reported them in the first place. "Never mind. Can you just confirm you know about the notes, you know, because someone should know about them?"

"Yes."

She kept watching, but he clammed up and it was clear the one word was all she was going to get. "Thanks."

She spent the time walking back to the office, plotting how she was going to get Camille to open up to her and not just about the notes.

CHAPTER SIXTEEN

Camille made sure none of the jurors were watching and stole a glance at her watch. This afternoon's mind-numbing argument about DNA evidence had already delayed testimony by a couple of hours, and it didn't look like they were going to be able to finish with the witness before she called a recess for the weekend. Camille listened carefully for just the right moment, and when Dr. Edmunds paused to consult his report, she said, "Counsel, I think this is a good stopping point."

Without waiting for a response, she turned to the jurors. "We will resume testimony at nine a.m. Monday morning. The usual precautions should be taken to avoid any news or conversations about this case. Do not speak to anyone about any aspect of the trial, including the testimony you have heard this week or your opinions about the evidence. Remember, you must wait until you have heard all of the evidence and both sides have rested before you begin your deliberations, which means no talking to each other about the outcome either. Have a good weekend."

The bailiff shouted, "All rise," and the minute the last juror filed out of the courtroom, she escaped to her office before the attorneys could trap her into a discussion about whatever point of contention they could dream up next. When she reached her office, she tore off her robe and examined her desk to see if there was anything she needed to deal with that couldn't wait until Monday.

The stack of mail looked innocuous enough, but she thumbed through it just to be sure, and was relieved when she didn't find any ominous messages encouraging her to quit her job. She'd shaken the missives off in front of West yesterday, and truthfully, they hadn't bothered her until the mysterious note sender included the photo and West's CPS file, both items making the threats more personal and damaging. In the past, when she'd received hate mail, it had always been very specific, with the author outlining the grievance and why he or she was convinced they'd been wronged. She might not agree with the message or the means of conveying it, but she could understand the frustration of being on the losing end of an adversarial position, especially when the loss meant being locked in prison for years.

But whoever was sending these notes wanted her gone and for no reason she could fathom. She hadn't been on the bench long enough to piss anyone off unless she counted the AUSAs in this case to whom she had dealt a daily tongue-lashing about how it appeared someone from their side was leaking evidence to the press. As much as she didn't care for Kyle Merrin, she couldn't imagine his strict law-and-order self would stoop to passing notes to try to get her to leave. No, Merrin was the type who would come right out and say it.

While she was thinking about it, she called the number for the marshal's service and asked to speak to Peter Donovan.

"Donovan here," the gruff voice answered.

"Marshal Donovan, it's Judge Avery. Just checking to see if there's been any progress into the investigation about the notes." She braced for a reference to the photograph of her kissing her law clerk. She'd considered not turning over the picture, but since the note was written on the back of it, she couldn't justify withholding it. Thankfully, there was no judgment in the tone of his response.

"Not much. Judge Blair received some suspicious letters before he left the bench, but they all specifically mentioned the Wilson case, so we don't think it's the same person. We're exploring some leads, but nothing I can share with you right now."

She wanted to say, you mean nothing you *will* share with me, but she knew how these things worked. Cops liked to keep everyone in the dark until they had a sure thing. "Please keep me posted." She paused, considering her next words. "I'd appreciate hearing an update no later than Monday."

"Judge, if you're concerned for your safety, we can assign someone to escort you this weekend."

"No, that won't be necessary," Camille said before he could go any further down that trail. As powerless as she felt about the situation, an armed guard would only make her feel more powerless. She had absolutely no desire to have a federal agent shadowing her every move, especially at her mother's event. "Updates will be fine. Thanks and have a good weekend." She cut the call short before he could say anything else, and walked out of her office to find Lloyd and West.

She hoped West was still planning to attend the party. She hadn't seen her all day and wouldn't be surprised if she'd made a quiet escape to spend her Friday night doing something more fun than attending a stuffy party. Who could blame her? Camille was only attending for appearances' sake. It wasn't that she didn't think MADD did good work, but standing around sipping drinks and eating food while people told stories about dead loved ones in order to raise money felt morbid. She could almost hear her brother scoffing at her for caring what anyone else thought, but his life choices had culminated in an untimely death, so there was that.

"Judge Avery?"

Camille turned, and Lloyd was standing behind her, looking ever eager. "Hi, Lloyd, are you ready to go? Have you seen West?" The last question had barely left her lips when Lloyd moved aside and Camille spotted West standing behind him. She was wearing a different suit. One that looked even better, if that were possible. The lightweight charcoal gray wool hugged her body with its trim, flattering cut. Camille was staring and cast about for words to distract her from drinking in the sight of West. She pointed to the door. "Ready to go?"

The night air was pleasantly cool, unusual for a week that had seen temperatures in the nineties. Camille was thankful for the light breeze, acutely conscious of the heat coursing through her as she accompanied West down the street. The setting sun provided the perfect cover for her to sneak glances at the way West's trim pants hugged her butt as they walked.

They'd just crossed Field Street, when a man stepped out of the shadows waving his arms. What happened next was quick and revealing. Lloyd stepped to the side, practically hugging the building on their right, while West positioned herself directly in front of Camille.

"I'm calling the cops," Lloyd shouted at the man as he jabbed at his phone.

West held up her hand. "Don't." She stepped closer to the man and stretched out an arm toward him. "Charlie, it's West. Are you okay?"

Camille watched the exchange with trepidation, finding it hard to believe West knew the raggedly dressed man towering over them. Wait a minute. She'd seen this guy before, talking to West. The morning she and Jaylyn had bumped into West downtown. "Do you know this man?"

"I do," West said, her voice quiet and low key. "He's a friend. Right, Charlie?"

The man nodded, his arms now at his sides. West pulled out her wallet. "I've missed seeing you this week." She handed him a bill. "My car windows are in pretty bad shape. Consider this a down payment for next week. Okay?"

The man looked down at the bill in West's hand and slowly reached out to grasp it. West stood perfectly still as he took the money and backed away, mumbling a soft thank you as he faded back into the shadows. When he was gone, West turned back to Camille. "Shall we keep walking?"

"What the hell was that?" Lloyd asked.

"A guy who's not going to a fancy party like we are."

"How long have you known him?" Camille asked, wanting to pivot from Lloyd's response.

"We talk most days. He's a veteran. I think he's probably schizophrenic and probably medicated some of the time and not others. He's a nice enough guy and always gives my car windows a mean washing."

Camille wanted to ask more. How did West meet him? How did they strike up a conversation? How long had she known him? But for some reason the questions felt intimate, like they would shed some light into the private places about West. Definitely not a conversation to have in front of Lloyd, so she settled on a simple, "Thanks for defusing the situation." She shot a glance at Lloyd, hoping he got the message that he'd been the reason the situation needed defusing. "Come on, let's go before all the good food is gone."

The Adolphus Hotel was one of the old, grand mainstays in Dallas, and Camille usually loved its rich feel, but tonight it felt oppressive. They'd barely made it in the door before several lawyers from big downtown firms approached, angling to get a word with her alone. Last year, she would have complied because big law meant big money and potential donations to her reelection campaign. But she no longer needed to glad-hand these lawyers in hopes they'd support her political ambitions. She was polite and firm as she skirted through the crowd with West and Lloyd at her side, hoping to reach the bar before being waylaid by her parents.

"Camille!"

Damn. Her mother stood to her right, surrounded by a group of women. They all looked impeccable, which made Camille conscious of her slightly mussed hair and the bags under her eyes. But her mother had probably spent the afternoon having a massage, a blowout, and her nails done and called it work since she considered appearance a crucial part of influence. "Hello, Mother." She waved an arm. "Looks like you have a great turnout."

"We do have an excellent turnout." She looked pointedly at her clerks. "Are you going to introduce me to your friends?"

Camille stifled a grimace. "Nancy Avery, this is West Fallon and Lloyd Garber, my law clerks. They graciously agreed to accompany me after a particularly grueling day at work. I promised them both a drink. We'll catch up with you in just a bit, okay?" She leaned in for the requisite just for show hug, and then steered West and Lloyd toward the bar.

"Doesn't your mother represent some of the Saudi royal family?" Lloyd asked, looking back over his shoulder as her mother wandered over to a new group of people.

"She does. I'm sure she'd love to tell you all about it. Just expect her to ask you for a big donation and don't be afraid to tell her no." Camille flicked her eyes in her mother's direction. "If you hurry, you might catch her in between sessions."

Lloyd didn't wait for her to say more before he took off across the room.

"Good job," West said.

"I take it you and Lloyd aren't the best of friends."

"He's okay."

"You mean, for an uptight, privileged guy."

"You kept him on."

West delivered the remark matter-of-factly and Camille didn't take offense. She'd done what she thought was the right thing at the time—trusting Stroud to loan her an intelligent clerk who would help her clear up her docket. Funny, if she'd seen West's résumé before she met her she would've ranked her as the top candidate because West was everything a judge could possibly want in a clerk: top of her class, well-rounded in clinic and law review experience, and universally liked by her professors. But none of that defined her. West was the perfect clerk but in a package she would've passed on if she'd been doing the hiring, and what a shame that would've been. How many other people and opportunities had she missed out on because she'd spent her life thinking things had to be a certain way to be right?

Her mother tapped the microphone at the podium and called the room to order. As she relayed her personal story about why MADD was so important to her, Camille looked over at West and wondered what she was thinking. Did she really want to be here or did she treat this as an obligation of her employment? Camille remembered comparing West to Sadie, her date from last weekend, and thinking Sadie would've made the better date for a function like this one. She'd been wrong. West was different from what she was used to, but she didn't fall short in any way. Handsome, polite, attentive, and intelligent—she was the perfect date.

Except West wasn't her date. While West listened to her mother's remarks, Camille allowed herself one more long, lingering look at the woman standing next to her before she let reality back in.

"Are you ready to go?" Camille asked.

West took the last sip of her beer and set the bottle on the table. "Sure, but if you need to stick around, I can head out on my own."

Camille shook her head. "No way. If I leave with you, I can make the excuse we have work to do at the office, but if I try to escape on my own, I'll never make it out alive."

West smiled. "You have been pretty popular tonight."

"Don't even. Popularity isn't all it's cracked up to be. Everyone who talked to me wanted something. You'd think I was Santa Claus."

"Yes, if Santa wore a midnight blue cocktail dress and had legs for days. Tell me you didn't wear that all day under your robe." Camille cast her eyes downward, and West half regretted the remark, but she wasn't going to take it back. It was true. Camille was hot and she'd been the center of attention all night. At least three times, West had considered ducking out, but had been mesmerized by the way Camille worked the room, only staying long enough in one place to keep people wanting more. Camille had probably raised more for MADD tonight than everyone on the board combined.

"You're very sweet, but I'm pretty sure it's the title, not the package that has everyone vying for my attention."

"Then let's get you out of here."

"Should we find Lloyd? I haven't seen him since we got here."

"He left about thirty minutes ago with Judge Stroud. But don't worry, he didn't go before he button-holed every partner at all the top ten firms in town."

"And you stayed?"

"I didn't want you to walk back alone." Had she been presumptuous to think Camille would want to walk back to the office with her? It wasn't late and the munchies the guys in suits had passed around the room weren't enough to constitute a full meal. For all she knew, Camille had a dinner date waiting.

"Again, that's very sweet. I'd appreciate the escort." Camille started walking, and West followed. When they reached the light at the corner near where her car was parked, she considered her options. In a few minutes, they'd be at the courthouse where Camille would go to her car, and she'd walk back to hers. They'd go their separate ways and Monday morning, they'd be back to judge and law clerk, instead of a couple dressed for a night on the town. She'd barely spent any time with Camille tonight, but strangely enough, she felt closer to her. Maybe it had something to do with meeting Camille's parents and seeing the ostensibly close relationship that struck her as cold and impersonal just below the surface. Whatever it was, the evening had left her with questions about Camille's personal life—her parents, her brother, her life growing up. Why did she become a lawyer, a judge? What were her dreams? How did she define success? If they kept walking, she feared she'd never have her answers and she really, really wanted them.

The light changed and Camille started to step into the street, but West called out, "Wait. Please."

Camille turned back and the shine of the streetlight illuminated her features. She was more beautiful than West could stand, and she couldn't imagine not taking the chance. "Let me drive you home. We can get dinner on the way. Remember you said if I gave your favorite pizza a chance, you'd let me pick the next time? Well, I know just the place. Come with me?"

She held out her hand and waited. One, two, three seconds passed. She spent them trying to interpret the changing expressions on Camille's face, but finally gave up and hoped for the best.

"Pizza sounds perfect." Camille reached back and took her hand. "Lead the way."

CHAPTER SEVENTEEN

"You're yawning," West said as she drove through the streets of downtown Dallas. "Are you sure you're up for dinner out?"

Camille stifled a second yawn. Now that she was out of the crowd of people vying for her attention, exhaustion had hit full force, but she didn't want to miss out on this opportunity to be alone with West. The last week of barely speaking to each other had left her feeling more bereft than she cared to admit. "Just a little drained from the crowd and the week in trial." An idea popped in her head, and she spoke before she could change her mind. "I might not be up for dinner out after all, but would you consider dinner in?"

"Tell me more about this plan."

"It's pretty simple, actually. Pizza to go. I'm sure I have a bottle of wine and some beer at my place, and I think it's clean enough for visitors, although this week's been such a whirlwind, I'm not entirely sure some of my clothes aren't strewn about the living room." She felt the slow burn of a blush as she thought about her clothes scattered around for a more salacious reason having nothing to do with poor housekeeping and everything to do with West. "But if you'd rather not, that's okay, I mean we can—"

"Your place, pizza, possibly imperfect housekeeping," West interrupted with a grin. "I'm in."

Thirty minutes later, pizza procured, Camille directed West to her condo. When they walked through the foyer, Camille looked around for any stray articles of clothing, wineglasses, or other debris from her haphazard week, and sighed with relief when everything was in relatively good order.

"You can set that in the kitchen and help yourself to anything in the fridge. I'll be right back." She didn't wait for an answer before taking off upstairs to her bedroom. Her mission was to change out of her dress into something more comfortable, but now that she was standing in her closet, contemplating her options, she began to think inviting West here, to her home, had been a crazy idea fraught with peril. She slid the hanger containing her favorite silk robe to the back of the closet, choosing instead a pair of yoga pants and a well-worn UT Law T-shirt. *Nothing sexy about that.* She changed quickly and started back downstairs.

The kitchen was visible from the landing, and she paused for a moment to watch West leaning back against the counter, drinking from a beer bottle. She'd shed her suit jacket, loosened her tie, and her shirt-sleeves were rolled up to her elbows. Her hair, that had been perfectly coiffed for the party, was now pleasantly mussed, with wispy tendrils curling around her ears and collar. Camille imagined running her hands through the dark waves. Was it thick and coarse or fine and soft? Would West welcome the touch? A week ago, she would've been certain of West's response, but after the wall she'd erected between them, did West still want her?

Camille descended the stairs, determined to set aside expectations of anything other than a friendly evening. She had no business asking for anything more.

"Do you like the stout?" Camille asked as she entered the kitchen.

West raised the bottle. "More love than like. I don't recognize the brand, but I love the name. Joe Mama's Milk. Perfection."

Camille laughed. "Leave it to Jaylyn. I mentioned you'd introduced me to a local stout, and she said I had to try this. A client from New York sent her a case. She doesn't normally care for beer, but she said she's become addicted to the stuff. Too bad you can't buy it around here."

"Definitely. Am I tasting coffee in this?"

"You are. Isn't it amazing?" Camille was standing beside West now. She wanted to say there were a lot more amazing things than the beer. The way West's eyes darkened when she drew close. The sexy ease of her casual stance, like she was unflappable and open to whatever path this evening might take. On some level, Camille had expected West might be sullen, still upset about having been pulled from the case, but she appeared to be relaxed and happy. "Are you hungry?"

The words tumbled out as a planned segue to something other than where her thoughts were headed, but they echoed in her head, ringing with innuendo. She started to overcorrect, to point to the box of pizza to clear up her faux pas, but before she could speak, West set the bottle down and pulled her close. So close.

"I'm starving," West breathed the words next to her ear, warm and inviting. She ran her hand down Camille's side, and she tilted her head back, inviting West closer. The kiss started the same as the one before. Soft, light brushes of skin leaving a trail of ignited nerve endings with each stroke. Camille groaned as West pressed harder, her lips, her tongue both insistent on tasting her completely. Wet, hot heat flooded through her belly and she kissed back, unwilling to resist any longer. Nothing else mattered at this moment—not the job, not the age difference, not their roles—only the desire burning through her soul and the longing to be consumed by it.

"Take me." West leaned back and gazed at her like she was trying to gauge the truth of what she'd just heard. Camille repeated the words. "Take me. Now."

This time West claimed her lips like they were lovers who'd kissed a thousand times, but knew each one could be the last. Camille surrendered to the heady glow. Her body was on fire, vibrating to her core with the desire to feel West's skin against her own. When they finally broke for air, Camille breathed a single word. "Bed."

She led the way upstairs to her bedroom. All thoughts about the condition of her housekeeping had vanished in the wake of West's kisses, but another form of trepidation crept in with each step closer to her room. This was the first time she'd brought anyone back to this condo, let alone this bedroom.

"Are you okay?"

She started at the sound of West's voice. They were at the top of the stairs, and she paused before walking toward her room. She had been saving this place. The condo, the career—they both represented new beginnings, setting down roots. Permanence. She hadn't brought anyone else back here because no one had fit her life for the long term.

No one was special enough to include in this chapter. If she walked down the hall with West right now, did that mean they had some sort of future together? Did she want them to?

"Is this what you want?"

West's words echoing her thoughts had to be a sign, a beacon guiding her to her destiny. But was her future down the hall or back the way they'd come? For a brief moment her mind flashed to the photograph of her and West kissing in the kitchenette at the courthouse. Was someone watching now? Did she care? The flood of arousal crowded out her ability to reason, and the only thing she could be sure of was if she didn't have West now, she'd regret it the rest of her life.

West ran her hand down Camille's arm and felt her shudder. Things had moved both fast and slow at the same time, but whatever the speed, she couldn't keep up. Camille had led the way up the stairs, sending strong signals sex was in their future, but now she was standing still, mere yards from the bed she said was their destination, and West wasn't sure where they were headed. She'd followed Camille's lead to this point, but what if the path led nowhere? Should she bow out gracefully and write Camille's invitation off to residual glow from the limelight she'd basked in earlier this evening?

"This is exactly what I want," Camille finally answered. "But only if you want it too."

West witnessed the mix of determination and doubt on Camille's face and answered by claiming her lips once again. She kissed and teased until Camille was limp in her arms and then told her what she needed to hear. "I want nothing more."

West followed Camille to her room, catching only slight details about her surroundings before they fell on the bed, a tangled twist of bodies unable to get close enough. West pulled Camille's T-shirt over her head, gasping when her lush, ample breasts were revealed. "You are so beautiful."

Camille grinned. "I bet you say that to all the judges."

"Only the truly hot ones." West raised a hand and started ticking off fingers. "Let me count them." She tapped one finger against her palm. "There's you and then there's…hmmm."

Camille grabbed the waistband of her trousers and pulled her close, her voice a sexy whisper. "You're hilarious."

"I'm right and you know it," West replied. She ran her hands down Camille's back, enjoying the way her body shivered at the touch. "Perfect."

"It would be more perfect if you were out of that suit."

"I thought you liked the suit," West teased her.

"Love it. Would love it more if it were on the floor."

West pushed up from the bed, slowly unbuttoning her pants and sliding down the zippered fly. She reached inside and ran her hand along the crease of her boxer brief, shuddering at the slight pressure, imagining Camille's hand there instead of her own.

"You're driving me crazy."

"That's the plan. Or, if you wanted, you could come along for the ride."

Camille answered by lying back and shimmying out of her pants, leaving her completely nude. West's entire body hummed with excitement as she watched Camille reach down and slide a finger through her glistening, hot sex. West swayed in place as Camille added more fingers to the play, and arched against her own touch. Each pass of her hand drove West insane, but she waited, knowing Camille was sending a message with this overt display of vulnerability, but when Camille moaned, West couldn't stand it any longer. She shucked off her clothes and walked to the edge of the bed, lowering her body between Camille's thighs.

West drew lazy circles with her tongue to slow the pace, drinking in the scent of Camille's arousal. Once Camille's breath steadied into a solid rhythm, West slid a finger through her wet center and curved upward, searching for friction. Camille bucked beneath her, and West varied the pace, licking harder, softer, faster, slower as Camille crested peak after peak at her command. When she finally sucked Camille's clit between her lips, she thrashed wildly in her arms. West drew the flat of her tongue along Camille's clit and thrust her fingers in and out of her sex to meet the intensity of her surging orgasm. When Camille screamed her pleasure, West curled around her and held her tightly through the shuddering aftershocks.

"Incredible," West whispered.

"You are." Camille's voice was breathy and faint.

"Let's call it a draw."

"Deal."

West tugged Camille closer, into the crook of her arm. "Can I get you anything? Water, beer? Pizza?"

"Only if you can levitate it up the stairs." Camille rolled onto her side and threw her arm over West's stomach. "Because no way in hell am I letting you out of this bed right now."

"Your call. I just thought you might be hungry after all that, uh, exertion."

Camille play-slapped her. "Oh, I'm very hungry, but everything I need is right here." She traced her fingers around West's breasts, taking care to keep her touch feather-light. She wanted to prolong the buildup, but after the incredible orgasm she'd just had, holding back was hard. When she skimmed West's nipples with the palm of her hand, West bucked into her touch.

"Talk about driving people crazy," West whispered in a jagged breath.

Camille answered by lowering her head and flicking her tongue around West's nipples, loving that they were already stiff with arousal. "Mmm," she murmured. "So good."

West's hand reached for hers and drew it downward until Camille's fingers felt the wet heat between West's legs. "Touch me," West begged.

Camille slid her fingers through the slick folds, loving the groans of pleasure each pass elicited. Since that night in the office when West had first kissed her, she'd imagined this moment, but never thought it could happen, never thought she would let it happen. West was the pursuer, and she'd run from the chase because it was the safe, sensible thing to do. Would she have run if she'd known it could feel this good? The answer was clear, and now that she'd been captured by West's spell, it was her turn to pursue, to catch, and to return the pleasure. Safe and sensible be damned.

At West's urging, Camille stroked with increased intensity while she licked and sucked West's breasts, reveling in the way their bodies melded into one giant ball of pleasure. When West's pelvis rocked in her hand, she amped up the pressure until West surrendered to the orgasm and fell limp in her arms.

❖

Camille woke to the smell of coffee, rolled over, and saw West standing in her bedroom doorway, naked except for the tray she held in her hands. "You are perfection." She rubbed her eyes. "I can't remember the last time I slept so hard."

"Sex does that to a person," West said. "Good sex, anyway."

She set the tray on the nightstand and settled on the edge of the bed. Camille reached an arm around her waist and pulled her close. "It's kind of a miracle I'm awake at all." Camille closed her eyes and replayed the night they'd shared. She'd never been with such an attentive lover, and she couldn't remember ever feeling so satisfied and yet so ready for more in her life.

"And this is why I brewed the strong stuff," West said, pouring them each a cup. "I see you not only stock great beer, but righteous coffee too."

"I think your good taste might be rubbing off on me. I used to go through the drive-through at Starbucks. Now, I'm spoiled."

"Heathen. Glad to hear you're turning your life around." West raised her cup. "To being spoiled."

"I'll drink to that," Camille said, savoring the bold brew. "Perfect. Thank you." She lowered the mug. "Thank you for everything. Last night was incredible." Camille read a look of hope in West's eyes as if she expected to hear more. Her words carried a hint of finality and farewell, and she regretted the way reality seeped into the intimacy between them, but there was nothing she could do. The lines they'd crossed last night would snap back into place on Monday morning whether she wanted them to or not.

Don't rush it. Enjoy the moment. Camille set her mug on the nightstand and reached for West's hand. She drew it to her lips, dropping tender kisses on her palm and her fingertips. "Talk to me."

"What do you want to talk about?"

"Tell me why you became a lawyer. And don't tell me you were following in Judge Blair's footsteps. You don't strike me as a follower."

West laughed and scooted closer on the bed. "You're right about that." She drank from her coffee, her eyes settled on a spot across the room as she relayed her story. "I told you I wound up in the system when I was a kid. I spent a lot of time in court and got to see a lot of lawyers at work. Good ones, bad ones—the whole range—but no matter how skilled or careless, they all had something in common. They spoke for people who couldn't or shouldn't speak for themselves. They took a stand and took charge." She looked down, and Camille followed her gaze, seeing the bed sheet clenched tightly in West's hand. "I wanted that. I wanted to be in charge of my own life."

Camille drew West into her arms. "And how do you feel about being a lawyer now that you're stuck doing a job you hate?"

West looked into her eyes. "I don't hate it. It's not what I would've chosen, but I admit Hank wasn't wrong when he said it was the best foundation an advocate can have. I guess there's something to be said for perspective." She ran a finger down the side of Camille's breast. "Besides, no one explained all the perks of the job, or I would have been on board way before now."

Camille knew she was teasing, but West's words set off alarms. She didn't regret the intimacy they'd shared—far from it—but she couldn't deny she'd transgressed boundaries that were in place for a reason. West was her employee, but more than that, she was supposed to be a mentor to West, teaching her, guiding her in her chosen field. Their roles were blurred enough now. What would happen if they continued down this path?

She couldn't wait around to find out. A moment ago, she'd felt very sensuous, lounging in bed, nude, freshly rested from a night of hot sex with her young lover, but suddenly, her naked body and West's doting presence were stark reminders of the sacrifices she'd have to make to have what she'd planned for her future.

"Camille?" West's eyes were narrowed in concern. "Are you okay?"

"West." Camille cleared her throat and pushed on, determined to be quick and clear. Like any good lawyer, she'd sorted the relevant points she wanted to make and was ready for a skilled and convincing argument, but when she finally opened her mouth all that came out was, "I can't."

Chapter Eighteen

West pounded through the rain like she was being chased by a pack of wolves. Several times she slipped and nearly fell into the already heavy Monday morning traffic along Greenville Avenue. In the still dark morning, if she slipped there was a strong chance she'd be mowed down by one of the oncoming cars zipping off to work. Who were these people in such a hurry to get to their jobs? Did they love their careers? Bet none of them were in love with bosses that didn't love them back.

Love. Holy shit. Talk about slipping. When had lust for the hot older woman she'd met by chance turn into something more substantial? It wasn't the sex, although the sex had been fantastic right up until the moment Camille cut it off. No, the passion she had for Camille had been growing steadily since the moment she'd walked into her office on her first day at work and watched her try to keep her cool while pretending they'd never met. Camille was smart, driven, and honorable—qualities West admired, qualities she possessed as well, so why shouldn't they make a perfect match?

The answer couldn't be as simple as different ages and experience. Both of those constructs had been easily overcome by countless others before them. It had to be something else. She'd tried to pull it out of Camille without success. Camille would only say she was sorry she'd crossed a line and whatever had happened between them was over, like saying she was done made it so. West got that Camille was hung up on the boss-employee thing, and West understood to a point, but her clerkship was temporary and Camille's pronouncement was permanent.

Her first instinct had been to go into the office on Sunday, write a letter of resignation, and leave it on Camille's desk. Problem solved. Except what she'd told Camille about the job Friday night had been true. Despite her intentions, she'd come to enjoy not just the work, but feeling she belonged somewhere, that she was part of something important. Her morning greeting from Ester, special treatment from Peter, and the opportunity to work a case from both sides—all of these gave her a sense of belonging and purpose she'd been searching for her entire life. She wasn't ready to give them up even if it meant spending the balance of the year working close to a woman she loved, but who might never love her back.

She pushed through the door of her apartment, and as she kicked off her soaking wet shoes, Bill appeared with an enormous towel in his hand. He shoved it at her. "Skinny people don't need to run, especially not in the pouring rain. It makes the rest of us look bad."

"Maybe skinny people are skinny because they run."

He cocked his head and then shook it. "Nope. At least that's not the case here. You only run when you're upset or trying to figure something out. Care to share which?"

West toweled her hair dry. "Not really."

"Are you going to work today?"

She squinted his way. "Why wouldn't I go to work today?"

"Dunno. You've been in a bit of a funk since you got home Saturday *morning*," he emphasized the last word. "I've been trying to give you some space, but if you want to talk, I'm here."

She wanted to tell him everything. How she'd gotten her hopes up and how being with Camille had exceeded all her expectations, but telling him that part meant telling the rest, and she didn't feel like choking her way through the story of Camille's rejection. "I'm good," she lied. "Going to grab a shower and then I'm out of here."

Fifteen minutes later, clean but not refreshed, West stood in front of her closet, trying to decide what to wear and wondering why everything seemed so much harder now. She brushed her way through her usual attire until her hand landed on the hanger holding the last of the three suits she'd purchased, ostensibly for the job, but realistically to impress Camille. *Look how well that turned out.* Before she could think it to death, she yanked the suit from the closet and picked a shirt to go with it. If she was going down, she may as well look good doing it.

❖

Camille was the first one in the office on Monday morning, and she headed directly to the kitchen. She switched on the coffeemaker and opened the cabinet. A big red plastic canister sat next to an air-tight glass jar of the coffee West supplied, and Camille stared between the two for a moment before pulling down the canister and measuring out enough of the grounds for a large pot.

While the coffeemaker spit and sizzled, she sank into one of the chairs at the small table. She'd barely slept all weekend. Friday night she'd made love to West, and Saturday and Sunday she'd lain awake regretting the way she'd handled their parting. Now she was facing a full, long day of conflict in the Wilson trial, and all she wanted to do was hide in her office with the door locked.

The coffee tasted horrible, but she drank it, the least of the punishment she deserved for the way she'd handled things with West. She should never have gotten involved, but she had and she couldn't bring herself to regret the intimacy they'd shared. West was charming, bright, handsome, and while they made love, Camille hadn't cared about any of the boundaries she'd erected to keep them apart. What had changed?

Her job was secure. She could dance naked on the roof of the courthouse and it was unlikely she'd be impeached. And if someone like the now retired Clarence Thomas could get confirmed in spite of a string of women testifying he'd sexually harassed them, then why should a perfectly innocent love between two consenting adults interfere with her advancement?

And there it was. She *did* love West. She didn't know when she'd fallen, but she had, and she'd fallen hard. But she'd thrown the possibility of a future with West away because she was worried about what other people might think. Damn it. She was a good attorney and had the chops to be an excellent jurist, especially now that she didn't have to be a politician as well. Why was she making things more difficult by placing her professional goals over her personal desires? How could she sit in judgment of others if she wasn't willing to examine her own life and measure the choices she'd made?

She stood and walked to the sink, tossing the foul tasting coffee down the drain. She was done with settling for anything less than the best, and she was going to remedy her last mistake the minute West arrived. She strode to her office full of purpose. If West wasn't in yet, she'd call her. She'd walk the halls until she found her, but she wasn't going to put on that robe until she made it clear to the woman she loved that they could figure out a way to make whatever this was work.

When she rounded the corner, Peter Donovan and a couple of other marshals she didn't recognize were hovering near Ester's desk. Ester was frowning, and the marshals' serious expressions told her the plan to find West was going to be delayed, but she vowed to make quick work of whatever it was they were here to say. "Marshal Donovan." She nodded at the others. "Do you have an update about the matter we discussed last week?"

Donovan shot a look at the other guys who now looked puzzled. "Judge Avery, perhaps we can talk in your office. Something else has come up and it needs your immediate attention, definitely before you resume trial this morning."

Camille sighed at his ominous proclamation and motioned for them to follow her. She invited them into her office, but didn't ask them to sit. "I came in early to get some work done, so I hope this won't take long."

Donovan launched in. "We've completed the bulk of our investigation about the press leaks in the Wilson case, and Judge Stroud asked us to brief you before the trial starts back up."

Camille stared at him, barely able to register he wasn't here to provide information about whoever had been delivering ominous notes imploring her to quit. "Excuse me, what?" She cleared her throat and tried again. "I wasn't aware I had authorized any sort of investigation into press leaks. Can you explain?"

Donovan shifted in place, clearly uncomfortable, but why? He looked at the two men with him and jerked his chin at the door. When they'd exited the room, Donovan pointed at one of the chairs in front of her desk. "May I?"

"Yes, of course," Camille answered. "Did you say Judge Stroud asked you to talk to me?"

"Yes, ma'am. He asked us to find out who was leaking sealed court documents to the local press outlets."

Camille bristled at the information. This was her court, not Stroud's. Leaks happened and, as pissed as she was that the leaks were happening on her watch, it was up to her to handle it, not Stroud. If she knew which side was leaking the information, she'd handle it with sanctions, not a potential criminal investigation led by the marshal service. What was Stroud's motivation for getting in the middle of her case? "I assume you learned something or you wouldn't be here this morning. Let's hear it."

Donovan avoided her gaze. "It appears several documents were emailed from this office to the local paper and a couple of the local TV news affiliates. The documents were sealed pleadings not otherwise available to the general public."

Camille shook her head, unable to believe that anyone in her office would have been careless with the pleadings let alone purposely provided sealed court documents directly to the press—a very serious allegation. Now she knew why the marshal's service was involved, but she still didn't know what had prompted Stroud to initiate the inquiry, although he'd been way too involved in her court since the day she'd started.

She looked back at Donovan, who was clearly uncomfortable to be the messenger, and asked the question even though she was certain she already knew the answer. "Who sent the email?"

"West Fallon."

West ran her hands down the front of the suit jacket and squared her shoulders before she pushed through the doors to the office suite, partly hoping court was back in session so she wouldn't have to confront Camille just yet. She was already second-guessing her decision to wear the suit since any confrontation would be easier if she were comfortable, but nothing about the situation with Camille was comfortable, no matter what she wore. Maybe the suit was the edge she needed to get Camille to stop concentrating on the reasons they shouldn't be together, and focus on her.

The minute she crossed the threshold, she knew something was wrong. Ester's eyes widened and cut to the right of her desk where Peter was standing with a couple of marshals West didn't recognize. Maybe they had some news about the whacko who'd been sending those notes to Camille. "Good morning, Ester," she said. Peter turned at the sound of her voice and she waved at him. "Good morning to you too. Any news?"

"West, we need to talk."

West heard the plaintive cord in his tone, but she couldn't make sense of it. She looked back at Ester and could tell she was upset, but not why. "What's going on?"

Peter reached for her arm. "Let's go to Judge Avery's office. We can talk there."

Certain Peter and his pals had a breakthrough in the threatening note case, West willingly led the way down the hall, anxious about seeing Camille for the first time since they'd made love. The door was partially open, and Peter motioned for her to go in. She was surprised to see Judge Stroud seated in front of Camille's desk, his face fixed into a stern expression. A dozen thoughts ran through her mind at once. Had Stroud found out they'd slept together? Was Camille in trouble for violating some arcane don't have sex with your clerk code?

She tried in vain to catch Camille's eye, but she was looking everywhere in the room but at her. West turned back to Peter, the only other friend she had in the room. "What's going on?"

"Have a seat, West," Stroud said, pointing at the chair next to him.

"I'm good, thanks." West felt an ambush coming and sitting seemed like a really poor defensive posture.

Stroud frowned. "Fine then. I'll get right to the point. It's come to our attention," he swept his arm to indicate the rest of the room, "that the press leaks in the Wilson case were made by you. Although no formal charges for obstruction of justice are pending at this point, it's my duty to advise you of your rights before we discuss this further."

West shook her head. Surely, she'd heard him wrong. Press leaks? Obstruction of justice? Her? The acid sting of nausea rose into her throat, and she grabbed the back of the chair to steady herself.

"West?"

She looked up into Camille's eyes and saw genuine concern. And pain. Was she the cause of this? West wished more than anything that she and Camille were the only ones in the room. "It's not true."

"West, don't say anything else," Camille said, her voice flat and quiet. "You have a right to a lawyer."

West smothered a laugh at the absurdity of the remark. Hell, she was a lawyer. If she weren't, things would be so much easier. Maybe if she'd met Camille under different circumstances, they could've fallen in love without all the complications. But none of that mattered right now. Camille thought she'd done something wrong and she hadn't. The question was why? She turned to Stroud. "What's the evidence?"

"Excuse me," he said, clearly annoyed at being questioned.

"You said I leaked sealed documents to the press. You must have evidence to make such an accusation. Witnesses, a paper trail, motivation?"

Stroud nodded. "We have all of those things. The marshals will be happy to share the evidence they've developed, but as to the motivation, I think your past is motivation enough. Everything that has been printed in the press has been designed to poison the jurors' minds against the defendant." He held up his hands. "I'm not saying I think the allegations are wrong, but Mr. Wilson is entitled to a fair trial, just like any other person accused of a crime." He leaned closer to West. "I can see how the horrible tragedy that resulted in your mother's death might motivate you to exact revenge in a similar case, but your motivation is misplaced."

He kept talking, but at the mention of her mother, his voice became a dull roar against the darkness that flooded West's brain. Why was he talking about her mother? Why did he know anything about her mother and the way she'd died? In desperation, she looked around the room for answers. Camille was the only one to face her directly.

"Gentlemen," she said, "I'd like a moment alone with West."

Peter nodded and walked to the door, but Judge Stroud remained seated. Camille gave him a pointed look and he frowned again. "I strongly advise against this."

"Point taken," Camille said. "Now, please excuse us."

Stroud slowly rose from his chair and glanced between them before stalking from the room. When the door finally shut behind him, West sank into the chair she'd refused earlier.

"Would you like some water?"

West looked up at Camille, suppressing another laugh at the oddness of the situation. A moment ago, she was being threatened with prosecution, and now the woman she loved was offering her a glass of water. Her head spun. "No. What I want is to know why in the hell you or anyone else thinks I would leak sealed documents?"

Camille folded her hands, her expression pained. "They have emails. Sent by you, from your computer." She paused as if deciding whether to say more and then rushed her words. "And what Stroud said about your mother. After the way she died, what happened to her…of course this trial would bring up feelings for you, make you want to act on them."

"How do you know all this?"

"I've read your file."

"My file? There shouldn't be anything about my mother in my personnel file." West heard her voice rising and struggled to tamp it down long enough to get some answers. "How is that even relevant?"

Camille was silent for a moment and West waited her out. Something was off and she was determined to find out what.

Finally, Camille answered. "It wasn't your personnel file. I've seen your CPS file. I know what happened to your mother."

The nausea was back, but West swallowed to keep it at bay. "You don't know anything." She glared at Camille who merely sat silent. West stood, too fast, and swayed against the chair back. Anger coursed through her like hot lava. She wanted to lash out, to shout that whatever Camille had read wasn't true, that it didn't affect her, that she didn't think about the impact of her mother's actions every single day. But she'd be lying.

She summoned all the strength she had and spoke her final words to Camille. "My mother killed herself. She chose drugs over everything—over a job, school, groceries, rent." She choked back a sob. "Over me.

"When she spent all the money we had shooting junk into her veins, she fucked her dealer for more. She died with a needle in her arm, and he went to prison. Did he get what he deserved? I don't know. It's not for me to decide. But she's better off dead than leading the life she did, and I'm better off without her. If you think I'd try to tank a case because of something that happened in my past, you don't know me at all, and you're not the woman I thought I loved."

Suddenly, she realized the real reason Camille had held her at a distance. Her past had come back to haunt her with a vengeance, inserted a wedge between her desires and satisfaction. Well, it was time she took control of her own destiny. She started toward the door. "And by the way, I quit."

West walked briskly to the front of the office where Stroud and Peter were standing near Ester's desk with Ester glaring at both of them. She reached down, gave Ester a hug, and whispered, "I tried," before walking past the two men.

"If you want to arrest me," she said. "You'll have to come find me. I'm sure you know where I live. It's all in my file." Angry and deflated, West stalked out of the office and didn't look back.

Chapter Nineteen

"It's been a week. Do you think you might ever wear real clothes again?" Bill asked as he walked in the door.

West rose from the couch just enough to chuck a pillow at him and sank back into the cushions. "Leave me alone."

"That line is getting old." He sat down beside her. "Besides, I'm a little worried this end of the couch is getting worn out. Maybe you could switch it up a bit and lie on the other side next week?"

West groaned inwardly at the thought of another week of this. Since she'd stormed out of Camille's office, her life had been in limbo. She'd gone home, tossed her suit in the back of her closet, and taken up residence on Bill's way too comfortable couch in front of the TV. The first couple of days her phone had blown up with messages, voice and text, mostly from Camille, imploring her to respond, saying she was sorry, saying she was wrong. The last time her cell battery died, West found the solution to her search for solitude and simply stopped charging it. Bill was the only human contact she'd had in a week, and it looked like she might be wearing him out. She just couldn't muster the energy to go back out in the world. Not yet.

"I'm sorry. I promise I'll figure out my life soon."

"It's whatever. You'll figure it out when you're ready. In fact, I might have some news that will help you along. But first," he grabbed the remote and turned on the television, "there's some news I think you should see."

He flipped through the channels until he landed on the local Eyewitness News. West watched a reporter talking to a man about an altercation with a roving pack of dogs. "Is this your idea of cheering me up? Because it's not working."

"Hold on, it's coming."

He turned up the volume, and seconds later, a banner across the screen read *Mistrial Declared in Darryl Wilson Trial*. West straightened up on the couch, eyes glued to the screen.

"After a week delay in the pending trial of Darryl Wilson, the defendant accused of providing a co-ed from Richards College with drugs that resulted in her death, Judge Camille Avery granted the defense counsel's motion for a mistrial. The motion was filed under seal, so we can only speculate about the reason for the mistrial, but a statement from the US Attorney's office said they are exploring their options for retrying Mr. Wilson and the case would likely be assigned to another judge."

When the anchor switched to the weather report, Bill turned down the volume. "What do you think about that?"

West's first thought was of Camille. Declaring a mistrial on her first federal trial was rough. She'd probably get an earful about the waste of taxpayer money and juror time from Stroud. The decision had to be based on the leaked documents, and the reassignment was likely because the leak had come from her office. Camille's last text was burned in her brain. *I was wrong. About everything.* Did everything include believing she'd been involved with the leaked documents?

"There's more," Bill said, breaking through her thoughts.

"What?" Not sure if she wanted to know, but unable to resist hearing every detail.

"Avery's other clerk, Garber, got the boot today."

Camille had fired Lloyd? West wasn't sure if she believed it. "Where did you hear that?"

"I have my sources."

West punched him in the side. "Spill."

"Okay, okay. Courthouse gossip. One of the attorneys at the office was in Avery's court today and said Lloyd was escorted out of the building by the marshals. That's all I know, but your judge is now down two clerks. Sure you don't want to give the couch a rest and go see her?"

West struggled to process the intel. Was Lloyd the one who leaked the documents? Had Camille figured it out, and was that the reason for the cryptic wrong about everything text? Maybe if she hadn't tuned out of life for the past week, she'd know more. West was desperate to find out. Or was she? Maybe she was better off in her bubble, away from the place and people that caused her pain. "What was the other thing?"

"Excuse me?"

"You said you had some news that might help me out. Please tell me it wasn't this, because I'm not going back there."

Bill shook his head. "Personally, I think you're making a mistake by not even talking to her, but what I was going to tell you is Lambda is hiring. Before you get all excited, it's a part-time briefing clerk position and you have to be admitted to the bar, but they'll accept résumés from graduates who sat for the exam in July. The money's not great, but it's a great place to work, and you'd be doing good things—"

She cut him off with a fierce hug. "Yes! Yes!"

"Hey, chill. It's not a sure thing. I can get you the interview, but the rest is up to you. With your grades and standing, you're probably set, but you can bet they'll ask why you decided to give up your clerk gig less than a month in."

Bill's words cooled her newfound excitement, but not entirely. Although she'd spent the past week in a steady funk, she'd had a few bouts of momentary panic wondering what she was going to do with her life. This summer her options had been endless, but now most of the sweet jobs would be taken, even the ones at the big law firms. More than once she'd speculated on what she would have done if she hadn't kept her promise to Hank, but so many of those doors were closed to her now. She didn't blame him, not in the least, but she'd about decided it was time to reach out to him, confess she'd quit the job he'd given her. She owed Hank an explanation of why she'd thrown away her clerkship.

Her first instinct was to call Camille to discuss her dilemma with her. Funny, since Camille was the reason she was in this position. If she'd clerked for any other judge, she might have faced conflicts, but none that forced her to decide between kissing her boss and keeping her job. She was better off facing Hank and his disappointment than crawling back to Camille and hoping for a do-over.

❖

Camille peered out the door viewer and sighed when she saw Jay standing on her front step. Jay wasn't likely to give up and go away, so she swung the door open and waved her in. "Do you want a glass of wine?" She raised the glass in her hand. "I just opened a bottle of red."

"Look who's being all hospitable. Can't be bothered to join her friends for brunch several weeks in a row, but when you show up at her door, you get free drinks."

Camille ignored the jibe, walked to the kitchen, and poured another glass of wine, but Jay was not to be deterred.

"I've conducted a poll of all our friends and the only person who's heard from you in the last week is Sadie. At first I was excited to hear you were still alive, but then she told me you phoned in the equivalent of a Dear Jane letter, so I'm thinking you might be dead after all. I mean, have you met her? Dr. Sadie Jackson, gorgeous, accomplished trauma surgeon?"

Camille glared at her, but sipped her wine instead of gracing her with a reply. She'd finally returned one of Sadie's several calls, thinking it was better to rip off the Band-Aid of possibility than leave her hanging. "It was hardly a Dear Jane. Besides, we'd only been on one date. I was doing the polite thing and letting her know that despite my very persistent friend, I wasn't really in the market for someone to date."

"Fine, but there's more. Why did I have to hear on the news that your first trial totally tanked? A mistrial right in the middle of testimony? That has to be a juicy story, but since you didn't bother coming to brunch yesterday, I had to come here to get the scoop. So spill."

Now Camille wished she'd ignored the doorbell since it would be a whole lot easier to explain her absence than the events of the past week. "Sit. This may take a while."

Camille took her through a summary of the case and the persistent leaks of information that had been contained in sealed court documents.

"But how did you find out documents were being leaked? Couldn't the press have just talked to the people who had knowledge of the contents? And that's not illegal unless it was one of the attorneys subject to your gag order."

"Yes and yes, but it turns out one of my clerks was leaking information to a wire service."

Jay set her glass down. "Tell me it wasn't the one you were lusting after. What's her name?"

"West," Camille said, irrationally annoyed Jay couldn't be bothered to remember her name. "No, it wasn't her. But she thinks I thought it was. And that's what caused—never mind. Anyway, no, it was the other one, Lloyd. The marshals are questioning him about his motives, but I'm not sure it matters. He actually had the gall to say he didn't get what the big deal was for exactly the reason you said—that everyone was telling the press their "why I hate Darryl Wilson" stories. I couldn't very well let the trial go forward when someone from my own office was obstructing justice."

"I see your point, but I heard the case is getting transferred to another judge. How does that affect your career plans?"

"It doesn't." At Jay's surprised look, Camille plunged on, relieved to finally give voice to the roller coaster of emotions she'd been feeling. "I'm no longer in the business of politics. From now on, I have one goal for my career. Do the right thing, no matter what. It's what I did in state court and it lost me my bench, but nothing could convince me to go back and change my mind. If I lose out on an appellate bench because I made the tough calls, then it wasn't meant to be. Those losses pale in comparison to what I sacrifice if I don't go with my gut."

Her speech skidded to a stop and Jay's eyes widened. "Someone's on a tear."

"Yeah, if only I could figure out how to translate all this good intention to my personal life."

"I'm guessing this has something to do with the clerk. West."

"We had sex. I thought she was involved with the leaks. She quit. She won't return my calls." Camille took another sip of wine after delivering the bullet point summary, bracing for a lecture from Jay about how she shouldn't have gotten involved with her clerk in the first place.

"That's rough," Jay said. "All of it. You really fell for her, didn't you?"

Fallen wasn't how Camille would describe how she felt. More like crashed and burned before she'd even gotten the chance to tell West she loved her. She wanted to confess the depth of her feelings, but Jay wasn't the one she should be telling, so she merely said, "It was more than that."

Jay nodded knowingly. She set her wineglass down and talked with both hands. "Then you should do something about it. Something big and bold. A grand gesture." She flicked her hands at Camille. "Quick before you lose your nerve."

For a second, Camille was roused by Jay's words, but then tried to imagine a scenario where West would be impressed by a flash mob, a declaration of love on a jumbotron, or any of the other wild ideas she was certain were reeling through Jay's head. No, those methods were more likely to send West running than revive their connection. What she needed was some spark to signal West might forgive her for doubting her, for doubting her own feelings, but even though Jay's excitement was contagious, she wasn't holding out hope.

Her phone buzzed, and for a second she imagined she'd conjured a reconnection with West, but when she looked at the screen, she saw a message from Peter Donovan instead. *Need to talk. Where are you?*

CHAPTER TWENTY

Camille fidgeted with the pens on her desk, trying hard not to look in the direction of the webcam the marshals had hidden in the bookshelf to her right. When Ester buzzed to tell her Stroud was waiting to see her, she forced calm, slow breaths, and told her to send him in.

Donovan and another marshal had come by her house last night after she shooed Jay out the door. Apparently, Lloyd had lasted all of an hour in custody before he spilled the truth about why he'd set West up to take the fall for the leaks in the Wilson case. The ultimate goal had been to make Camille look incompetent, first for agreeing to keep a clerk that was so clearly biased, and second for failing to notice that same clerk was the source of the leak. According to Lloyd, the plan to undermine Camille had been Stroud's idea, and he'd been loaned to Camille to find opportunities to bring the plan to fruition.

"Lloyd told us he planted the notes you received, but Stroud wrote them," Donovan said. "Stroud also gave him the copy of West's CPS file that he left on your desk." Donovan cleared his throat. "And it was Lloyd who took the picture of you and West."

Camille resisted the urge to try to explain her indiscretion. Justifying her feelings to strangers was the old way of doing things, and she'd meant what she said to Jay about her new perspective. "If you have Lloyd's statement, I'm not sure what you want from me."

"You know as well as I do a confession is a helluva lot better than a statement from an accomplice. Just have a conversation with him and see if he trips up on anything. We'll be watching the whole time. We're not going to let anything happen to you."

Watching the whole time. Camille wasn't sure if the virtual presence of law enforcement in the privacy of her office made her feel more secure or more vulnerable, but as Stroud took his seat, she concluded it didn't matter now. All she wanted to do was put this chapter of her life behind her and figure out how to win back West.

"Camille, dear, I came as soon as I could. I've had so many calls from the press about these unfortunate matters. First West, then Lloyd. I can't get a straight answer from the marshals about why they arrested Lloyd when it's clear West was the one leaking information to the press."

Camille relaxed at bit. The fact that he'd plunged right into the details of Lloyd's arrest told her he was at least slightly worried about whether his role would be revealed. "Actually, Barry," she leaned forward to give her words a conspiratorial flavor, "Lloyd set West up. He was the one funneling stories to the press. He confessed. Guess we should have looked into that a little more carefully before accusing West." She sat back and watched his face take on a pinched look.

"Are you sure? I find it hard to believe the marshals wouldn't have told me about this development."

"Oh, I'm not surprised. He's saying all kinds of things. I'm sure they're taking their time to investigate before they make additional arrests."

"I see," Stroud said. Camille let the silence hang between them, certain he wouldn't be able to resist asking more. She didn't wait long.

"I don't suppose the marshals have shared any of the allegations with you, have they?"

Camille gave him what she hoped was a knowing smile. "Oh, they most certainly have, which makes sense since they directly involve me and my safety."

"Have you spoken with your parents about this?"

The question threw her for a second and she blurted out, "Why?"

"Because I'm sure they'd have some advice for you, especially if your well-being is at stake." Stroud reached a hand across the desk. "Camille, I didn't want to be the one to bring this up, but maybe this job isn't worth the risk. You're an accomplished lawyer. You could secure a job wherever you wanted. Why put yourself in the public eye to risk embarrassment again, especially when you don't know if the person threatening you might actually be capable of causing you harm?"

The subtle threat sent a chill up her spine, and Camille pushed her chair back to gain some distance. "I know of very few people who have the ability to put their hands on an unredacted CPS file, and Lloyd isn't one of them. Would you like to tell me why you had him deliver West's file to my office?"

"I don't know what you're talking about."

"You do. I know you do," she said, mustering confidence she didn't feel. "And Lloyd told the marshals you gave him the file with instructions to leave it on my desk."

Stroud's eyes narrowed, his pupils steely glints of disdain. "I never understood what Blair saw in that trash. I suppose she was a charity case to him, something to make him feel like a big man, but she never even pretended to appreciate the chances he gave her. And you? Your parents would die if they knew you were sleeping with your law clerk, especially one with her lack of pedigree."

The personal attack took her off guard. "So this is about West?"

"No, Camille, this is about you. You never should have gotten this bench. There are others with more experience. Others who didn't spend the last year in the news because of their poor judgment."

Camille's memory wound back to the conversation she'd had with him the day she started. "Like Mark Hollis? Is that why you did all this—sent me the notes, set me up to look like I didn't know what was going on in my own court—so you could get me to resign and your buddy Mark could get the job?"

"Too bad it didn't work."

It wasn't quite a yes, but it definitely wasn't a denial, and it would have to do because Camille was done talking to this man. "I think it's time for you to leave my office."

He didn't move. "No one will ever believe I did anything to you."

Bingo. It was like he was reading the standard script of the guilty as charged. "I predict you're wrong about that. Now get the hell out of my office."

She saw the marshals corner him as he crossed the threshold. This wouldn't be the end of the investigation—there would be lawyers and law-enforcement interviews and court dates—but she hoped Stroud's demise would clear the way to a new beginning for her and that West would be part of it.

❖

West sat in the dining room at the Blairs' house picking at her food. She'd called Diane hoping to schedule a quick visit with Hank, but Diane had insisted she come for dinner. She didn't have the heart to say no.

When she saw Hank, Diane's insistence made sense. His physical condition had improved exponentially, and he took a lot of pleasure in showing off his ability to walk with a cane. West was relieved to see him getting around on his own, and hoped it would buffer the impact of her announcement.

"I quit the clerkship," she blurted out between bites of mashed potatoes.

Both Hank and Diane turned toward her, neither showing any signs of surprise. "I know," Hank said.

"Who told you?"

"Ester."

West sighed. She should've known Ester would call and give him all the courthouse news. "I didn't have a choice."

Hank set his fork down and looked at Diane. West looked between them. "It's okay. You can say whatever you need to say in front of Diane. I'm fully prepared for you to be pissed."

"I hate that word," Hank said. "But let's talk about choices. You absolutely did have a choice. You always have a choice. I don't know every detail about what happened, but it sounds to me like you took off when things got rough. I've never known you to do that before."

"You don't know what it was like. They were accusing me of violating a court order, breaking the law. And somehow Camille had my CPS file and they were discussing my past—" She stopped mid sentence, conscious of the desperate ring of her rising voice. In the pause, Diane excused herself to check on dessert, and West focused on steadying her breath. She needed to sound more rational if she was going to make him understand.

"Tell me about Camille," he said. "Do you think she's a good judge?"

West eyed him closely, trying to decide if his use of her first name was for her benefit. "I guess."

"You guess?"

West considered the question. Camille was a good judge—fair, open, and smart. But she was having a hard time separating Camille the judge from Camille the lover, and the lover had shut her out. "I guess I can't really answer because I'm kind of biased." She rushed the next words before she lost her nerve. "I fell in love with her."

Hank chuckled. "I had a feeling there was something more to it."

His reaction was the complete opposite of what she'd expected. "Why are you laughing?"

"Because just when I think you can't surprise me again, you do. Although I bet you surprised yourself even more. Am I right?"

Was he? Falling in love with Camille certainly hadn't been expected. When she first met Camille, she'd imagined one of her usual hookups, but nothing more substantial. The falling part took place in tiny increments of shared interest, deep conversation, and slow-building intimacy. The connection they'd shared was like nothing she'd ever experienced, and it was the best thing that had ever happened to her, which was probably why she couldn't shake the loss. "I don't know what to do."

Hank reached for the bowl of green beans. "Trust your instincts. They've carried you this far, and you've come a long way from the rebellious kid I first met."

He continued eating as if nothing had happened. She'd spent the entire day practicing all the things she'd say in response to his epic scolding, but he seemed almost ambivalent to the bombshells she'd dropped. She supposed she should be happy to be off the hook, but instead she felt deflated. "I'm sorry I quit the job without talking to you about it."

Hank set his fork down. "I think I'm the one who owes you an apology. I never should've held you to that promise. After all you'd been through, I took the only thing you had left—control—and that wasn't right."

West placed a hand over his. "It's okay." And it was. But for her promise to Hank, she might never have met Camille, and as painful as losing her was, West wasn't ready to say she wished it hadn't happened. But Hank's belief that she'd figure it out was misplaced because if she'd had the guts to move past what had happened, she would've done it by now. It was time for her to move on to new things and hope that someday she'd meet another woman like Camille who made her feel special, wanted, and loved.

"I have a lead on a new job." She told him all about the work with the regional office of Lambda Legal. "The interview went well, but they have a few other candidates, and any job offer is pending bar exam results."

"Those should be here any day now, right?"

"Yes. I guess it wasn't very smart to sit for the Alabama bar, but this job doesn't require a Texas license since most of the work is behind the scenes. I'm thinking I might sit for the Texas bar in February."

"Good plan. Let me know if there's anyone I can call to help you out."

"I appreciate the offer, but if it's all the same to you, I'd rather do this on my own." She watched his face for signs she'd hurt his feelings, but pride was the only emotion she saw reflected back.

"I have only one request."

West braced for another promise she wasn't sure she could keep. "What is it?"

"When you get the results, may I swear you in? It's one of the few privileges I still have now that I'm retired. We can do it here, in my study. Very low-key."

West sighed with relief. She hadn't thought through the logistics of being sworn in, and she sure didn't want to drive all the way back to Alabama to make it happen. "Deal."

"Now that you've got your new career sorted out, what are you going to do about the other thing?"

"Other thing?" she asked. He stared hard for a moment before she realized he was talking about Camille. "Uh, I don't have a clue. Probably nothing."

"Look, I understand quitting a job that wasn't for you, but quitting people you love because they make a mistake?" He shook his head. "You're going to have a hard time finding someone to love if you're that much of a hard-ass."

"I tried. I was the one who pushed it. She never wanted more, and definitely never out in the open." West winced as she remembered the confrontation in front of Stroud and the marshals. She'd desperately wanted Camille, her lover, to stand up for her, but she wouldn't because doing so would've revealed the depth of their relationship. "Honestly, I don't even know what I would say to her at this point."

Hank looked at his watch. "Well, you might want to give that some thought because she'll be here in about ten minutes."

Camille stood at the door and knocked, but her focus was inward, as she remembered the day she and West had stood outside this very house, and West had handed over her phone number in a shameless display of flirtation.

She'd seen so many sides of West since then. Smart, cool, sexy, even a little shy at times. She'd give anything to see any of those facets again instead of the cold, hard silence she'd experienced since West had stormed out of her office the week before.

The door opened and she looked up, expecting to see Diane Blair, but like a cruel mind trick, West was standing in front of her. She started to reach out, but another part of her brain kicked in to say it wasn't, couldn't be real.

"Why are you here?" West asked.

Camille stared at the doorway, at West, who was very real. Her question had been delivered in a quiet, almost painful voice. "I wasn't sure I'd ever see you again."

West stepped outside, closed the door behind her, and stood across from her on the porch. The night air was cool and crisp and West shivered against the cold, or was it discomfort from this chance meeting? Camille had spent a lot of time imagining what would happen if she ran into West. Every version had a slightly different twist, but all of them ended well. Judging by the waves of animosity coming from West now, her optimism had been misplaced, so she said the only thing she thought West wanted to hear. “I’m sorry. I never should’ve violated your privacy. I never should’ve doubted you.”

West nodded but didn’t speak, and Camille took small comfort that West didn’t reject her altogether. She fumbled for something else to prolong the contact, but before she could string together more words, the door opened.

“What can I do to get you two to come in from the cold?” Diane asked, her cheerful voice like a blaring horn in the silence between them.

“I have to go,” West said, already on the move.

Camille started to yell for her to stop, to grab her by the hand, and pull West back into her arms, but she did none of those things. West had to come to her because she wanted to, not because she was being pushed or pulled. Powerless to stop her, Camille watched West fade into the distance.

“Camille?”

Diane watched her watching West. Once, she would’ve worried about someone seeing her so vulnerable, but surprisingly, she didn’t care that Diane had heard or seen everything that had just happened between her and West. The realization was liberating and she liked it.

She followed Diane into the dining room where Judge Blair was seated at the head of the table. He looked so much better than when she’d visited him weeks ago and she said so.

“It’s kind of amazing what you can accomplish when you only have one goal,” he said. “Thanks for coming by.”

“I should’ve come later. I wasn’t thinking about it being dinner time.” She’d called Diane this afternoon to let her know that the marshals had concluded their investigation into the threatening notes. She’d expected Diane to pass the message along, and that would be the end of it, but he’d insisted she come out to the house and tell him everything in detail. Considering how dramatically his speaking had improved since she’d seen him last, she wondered why they couldn’t have just spoken on the phone.

“Nonsense. Are you hungry? There’s still some dinner left, and Diane made a lemon icebox pie for dessert.”

Camille shook her head. Any appetite she'd had vanished at West's rejection. "No, thank you. I can't stay long. I have a lot of work to do still."

"And you like the work? You're enjoying it?"

His questions were innocuous on the surface, but they seemed loaded and full of mines. "I'm finding that I need to be better about balance," she said, quickly changing the subject. "Would you like to hear what happened with the investigation?"

"Yes, thanks. And I appreciate you indulging me by coming all this way."

She reached in her bag and pulled out a file. "The marshals provided me with this draft of the report." She handed over a document. "You can keep that copy. They attempted to interview Stroud after he left my office this morning, but he told them to talk to his lawyer and he left the building. They obtained a warrant based on Lloyd's statements and Stroud's conversation with me and contacted his counsel about an hour ago to make arrangements for Stroud to turn himself in."

"You don't sound happy."

"Professionally, I get why it's not good policy to throw a sitting federal judge in handcuffs, but personally, I'd like to tighten the steel around his wrists myself. I'm just glad it's over."

"You've had a rough first start. Threats, a mistrial."

"Don't forget one of my law clerks obstructed justice."

"And the one I made you promise to keep walked out on you."

Camille thought she heard an extra layer of meaning behind his words. Had West told him anything about their relationship? Relationship was probably too strong a term for what she and West had shared, but it was exactly the right word for what she wanted. Would he think she was a horrible person for falling in love with West after he'd entrusted her with West's career?

He was staring, waiting for her reaction to his statement. She had a choice. She could act like West was nothing more than an employee. She could say she was disappointed the professional relationship hadn't worked out, but she wished West well in her future endeavors. Those were the proper things to say and do. The safe things. But to do so was to deny her feelings, and more importantly, to deny West's role in awakening them. Camille was just beginning to realize she'd been filling her life with titles and trappings, but with all her accomplishments, she was still empty inside. Until West.

West might never want her again, but she wasn't ready to stop trying to win her back, and the first step was taking a risk. She took a deep breath. "I want her back. Not to be my clerk." She scrutinized his face, searching for signs her next words weren't welcome, but then decided it didn't matter. She had to speak the truth so she plunged in full force. "I know you're like a father to her, and you're probably very protective. I don't know what she told you, but I never meant to hurt her and I'll spend the rest of my life making it up to her. I'm in love with her, and I'll do anything to get her back."

She stopped talking and waited. For shock, for admonishment, but all she got was a big smile.

"Thank you for telling me. I appreciate your honesty," he said. "Now, as for getting you two back together, I have the perfect plan."

CHAPTER TWENTY-ONE

"You look great," Bill said, "but I think you should wear a suit."

West looked down at her outfit. She had on her best chinos and her favorite Wembley tie. "Dude, I'm not wearing a suit. This is not a super formal thing. It's at their house. I'm only bringing you along because Diane made cake and I know how much you love cake. PS, I'm making you drive because Hank will probably break out some of his killer scotch."

"You say that, but I know you're bringing me because you love me for getting you in the door at Lambda." Bill danced around waving his hands in the air. "You love me, you really love me."

"Quit it." She shot him a fierce look, but it didn't work and soon they were both laughing hysterically.

It felt good to laugh. She was still in a funk over losing Camille, and seeing her at Hank's house had only made matters worse. Camille had managed to look exhausted, anxious, and alluring at the same time. West had driven around the block three times, and on each pass, she'd almost stopped and gone back inside, but she didn't know what to say, so on the final lap, she kept going, away from Camille, away from risking her heart.

But today was about moving forward. Yesterday, she'd received her bar exam results, and the call from Lambda Legal offering her the job came just hours later. She'd considered buying a lottery ticket, but didn't want to push her luck. She decided to take her professional successes and run with them. She didn't need a personal life to be happy.

The first thing she noticed when Bill pulled up in front of Hank's was the line of cars parked in front of his house. She looked up and down the street for signs of people, but there was no one in sight.

"Looks like someone's having a party," Bill said as he eased his Audi between a couple of other cars.

"Yeah, I guess." West got out of the car and walked toward the house with a growing sense of unease. She'd barely reached the front step before the door opened.

"West!" Diane called out. "We were beginning to wonder if you were going to make it. Come on in. Everyone's in the study."

Everyone? West turned back, searching for Bill. He gave her a knowing smile and urged her along.

"You heard the lady." He reached for her hand with a mock bow. "Your audience awaits." He hustled her down the hall before she could protest, and when she reached the door of the study, the room was crowded with familiar faces. Hank was leaning against his desk, and surrounding him were Ester, Peter, Sam from the cafe at the courthouse, and a few court clerks and bailiffs she'd gotten to know over the years. If Bill had filled her in on the surprise, she would've bailed, but standing here now with all these people who'd been with her on this journey, her heart swelled. She tapped her hand on her heart and ducked her head to hide the tears of gratitude.

Hank gave a little speech thanking everyone for being there to witness this important occasion, and then said he'd always known she'd be a fantastic litigator because she'd argued with him from the moment they met. While everyone laughed at his joke, West looked around the room, drinking in the love and support she saw reflected back at her. She turned to whisper thanks to Bill, but stopped mid-word when she saw Camille standing in his place.

Camille looked as stunning as ever and more rested and at ease than when West had seen her last. West stood still, not knowing what to say, but Camille tapped her on the shoulder and pointed at Hank who was smiling at them both. In that instant, West knew he was responsible for bringing them together today, but before she could figure out the why behind his move, he called her over and asked her to raise her right hand while he administered the oath.

She could hear the tremble in her voice, but her trepidation had nothing to do with the words and everything to do with Camille standing across the room, watching her with an intense gaze. West forced herself to focus on the words Hank was asking her to repeat: *with all good fidelity...use no falsehood...support the constitution.* When the applause started, she finally allowed herself to breathe, and the first person she turned to was Camille.

But Camille was on the move, gently pushing past the others to walk to the center of the room. She stood there until the applause died down and then held up a hand.

"My name is Camille Avery. Judge Blair invited me to take part in this very special event and has graciously allowed me to say a few words.

"Unlike most of you, I haven't known West for many years. However, I've had the privilege of working with her over the past month and have personally witnessed the integrity and industry she'll bring to the profession.

"But I'm not standing in front of you today to tell you about what a great person West is and what a brilliant lawyer I think she will become. I have a very selfish reason for this little speech, and it has to do with what Judge Blair said earlier about some occasions being so important that it's necessary to have witnesses who can attest to what happened—to make it real."

Camille stepped closer to West but kept her voice loud enough for everyone to hear. "So, West, I'm here to say, in front of your friends and family, that I'm in love with you. I started falling in love with you the moment we met, but I was too caught up with the shoulds and shouldn'ts of my career to leave room for all the possibilities a future with you might hold. I'm sorry for that, but if you'll have me, I'd like the chance to try again, the chance to build a future with you." She paused, her eyes glistening with tears. "I love you, West Fallon."

The room fell silent, and West felt everyone staring at her, waiting for her response. She'd come here today, optimistic about her professional future, but pessimistic about her chance at ever finding the kind of love she felt for Camille. Now Camille was standing in front of her—in front of everyone—baring her heart and promising more than West had ever allowed herself to dream possible.

Hank's advice echoed in her ear. She had a choice to make, and only one was the right one, only one would allow her to claim the life she'd hoped for, but had never been sure she truly deserved.

"I love you too." And with those words, West walked into the arms of her lover, intent on staying there for the rest of her life.

❖

Camille glanced out the French doors that opened into the Blairs' backyard and spotted West sitting alone on the porch swing. For a second, she was gripped with uncertainty, but she mentally replayed West's declaration of love several times to give her courage and pushed through the doors. "I brought you a piece of cake."

West looked up and Camille witnessed a jumble of emotions in her half smile and teary eyes. She set the cake plate on the table beside the swing and knelt in front of West. "Are you okay?"

"Yes." West uttered the muffled word as she wiped her eyes.

Camille wanted to pull her into her arms, but hesitated. Maybe the grand gesture had been a little too grand. She'd thought telling West she loved her in front of the people important to her was the perfect way to prove her feelings were genuine, but maybe she'd put West in the embarrassing position of accepting something she didn't want any more just to save face.

She passed West a napkin. "It's okay if you want to take it back. I did kind of ambush you. I meant everything I said and I'll wait for you if you need more time, but if you want me to go, then I—"

West put a finger against Camille's lips and grinned through her tears. "It's a good thing you're a judge and not a litigator 'cause you don't really know how to quit when you're ahead." She pulled Camille up beside her. "I meant everything I said too. I'm just a little overwhelmed. There was a time in my life when I never thought any of this was possible. Those doubts will probably always creep in from time to time."

Camille's heart ached that West would ever doubt she deserved the best life had to offer, or the love she had to give. She put her arms around her and hugged tightly. "Oh, sweetheart, when the doubts sneak in, I'll just hold you close and tell you I love you every day for the rest of your life."

West tilted her head and just before they kissed to seal the deal, she murmured against Camille's lips, "That would be perfect."

THE END

About the Author

Carsen Taite's goal as an author is to spin tales with plot lines as interesting as the cases she encountered in her career as a criminal defense lawyer. She is the award-winning author of over a dozen novels of romantic intrigue, including the Luca Bennett Bounty Hunter series and the Lone Star Law series. Learn more at www.carsentaite.com.

Books Available from Bold Strokes Books

A Lamentation of Swans by Valerie Bronwen. Ariel Montgomery returns to Sea Oats to try to save her broken marriage but soon finds herself also fighting to save her own life and catch a murderer. (978-1-62639-828-3)

Between Sand and Stardust by Tina Michele. Are the lifelong bonds of love strong enough to conquer time, distance, and heartache when Haven Thorne and Willa Bennette are given another chance at forever? (978-1-62639-940-2)

Freedom to Love by Ronica Black. What happens when the woman who spent her lifetime worrying about caring for her family, finally finds the freedom to love without borders? (978-1-63555-001-6)

House of Fate by Barbara Ann Wright. Two women must throw off the lives they've known as a guardian and an assassin and save two rival houses before their secrets tear the galaxy apart. (978-1-62639-780-4)

Planning for Love by Erin Dutton. Could true love be the one thing that wedding coordinator Faith McKenna didn't plan for? (978-1-62639-954-9)

Sidebar by Carsen Taite. Judge Camille Avery and her clerk, attorney West Fallon, agree on little except their mutual attraction, but can their relationship and their careers survive a headline-grabbing case? (978-1-62639-752-1)

Sweet Boy and Wild One by T. L. Hayes. When Rachel Cole meets soulful singer Bobby Layton at an open mic, she is immediately in thrall. What she soon discovers will rock her world in ways she never imagined. (978-1-62639-963-1)

To Be Determined by Mardi Alexander and Laurie Eichler. Charlie Dickerson escapes her life in the US to rescue Australian wildlife with Pip Atkins, but can they save each other? (978-1-62639-946-4)

True Colors by Yolanda Wallace. Blogger Robby Rawlins plans to use First Daughter Taylor Crenshaw to get ahead, but she never planned on falling in love with her in the process. (978-1-62639-927-3)

Unexpected by Jenny Frame. When Dale McGuire falls for Rebecca Harper, the mother of the son she never knew she had, will Rebecca's troubled past stop them from making the family they both truly crave? (978-1-62639-942-6)

Canvas for Love by Charlotte Greene. When ghosts from Amelia's past threaten to undermine their relationship, Chloé must navigate the greatest romance of her life without losing sight of who she is. (978-1-62639-944-0)

Heart Stop by Radclyffe. Two women, one with a damaged body, the other a damaged spirit, challenge each other to dare to live again. (978-1-62639-899-3)

Repercussions by Jessica L. Webb. Someone planted information in Edie Black's brain and now they want it back, but with the protection of shy former soldier Skye Kenny, Edie has a chance at life and love. (978-1-62639-925-9)

Spark by Catherine Friend. Jamie's life is turned upside down when her consciousness travels back to 1560 and lands in the body of one of Queen Elizabeth I's ladies-in-waiting…or has she totally lost her grip on reality? (978-1-62639-930-3)

Taking Sides by Kathleen Knowles. When passion and politics collide, can love survive? (978-1-62639-876-4)

Thorns of the Past by Gun Brooke. Former cop Darcy Flynn's heart broke when her career on the force ended in disgrace, but perhaps saving Sabrina Hawk's life will mend it in more ways than one. (978-1-62639-857-3)

You Make Me Tremble by Karis Walsh. Seismologist Casey Radnor comes to the San Juan Islands to study an earthquake but finds her heart shaken by passion when she meets animal rescuer Iris Mallery (978-1-62639-901-3)

Complications by MJ Williamz. Two women battle for the heart of one. (978-1-62639-769-9)

Crossing the Wide Forever by Missouri Vaun. As Cody Walsh and Lillie Ellis face the perils of the untamed West, they discover that love's uncharted frontier isn't for the weak in spirit or the faint of heart. (978-1-62639-851-1)

Fake It Till You Make It by M. Ullrich. Lies will lead to trouble, but can they lead to love? (978-1-62639-923-5)

Girls Next Door by Sandy Lowe and Stacia Seaman eds.. Best-selling romance authors tell it from the heart—sexy, romantic stories of falling for the girls next door. (978-1-62639-916-7)

Pursuit by Jackie D. The pursuit of the most dangerous terrorist in America will crack the lines of friendship and love, and not everyone will make it out under the weight of duty and service. (978-1-62639-903-7)

Shameless by Brit Ryder. Confident Emery Pearson knows exactly what she's looking for in a no-strings-attached hookup, but can a spontaneous interlude open her heart to more? (978-1-63555-006-1)

The Practitioner by Ronica Black. Sometimes love comes calling whether you're ready for it or not. (978-1-62639-948-8)

Unlikely Match by Fiona Riley. When an ambitious PR exec and her super-rich coding geek-girl client fall in love, they learn that giving something up may be the only way to have everything. (978-1-62639-891-7)

Where Love Leads by Erin McKenzie. A high school counselor and the mom of her new student bond in support of the troubled girl, never expecting deeper feelings to emerge, testing the boundaries of their relationship. (978-1-62639-991-4)

Forsaken Trust by Meredith Doench. When four women are murdered, Agent Luce Hansen must regain trust in her most valuable investigative tool—herself—to catch the killer. (978-1-62639-737-8)

Her Best Friend's Sister by Meghan O'Brien. For fifteen years, Claire Barker has nursed a massive crush on her best friend's older sister. What happens when all her wildest fantasies come true? (978-1-62639-861-0)

Letter of the Law by Carsen Taite. Will federal prosecutor Bianca Cruz take a chance at love with horse breeder Jade Vargas, whose dark family ties threaten everything Bianca has worked to protect—including her child? (978-1-62639-750-7)

New Life by Jan Gayle. Trigena and Karrie are having a baby, but the stress of becoming a mother and the impact on their relationship might be too much for Trigena. (978-1-62639-878-8)

Royal Rebel by Jenny Frame. Charity director Lennox King sees through the party girl image Princess Roza has cultivated, but will Lennox's past indiscretions and Roza's responsibilities make their love impossible? (978-1-62639-893-1)

Unbroken by Donna K. Ford. When Kayla and Jackie, two women with every reason to reject Happy Ever After, fall in love, will they have the courage to overcome their pasts and rewrite their stories? (978-1-62639-921-1)

Where the Light Glows by Dena Blake. Mel Thomas doesn't realize just how unhappy she is in her marriage until she meets Izzy Calabrese. Will she have the courage to overcome her insecurities and follow her heart? (978-1-62639-958-7)

Escape in Time by Robyn Nyx. Working in the past is hell on your future. (978-1-62639-855-9)

Forget-Me-Not by Kris Bryant. Is love worth walking away from the only life you've ever dreamed of? (978-1-62639-865-8)

Highland Fling by Anna Larner. On vacation in the Scottish Highlands, Eve Eddison falls for the enigmatic forestry officer Moira Burns, despite Eve's best friend's campaign to convince her that Moira will break her heart. (978-1-62639-853-5)

Phoenix Rising by Rebecca Harwell. As Storm's Quarry faces invasion from a powerful neighbor, a mysterious newcomer with powers equal to Nadya's challenges everything she believes about herself and her future. (978-1-62639-913-6)

Soul Survivor by I. Beacham. Sam and Joey have given up on hope, but when fate brings them together it gives them a chance to change each other's life and make dreams come true. (978-1-62639-882-5)

Strawberry Summer by Melissa Brayden. When Margaret Beringer's first love Courtney Carrington returns to their small town, she must grapple with their troubled past and fight the temptation for a very delicious future. (978-1-62639-867-2)

The Girl on the Edge of Summer by J.M. Redmann. Micky Knight accepts two cases, but neither is the easy investigation it appears. The past is never past—and young girls lead complicated, even dangerous lives. (978-1-62639-687-6)

Unknown Horizons by CJ Birch. The moment Lieutenant Alison Ash steps aboard the Persephone, she knows her life will never be the same. (978-1-62639-938-9)